I0587911

TAKE IT OFF
THE MENU

A Mile High Matched Novel

CHRISTINA HOVLAND

For rights information, please contact:
Prospect Agency
551 Valley Road, PMB 377
Upper Montclair, NJ 07043
(718) 788-3217

Holly Ingraham, Development Editor
Tamara Beard of Wrapped Up in Writing, Copy Editor & Proofreader
Shasta Schafer, Final Proofreader
First Edition August 2019

This book is dedicated to all my English Lit teachers who nurtured my love of storytelling.

(Except for the one in 7th grade who wrote on my report card that I needed "improved self-discipline." She is excluded from this dedication for obvious reasons.)

Praise for Christina Hovland

Going Down on One Knee

"Humor, witty dialogue, **delightfully crafted characters**, and a unique premise combine to make *Going Down on One Knee* a treasure!" — *InD'tale Magazine*

"An **utterly charming** opposites-attract-story. Hovland perfectly balances simmering sexual tension with a surprising amount of emotion, and the stomach-flip-causing ending is the perfect example of **why I read and love romance**."
  - *New York Times Bestselling Author, Lauren Layne*

"I wasn't expecting to **laugh** as much as I did. ... Anyone looking for a **light, funny story** will find it here in Christina Hovland's *Going Down on One Knee*." - *Romantically Inclined Reviews*

"If you are a fan of **opposites attract stories** that make you laugh one minute, and swoon the next, you'll not go wrong with one of her books. Well done, Christina Hovland! Very, very well done." - *The Reading Cafe Reviews*

"A delightful blend of **witty humor and romance**!" - *Jenn (YeahOrNeighReviews)*

"Brek and Velma. He exudes tranquility. She exudes tension. The chemistry between them is **palpable without being forced**." - *Avidez Literary*

"This is **so much more than a romance novel**. It literally describes how life is. You have to let go to find yourself. " - *Reckless Readers*

Blow Me Away

"Blow Me Away is the perfect beach read: low on angst, **high on humor** and good-hearted." — *Reedsy Discovery*

"I don't know the best way to describe this book or these characters in a way that will do them justice. **Just read the book** and enjoy the madness!!" - *Nerdy Dirty & Flirty Book Blog*

"Oh. My. Word. Blow Me Away was an absolute blast! **I seriously loved every second of it.**" - *Anna's Herding Cats Book Reviews*

"A hilarious romantic comedy with colorful characters, a **witty banter** and sparkling wit!"- *Aaly & The Books*

"I have not had that much fun reading in a long time." - *Read.Review.Repeat Blog*

The Honeymoon Trap

"*The Honeymoon Trap* is adorable, clever, funny—in short, completely charming." - Serena Bell, *USA Today* bestselling author of *Do Over*

Chapter One
TWO DAYS BEFORE THE WEDDING

"LOTHARIO, STOP HUMPING THE ANGORA," Marlee Medford—soon-to-be Bishop—stepped onto the patio of her Denver townhome. Her pure-white-haired chihuahua tipped his head to the side, stopped humping her fiancé's angora sweater that had fallen to the ground, and whined.

Leaves from their two aspen trees rustled beside her—red and orange and ready to break free from their branches in preparation for winter.

She snatched the sweater, brushed a couple of fallen leaves from the sleeve, and hung it over the arm of the empty chair next to Scotty. He was immersed in his phone, apparently oblivious to the defiling of his clothes.

Lothario had a thing for Scotty's shirts, and it drove Scotty absolutely nuts. Aside from Scotty's clothing, Lothario literally humped anything that moved. Except Marlee. She'd put a stop to that early on. One would've thought Lothario's recent unfortunate experience with a moving bicycle tire would've stopped the behavior, but all it got him was a cast on his right leg and a rededication to defiling all things.

She turned her focus from the dog to Scotty. He had his serious face on that morning.

"Hey, sweetie." She squeezed his shoulders and kissed his cheek before sitting next to him with her morning coffee. "I've only got a second. I have a bajillion things to do today for the wedding."

Their wedding.

Their forty-eight-hours-away nuptials.

"Leelee." He set his phone down beside his coffee mug. "We need to talk about the wedding."

"Okay." She squeezed his hands. "What's up?"

"I don't want to do it." He glanced to the side, not meeting her eyes.

That wasn't exactly a choice anymore. Not with four hundred of their closest friends coming to Denver for their wedding.

"We're not getting married, Leelee." He heaved a huge breath. "I'm sorry."

She dropped his hands. *What?*

"We're not getting married?" she asked.

"No." He shook his head. "I'm so sorry."

He was sorry? *He* was sorry?

Marlee's stomach dropped.

"It's been this way for a while." Scotty's eyes were kind as he spoke. "I've been thinking we should take a break, but with the wedding planning and your dad, I figured we'd see it through." He sighed. "It was the wrong decision."

He'd asked her to sit on their patio with him and have a cup of morning coffee so he could end their relationship? What. The. Hell?

No. This was just cold feet. They'd get through it.

"I know we haven't exactly been connecting lately, but that's totally normal. We're in a committed, long-term relationship. It's not supposed to be exciting," Marlee said. It's not like she hadn't noticed the lack of spark. "We're just supposed to stick with it, so we have someone to grow old with, right?"

They'd settled into a routine with each other that was just about as comfortable as lukewarm bathwater. Not awful. Definitely not great. Once they were married, things would heat up again. They'd get back to Jacuzzi level.

"I don't just want someone to grow old with." Scotty gulped. "I want someone who lights a fire inside of me. Like we used to do for each other."

"Look, if you want a fire, I can try to cook something." Marlee was the queen of burning the shit out of anything she tried to make.

He chuckled. Then his expression broke. "I think we should stop now, while we still like each other. Not wait until we can't stand to be in the same room together."

While she waited for her heart to break, she focused on the milky brown liquid in her mug. Her best friends had flown in from all over the country. Her family owned two of Denver's most prized sports teams, so the wedding had even made headlines in the *Denver Post*. The breakup would undoubtedly be devastatingly public. The panic she felt wasn't from all that, though. She felt like she'd been dropped out of a plane but landed on a mountain of soft pillows. What she was feeling was…relief. Relief that was starting to make her panic. And that didn't even make any sense.

"Marlee?" Scotty kept his focus on her. "Say something."

Her gaze caught Lothario pulling Scotty's sweater off the chair again. "Seriously, stop having sex with Scotty's sweater."

"That's not what I wanted you to say." Scotty rubbed his forehead.

"What do you want me to say?" Marlee asked. "It's fine?"

"Just say what you're feeling."

Staring at him, she really tried to see the man she'd fallen in love with. But that man was gone—he had been for a while —and she wasn't the woman he'd fallen in love with, either.

She opened her mouth to speak. Then she closed it again.

How was she supposed to be done with the guy who had been there for her since she was twenty? They'd spent a decade together. A decent decade. There were good parts to that decade.

"Scotty, I…"

Her throat started to close up, her chest went tight—and not from an asthma attack. No. This was the panic portion of their breakup.

"You said you loved me more," she said on a breath. Just last night, he'd said that very thing.

He dropped his gaze to the table, not responding.

They sat together in the silence of their broken relationship.

"I meant it. I just don't think you love me very much anymore, either," he finally said.

No, not really, but she figured they'd get back to that. She'd figured that's what a relationship was—two people who fell in and out of love over and over again. They just hadn't gotten around to falling back in love yet.

Marlee couldn't draw a breath. Four hundred guests to notify. The task would be mammoth. She had to call her wedding planner ASAP. Her lungs had seemingly collapsed against her ribs, the pillows of relief deflating to spikes of *holy shit*.

Keep it together, Marlee.

"You want a relationship break, or you want to move on?" she asked. Clarification at this point was a good thing.

A relationship break would be like twenty-four hours, and then they'd still have a wedding. The moving on? Totally different. Besides, wasn't a break just something people said to ease the bandage from the wound of an eventual breakup?

A vein in his forehead pulsed. It always did when he was agitated. Which she did not understand at all at the moment, given that he was the one messing everything up.

He didn't say anything. He didn't have to.

"This isn't a break," she said. Scotty was way too decisive for that. "You're ending us."

It wasn't a question, because she knew the answer.

"Yes." The word hung in the air around Scotty's lips.

"Seriously, Lothario, leave the sweater alone," she said firmly. The dog clearly had no idea her life was in a free fall and it was not the time to have a fling with angora. He was getting more action during her breakup than she'd had in weeks.

There seemed to be no feeling in her body. She couldn't get her limbs to move. Her lips were numb. Her fingertips had no feeling.

This was happening.

What was she going to do about all the filet mignon they'd already purchased for the reception? The cake she'd picked out? The final hair trial with her stylist scheduled for that afternoon? She glanced toward the French doors of their townhome, itching to get inside and start making the calls that needed to happen. And what did that say about the state of their relationship?

"There are four hundred people coming." She leaned forward, pressing her palms against the glass-topped patio table. "You didn't think to tell me this yesterday? Or last week? Or last month? Or whenever it hit you that you didn't want to spend forever with me?" She stabbed her finger at her own chest.

"It's not that cut and dry." Scotty fidgeted with his mug. "I had to get my own feelings straight." He shook his head, then quickly added, "But there's not anyone else, I promise."

She stared at him like he'd shown up to their wedding in Bermuda shorts and a Hawaiian shirt.

Of course, there was no one else. They worked together, lived together, exercised together—okay, he hit the weights, she scrolled through her phone while she walked on the treadmill. In any case, *duh*, he didn't have someone else. He wouldn't have time for that.

"I'm sorry, Leelee." He studied his coffee. "So sorry. I think we've both been feeling a little lost in the relationship for a while now," Scotty continued like he needed to keep explaining something that really didn't need explaining. "I know you feel it, too."

He wasn't wrong—the little flare that had started their fling dimmed way past the ember stage years after they'd entered full-blown relationship status. But then he'd proposed. And they'd—she'd—planned an elaborate wedding. Scotty worked with her father. Her father who would not be happy about the amount of cash he'd already poured into Denver society's event of the season.

"What are you going to do for a job?" Marlee asked as gently as she could. It's not like Scotty could keep working for her father after they split. She'd gotten him the job as vice president of operations and personally worked as director of events in the office. It'd be way too awkward for them to continue working there together. He'd have to sort out his job, and they'd have to figure out what to do with the townhome they'd purchased together. The logistics were starting to tug at a migraine brewing behind her eyes.

Scotty gave her his what-are-you-talking-about look. "I'll still work for your dad."

For a really smart guy, Scotty was being very dense.

"Even after we break up?" she asked.

"Yeah, Marlee, it's my job."

No, that wouldn't work. It was the job he got because he was with her. "But I work there."

"And?"

"And we won't be a couple. I don't think Dad will be okay with—"

"He's fine. We discussed it yesterday."

Wait. What?

There was that free fall feeling again.

"You told him we were breaking up before you told me?" Her cheeks heated, but not with embarrassment. "You knew you were ending things yesterday? And you didn't mention it?"

"Leelee." Scotty used that tone that never failed to piss her off. "He's my boss. He's my friend. Of course, I talked with him."

Her blood pounded through her heart, echoing in her eardrums. "You told him before you told me? And if he'd have said you couldn't keep the job, would we be getting married?"

She'd never have known.

Scotty pinched his lips into a flat line.

So that's how it was. This was all amicable, but if Dad would have said no, then Marlee would be getting married to a guy who didn't really love her.

The moral of this story? Never trust someone who says they love you more.

"You and I… We haven't connected in a while," Scotty said again.

She was sad, too. Sad that she understood about the not connecting. Their lives were more than intertwined, but their hearts? Once upon a time, they had been. Lately? Not so much.

Maybe that's why the breakup didn't burn the way it should've. The wound had broken open and healed long ago.

"You're right. We haven't connected lately," she finally said.

They hadn't. And she'd tried. Tried hard to catch his attention the way she used to, but after so much time together, things just… They just felt like one of those drums that you strike with the top of your palm. So, instead of a good tap, the sound was more of a thud.

She blew a breath into her cheeks. Scotty hated when she

did that—it annoyed the ever-loving snot out of him. But what Scotty thought didn't matter anymore. The breath escaped her lips slowly.

"When are you leaving?" she asked. Wasn't that the way this worked? The one who called it off was the one to leave?

"I'm not leaving. We'll sort through the logistics together. No need to rush."

Okay, so she would be the one leaving. At least for now, until she could figure out the legalities of homeownership after a breakup.

"I'll start making calls to cancel the ceremony and reception." She paused, waiting for that feeling of dread to take over like it should. A relationship was dying, but all she could think about was what she should do about the food that had been purchased.

"I'm sorry." His forehead relaxed, and he stared at his reflection in the table.

Her chair scraped against the concrete patio as she pushed from the table. "Me, too."

The soles of her bare feet padded across the cold concrete, through the door, past the kitchen. Lothario followed her inside, his cast thumping with each step. She paused at the bottom of the stairway, her gaze snagging on the open office door. He'd moved in there over a month ago. Sworn it was because he wanted their wedding night to be special, a little time apart in the bedroom would heat things up again. She'd thought it was odd at the time, but she'd gone along with it because... Why had she gone along with it? Right. Because she was thigh-deep in wedding planning and didn't have a thought to give about the *why* of Scotty's decision.

His decision to break up.

The pull of gravity seemed stronger than it had thirty seconds before. Oh God. They were really over. All her limbs doubled in weight. She gripped the railing, hefting herself up the beige carpeting of the staircase. There wasn't time for a breakdown. There were calls to make. Hurrying to the bedroom, she closed and locked the door.

"This is fine. Everything is fine," she said to Lothario. "We're going to stay at a hotel for a little while. Just until we figure everything out."

She grabbed her cell from her nightstand. Her father had called twice. She ignored his voicemails. "Hey, Siri, call Sadie."

Marlee fell to the edge of the bed, tucking her feet under herself. Sadie, former maid of honor, picked up on the second ring. "Soon you'll be Mrs.—"

"I'm not getting married. Scotty called it off and I'm about twenty minutes from a full-blown meltdown, so if you could come help me pack a few bags, that would be amazing." The words spilled from her lips.

"Uh," Sadie said. Shocked Sadie's silence filled the line.

"Sadie?" Marlee finally asked.

"Coming," Sadie said. "I'm coming. Literally calling a car right now."

"'kay." Marlee hung up the phone without saying anything else because she was afraid of what she'd say if she kept talking. She pressed her forehead to the phone screen. She needed a list. Lists were good for the times when a fiancé called off a wedding with less than two days to go. Yes, she'd make a list right after she got her bags together.

She pulled out the suitcases she'd been packing for their honeymoon and dumped the contents of each on the bedspread. There wouldn't be a honeymoon now. No need for swimsuits and summer wraps for an autumn in Denver. Hurrying to the closet, she started pulling clothes from hangers and tossing them into a suitcase.

She should fold them.

There wasn't time to fold them.

She needed to get everything together. Then she needed

to call Aspen, her wedding planner, so she could start the cancellation calls. That should happen first. Cell in hand, Marlee pulled up Aspen's number. She tried to force her fingers to tap on the phone number, her gaze catching the diamond engagement ring Scotty had slipped on to her left hand.

She couldn't bring herself to make the call. This was ridiculous. Yes, she was sad Scotty had called things off. Yes, she was disappointed in his timing. But no, this would not wreck her.

Still, she couldn't bring herself to make the call.

She pulled off the ring, dropping it on the nightstand. Then she pressed the message button and tapped out a note to Aspen. *Wedding not happening. Need to cancel everything. Call Scotty, he can handle this. He broke it off.*

There. That was better. Scotty could deal with the aftermath.

Since he loved her more and all that.

The garage underneath her bedroom opened. She moved to the window. Scotty backed out of the driveway in his black Sport BMW.

She did the cheek thing again, blowing out air through her lips.

Her phone pinged with a response, but she didn't read it. She held the off button until the screen went black. Then she shoved clothes into her suitcases. Sadie would be here in just a little bit and she only had to hold out until then.

Clearing her mind while she packed, she did her best to ignore thoughts of anything other than the task in front of her.

"Marlee?" Sadie's voice carried through the foyer and up the stairs to the master bedroom. Lothario yipped and jumped from the bed, limping through the doorway on his tripod legs.

"Up here." Marlee's voice cracked on the last word. Unacceptable. She coughed. "Here. I'm in the bedroom."

"I brought help," Sadie hollered.

Marlee met her at the doorway.

Sadie wrapped her in a hug. "I brought Eli to kill Scotty for you, but we passed him on the street. Eli will be lifting all the heavy things instead."

Marlee looked over Sadie's shoulder to where Sadie's brother, Eli, stood on the top stair. His talent as a chef would now be wasted since he wouldn't be catering the wedding anymore.

"Hey, Mar." He said her nickname so softly it hardly seemed fitting coming from a guy who looked like he had driven there from a UFC fight. A cross between Joe Manganiello and Jason Mamoa, Eli had the tall, dark, and scary-as-hell bit down. The scary-as-hell bit was only to those who didn't know him. Everyone who really knew him knew he was all pudding and marshmallow fluff inside.

"I'm here to lug suitcases and crack skulls, whatever you need," he said.

"Thanks." She cleared the emotion that was starting to lodge in her throat. No emotions. Scotty didn't deserve them.

"You're on Marlee duty." Sadie released Marlee from her hug and shoved her toward Eli. "I'm on getting-everything-sorted duty. Becca and Kellie are on their way."

Eli pulled Marlee in for a hug and…well…this was nice. She had her friends, she'd be fine. So why were her eyes leaking all over Eli's gray tee? She started to pull back, a hiccup wrestling its way out. She'd left tear-stained mascara smudges all over his shoulder.

There was no reason to cry. She was practically already over Scotty. He'd done her a favor.

"Hey." Eli's thumbs wiped her tears from her cheeks. "Let's let Sadie deal with the packing. Aspen already called to cancel everything, so she's got that covered."

"I need a place to live for a while." Marlee swallowed another hiccup before it could escape. "I was thinking a hotel. And I'd like to get out of here before my parents show up. Dad will talk about what a great guy Scotty is, and Mom will make the breakup all about herself."

Her parents meant well, but they were nothing if not predictable.

"Why are you the one leaving?" Eli asked, his thumbs resting on both sides of her cheeks.

"Because I know he won't." And when was the last time Scotty had comforted her when she was upset?

"Then we'll start with finding the hotel." Eli pulled her in for another hug. "And evacuate to it after."

She nodded. This was good. Sadie and Eli had a plan. They'd probably even written it down somewhere. The release of years of wedding planning, the official death of her relationship with Scotty—it had all just bubbled up in her chest and flowed out of her eyelids. That's all.

She wiped at her cheeks with the backs of her hands. "I'm a mess."

"You're practically part of the family. We're here for you," Eli whispered against the top of her hair. Then he let her cry all over his shoulder. He didn't even balk when she snorted. Somehow, he managed to produce a handful of tissues she could only believe Sadie had slipped to him.

He shifted, readjusting her in his embrace. One thing Marlee had never noticed about Eli before was how really nice he smelled. Not cologne, per se. That morning, he smelled like pancakes and bacon and man. Eli shifted again.

"Were you working this morning?" she asked.

"Yeah, we catered a thing before Sadie caught me." His voice was comforting, warm syrup over pancakes.

"You smell really nice," she said through a sniffle. "Like breakfast."

He shifted again.

"Sorry." She pulled back. "I'm making you uncomfortable." Probably because she was smelling him up.

"It's not you." He rubbed the spot between her shoulder blades with his palm. "But what do I need to do to get your dog to stop humping my shoe?"

She looked down and, sure enough, Lothario was going to town on one of Eli's trainers.

"Shit." She leaned down and lifted the pup. "This is Lothario."

"We've met." Eli nodded toward her lecherous dog. "Nice to put a name to the feeling in my toes."

"I'll just…uh…I'll just put him outside." Squirming dog in hand, she hurried down the stairs and dropped him off on the patio. She pointed at him. "Stay."

He whined.

"And no humping Eli," she continued.

"Listen to your mom, kid," Eli said from behind her.

She closed the door. "Can I get you coffee? Tea?" *Deep breaths, Marlee.* "Vodka?"

"Tell you what, you grab a cup of whatever you'd like, and I'll start looking for a hotel."

Everything was going to be fine.

No wedding. No fiancé. But things would be fine.

Just. Fine.

Chapter Two

THERE WAS NOT a single vacant hotel room in Denver. Eli hung up the phone after talking to the front desk clerk of yet another downtown hotel. The online booking companies had nothing, but he'd hoped if he called around, something would maybe pop up.

No, a huge outdoors show had booked everything east of Breckenridge. The block of rooms Marlee had reserved for wedding guests was totally filled.

He glanced to the former bride-to-be perched on the other side of the sofa with her notepad. She was, apparently, a quick crier. On it and then over it. Sadie was packing. He made calls and Marlee made lists.

"We're here," Becca called from the front door.

Kellie followed her into the living room with an armful of collapsed cardboard boxes and packing tape. She gasped. "Eli's here."

"If it's Eli serious, it's worse than I thought." Becca helped Kellie get more boxes through the doorway.

Yes, Eli was there. He'd spent a good part of his senior year of high school playing referee as these girls navigated their freshman year. They officially made up the rest of Sadie's girl posse, and they'd all moved away from Denver. Marlee was the only one who had stuck around. They were back for the now-not-happening wedding.

He might grump about them suffocating him, but deep down, he actually did enjoy having them around. Most of the time. Especially now that he wasn't personally responsible for their well-being.

"Hey." Marlee padded over to them and did the thing where they hugged and commiserated on what assholes men could be. Frankly, he could relate. Men really could be assholes. Scotty was a perfect example. What kind of a dick called off a wedding with two days to go? Not that Eli had his sights on marriage—hell no—he was perfectly content looking out for number one and number one alone. That was a lesson he'd learned long before he even graduated high school. But once Scotty had slid that ring on Marlee's finger, he should've been prepared to follow through. Not be a dick and call it off with the day in sight and the dinner all but plated.

"Is the rest of the bridal party coming?" Becca asked.

"You mean Scotty's sisters?" Marlee wrinkled her nose. "That's a negative." She pursed her lips into a thin line but then quickly covered it with a smile. "Eli's helping me find a hotel."

"With no luck," he added. "But you can stay at my place until the convention is over." Sadie was already sleeping in his bedroom, but he'd use a sleeping bag so Marlee could take the sofa bed.

"There's a convention?" Kellie asked.

"Some outdoor thing." He shrugged.

"Okay, you'll think I'm crazy, but you should go on your honeymoon," Sadie suggested, marching down the stairs to join the party. "Leave Scotty behind to deal with the fallout and take one of us along instead."

"By one of us, she means all of us." Kellie ran a length of tape along the side of a box.

Nope. Not Eli. All of us meant all of them.

"Going on your honeymoon after calling off the wedding is so cliché." Becca went to work folding another length of corrugated cardboard for Kellie to tape. "Let's go someplace else."

"You know where they have hotel rooms?" Kellie asked. "Vegas."

Shit.

"I'm not going to Vegas." Marlee fidgeted with one of the boxes.

"I'm with Mar on this one," Eli said.

"Getting out of town for the weekend isn't a bad idea," Becca mused. "I mean, of all the places to go after an epic breakup, Vegas is an excellent choice."

"The breakup wasn't epic. No one threw glassware," Marlee mumbled.

Broken glass was a requirement for "epic"?

There was the time Marlee and her senior-year boyfriend had called it quits, and she and the girls had covered his prized '69 Chevy Camaro Super Sport in toilet paper. Eli had thought that was pretty epic. He'd also been the one to explain to the police that his sister and her friends were not, in fact, perpetual rule breakers. Then he'd been the one to threaten to take away all their mascara if they ever pulled shit like that again.

"But you wanted to throw something," Kellie said. "I know you wanted to. Right at his head."

"Not really." Marlee dropped to the sofa beside Eli. "We grew apart."

The side of her thigh touched the fabric of Eli's jeans, her warmth seeping straight into his skin. In the good way when one actually likes someone and doesn't mind their thighs touching.

"I mean," Marlee continued, "at this point, I *do* think a quick divorce would be easier than cancelling it all, but Scotty's right, things between us haven't been awesome for a long time. I just hadn't realized it yet. Not out loud."

One thing about Marlee? She was a toucher. Always had been. So it wasn't a shock to him when she dropped her hand against his and pulled her calves underneath herself. No, that wasn't the shock. The shock was that he liked how at ease she was with him. How her hand felt on him. It was one of those endearing Marlee things that helped make her everyone's friend. Everyone loved Marlee. He wasn't that kind of person. He had his friends, but he didn't have the gravitational pull of Marlee.

It's not that he was standoffish. But he wasn't obtuse. He worked out a lot of frustration at the gym. He was six-foot-four, and the amount of space he took up—he'd been told—could sometimes be interpreted as intimidating. Hell, Sadie had told him just that morning she needed to use him as their bouncer if Scotty did anything stupid.

"Let's do this," Kellie suggested. "Finish packing up the basics, grab breakfast, and figure out what comes next."

"When's the last time you ate?" Eli asked Marlee as gently as he could. He may not be able to swing a hotel room, but he did have the skill set required to whip up a decent meal. "You know what? Never mind. Don't answer that. I'll make breakfast."

"Awesome." Kellie held out her knuckles for a fist bump.

He met it.

Becca started taping together boxes. "It'll be just like when we were kids."

His gut twinged at the thought. Not that he'd minded helping his parents out when he was a teenager—he was the oldest and, in their family, that meant it came with the territory—but his mom had gotten sick, and his dad had worked crazy hours, and that meant Eli had taken care of his four little sisters and, by default, their friends. The stress of that year still raised his blood pressure, and he'd sworn he would never repeat it. Would never put himself in another situation where he was solely responsible for anyone's well-being.

"Marlee, you should help Eli." Becca was already headed upstairs with Sadie. "And by help, I mean you should do nothing and let us all take care of you."

"I'm not going to let you guys do it all." Marlee started to stand.

Eli caught her hand and pulled her back to the couch. "We've got our orders."

"I'd like pancakes." Kellie followed Becca up the stairs. "Pancakes are my favorite."

Eli headed to the kitchen and pulled open the Sub-Zero refrigerator that blended in with her maple cabinets. He drooled only a little at the brands and the luxury of Marlee's appliances. The La Cornue range just begged to be fired up. Petted. Appreciated for the work of art it was. As a professional, a kitchen like this practically made his fingers itch to bake something.

But he wasn't there to eye-fuck her appliances. He stuck his head in the door of the fridge and paused. One jar of pickles. Two tablespoons of ketchup left in a plastic squeeze bottle. A couple of Styrofoam takeout boxes.

This was like the biggest middle finger to a brilliant appliance that he'd ever seen.

"We usually order in, it's just easier," Marlee said from behind him.

He glanced over his shoulder to where she peered into the refrigerator, her palm resting against his upper back.

He denied his body's desire to lean into her hand. To dive into the perpetual kindness in her eyes, the soft look she got when her gaze focused on his, the way her little touches didn't bother him—when they would have from anyone else.

His attention turned back to the pickles and away from

her continual touch. This would absolutely not work. Channel Ten News had called him a genius in the kitchen. A master of turning nothing into something. One of the national cooking shows had even approached him about doing one of their segments that relied on a chef being able to turn a pot of coffee, whipping cream, and a pork loin into a three-course meal.

He could not, however, turn a jar of pickles—he reached for it and turned it over in his palm—nix that, a jar of *expired* pickles, into a breakfast worthy of Kellie's fist bump.

"We're going out to find ingredients." He stood, closed the door, and set the jar on the countertop next to the stainless-steel sink. "Then, as part of your getting over Scotty, I'm going to teach you to cook."

"I'm already over Scotty," Marlee insisted, but the light didn't quite reach her eyes.

He didn't buy it. He gave her a look that, he hoped, broadcasted just that.

"There's a King Soopers just around the corner." Marlee moved to let Lothario back into the house. "We can hit that for supplies. And I *am* over Scotty." Her voice cracked a little at the end. She cleared her throat.

He leveled a you're-full-of-it stare at her.

"Fine. It's a work in progress." She tilted her head to the side, daring him to question her any further.

He wouldn't, because unlike her ex, he wasn't a dick about things.

Lothario trotted beside her to the front door. "Are you driving or am I?"

"I'll drive." He already had the keys to his Jeep Cherokee in his hand.

"Perfect." She turned the door handle and pulled it open. Lothario began to follow her outside.

Eli scratched at his ear in confusion. "Mar, you're you, and I know you can convince people to look away from most anything"—it was part of that talent she held that drew people to her—"but even *you* can't bring a dog into the grocery store."

He wasn't besties with the health inspector, but he knew the rules—no pets.

Marlee rolled her eyes. "Lothario goes where I go." She pulled a red vest from her purse and Velcro'd it around the mutt. "He's my medical alert dog."

Eli had seen a lot of things. He'd never in his life seen a medical alert vest on a chihuahua. He shook the dust bunnies that seemed to settle in his ears.

She wasn't serious. No way was she serious.

"A medical alert dog?" he questioned.

"Well, he's not just pretty." She smiled down at the pup. "Although, he is definitely a pretty doggie."

Lothario puffed up at the compliment.

"Are you just making this up?" he asked. Marlee was one of those people who could convince a man to pay an extra ten dollars for a bottle of water when he wasn't even thirsty.

"Of course not. I have asthma, he lets me know if I'm about to have an attack." She made kissy faces at Lothario. "Don't you?"

Eli wasn't buying it. She was screwing with him. "Does it work?"

"Yeah, he does his job really well." Marlee clipped a leash onto Lothario's collar and stood. "He's trained to tell me if I start wheezing."

Eli wasn't mistaken. She was definitely screwing with him. "You don't notice if you're wheezing?"

"Not when I'm asleep."

Then Scotty didn't notice she was wheezing? The guy was losing punches left and right on his fiancé card.

One thing though. Eli held up an index finger. "So you can train the dog to alert you when you can't breathe, but you can't get him to stop defiling shoes?"

"It's only your shoes," Marlee said like it wasn't a big deal. "He also likes Scotty's shirts." She took a deep breath. "And pretty much anything that moves. Especially bicycles… Hence the leg. That's a touchy subject, though, so we don't talk about it around him."

Of course, because Lothario was a super smart wheezing-detection device. One wouldn't want to offend him.

"A bicycle? And it was moving?" Eli raised his eyebrows in her direction. His own dick retreated into his boxers at the idea.

Not that he hadn't noticed the cast on the little dude's leg. He'd just assumed it had come from getting caught on the wrong side of a pair of Sketchers. Not the rubber on a bicycle tire.

"But he won't do that when his vest is on. He knows he's working now," Marlee assured, setting Lothario beside her. He stood at attention as if illustrating her point.

Eli, and his shoes, didn't buy the innocent act of the chihuahua.

"Why don't you leave his vest on all the time then?" That's what Eli would do—out of respect for his shoes, sweaters, and non-motorized transportation, if nothing else.

"He deserves a break sometimes." Marlee opened the door and headed outside. "No one wants to work all the time. You understand that."

Of course, he did. Eli could use a break, too, come to think of it. "He'll only tell you if you're wheezing when he's wearing the shirt thing?"

"That'd be ridiculous. He'll always tell me, but he knows he has to behave like a professional when he's in uniform."

"How much does one of these dogs cost?" Eli asked, pulling the door shut behind them.

She lifted a shoulder. "Not much, around sixty."

Sixty? The gears in Eli's mind cranked.

He stared at her blankly. "Sixty thousand?"

Yeah, definitely, the ridiculous part of the dog was that he only stopped defiling things when he wore his vest—not the fact she'd dropped enough on him to buy a new car.

"Training is expensive." There was that *duh* voice again. "Are we grabbing stuff for breakfast or what?"

Definitely grabbing stuff for breakfast. And apparently, taking along the dog.

Chapter Three

MARLEE HAD SPENT many Saturday mornings with Eli and Sadie and their family. She was very familiar with teenaged Eli's pancake-making skills, and over the years, he'd clearly honed them further.

After a quick trip to the market, Eli had all they needed to make breakfast. Her bedroom was nearly all boxed up, and she was now being fed by the man Denver's *5280* magazine called "the most up-and-coming chef of his generation."

Except he was making her help.

And Marlee didn't cook.

Like, at all.

She preferred to use the telephone to call for takeout. The kitchen at the townhouse was more for show than function. Her interior decorator had never really understood that. She totally earned her commission, though, because the flinger thing Marlee found in the drawer was really cute. The handle had adorable yellow sunflowers—Marlee's favorite.

"Mar?" Eli asked.

She glanced toward him and raised her eyebrows. "Yeah?"

He pointedly moved his gaze to the skillet in front of her.

The bubbles on the pancake burst through the batter, starting at the edge and moving toward the center.

"On it." She focused. Waiting.

Eli's instructions were to wait until the batter bubbled in the center and then she should flip it. That was way easier said than done. So far, she'd burned two batches by not flipping quickly enough and she'd flopped batter everywhere once. He'd said she flipped too soon. Clearly, by the batter splatters all over the stovetop. Meanwhile, he cracked eggs into a pan and fried up bacon like it was the easiest thing in the world.

She happened to know it wasn't. He had tried to teach her to cook eggs and bacon first, but there had been shells in her scrambled eggs and the whole batch had stuck to the non-stick coating. The bacon wasn't quite done when she'd pulled it off the burner. Apparently, bacon was not like steak where rare was a good thing.

Eli slipped behind her, close enough that it felt really nice.

She stilled. What was she supposed to do with his proximity? The bridal etiquette books said nothing about jilted brides and the appropriate amount of time before they could find comfort in another man's presence. Was this one of the stages of a breakup? She had no idea, but two hours likely wasn't long enough. She was barely single. The ink on her not-a-divorce wasn't even dry.

This was ridiculous. Eli watching from behind was fine. He wasn't touching her or anything. She turned her attention to the pancake.

His fingers curled around hers on the spatula.

Well, hell. Her heart beating faster and all the little nerve endings in her skin perking up only happened because Scotty hadn't really touched her in weeks. Not since he'd moved downstairs.

"Now," Eli said into the air around her earlobe. It felt intimate and right when it was absolutely wrong.

He used her hand to slip the yellow flinger part of the spatula under the batter. Her shoulders hunched, her chin dipped, and Eli was all about control of the flipping.

"It's all in the wrist," he continued on like he wasn't turning her into a puddle of pancake batter that Lothario would have to lick off the floor. "Relax your wrist."

She gave relaxing her wrist her best effort. With Eli's help, they flipped the golden-brown, perfect pancake.

"I did it." She turned around and froze.

Their hands still held the spatula and the pancake continued to cook behind her, but Eli was right *there*. Right in her space. And he was cooking for her. And teaching her how to cook. And her stomach was fluttering. And her bottom lip felt full. And he had the smallest splatter of batter on his cheek from when she'd flipped and then flopped before.

She wiped the batter off with the edge of her thumb.

He stepped back, clearly startled.

"Sorry." She held up her hand. The one with the batter splatter.

He massaged his jaw with his palm and fingertips, apparently testing for additional splatterage.

"I got it all," Marlee assured him.

"Uh." Eli handed over the spatula, an odd expression on his face. "Pancake's done."

"Yeah." Marlee moved the pancake to a plate, only creating the tiniest of rips in the process. "I did it." She waved the flinging part of the spatula, whacking Eli in the nose. "Oh my gosh." She dropped the spatula. It hit the tile with a clank.

Eli held his nose. "I'm fine. Just an accident."

Marlee bent to grab the utensil, ready to crawl into the empty pantry and pretend to search for…whatever else went into making breakfast. She grabbed the spatula and stood, bonking her head right on the oven handle. "Ow."

She rubbed at the spot, the kitchen tilting a little.

Eli steadied her, his hands on either side of her shoulders.

"Maybe you should eat something. Before you give one of us a concussion."

"Yeah." She pressed the sensitive spot at the top of her skull.

"Are you okay?" he asked.

"I'm fine." Her eyes met his, and darn it all, he really looked concerned. Which was nice. Nice to have someone look concerned. No one ever looked concerned about her. Not really. Not lately. The day was not a good one, for sure, but Eli was there for her—so little wins for the win.

"Grab a drink, go sit, and I'll get you a plate." Eli was already adding the slightly torn pancake to a plate and moving to the eggs. He handed it over, but she set it aside.

She hugged him. She couldn't help it. "Thank you."

Then something happened. Eli Howard hugged her back. And it wasn't because she was crying and jilted, it wasn't because she'd hit her head. Eli Howard hugged her back and she had no idea why, other than the fact that he was just a nice guy. "Anytime, Mar."

"Leelee?" Scotty called from the foyer.

Was it her imagination or did Eli pull her tighter for just a split second?

"Leelee?" Scotty's voice went a teensy bit higher. He'd apparently made it to the kitchen.

She pulled away from Eli and turned to face her ex. Her ex who looked like he was ready to bite Eli's head off like a torn-up pancake.

Little wins were just not going to cut it today. She couldn't open her lips to respond.

"Wow, you have company." Scotty opened his eyes bigger in Marlee's general direction. She knew his mannerisms, knew he wasn't jazzed that Eli was making himself at home in their kitchen. Wasn't happy that she'd splattered batter every-where. Scotty liked his space to be a calm oasis.

Well, whatever.

"I didn't realize you were having friends over." He shifted his gaze toward her group of friends shuffling into the kitchen from the stairs.

"They're my friends, so…" She forked a bite of pancake and shoved it in her mouth.

He focused on her and only her, like he used to long ago. Long before they'd gotten so comfortable with each other. Dated. Fallen in love. Planned a wedding.

"I'll get my bag and get out of here," he said only to her.

He was getting his bag? She choked on the soft cake. A little kernel of hope grew in her chest that she wouldn't have to be the one to leave after all.

"You're moving out?" That would be fantastic. Her Gucci collection was so much happier with tons of breathing room in her walk-in closet instead of crammed together in a box. "That's great that you're leaving. I mean, not great that you're leaving." She took a breath. "It's great that you're being reasonable about this and letting me have the house."

He didn't say anything.

No one else said anything.

"You are leaving, right?"

"Maybe we should do this where there's not an audience," he said in response to her question, as though that were actually an answer.

"I think an audience is great." Eli crossed his arms, sunflower-yellow spatula in hand. If anyone could pull off that look, he could. "Witnesses and all that."

Marlee may not have been on her A-game all morning. Heck, she hadn't even been on her D-game. But the way Eli held the spatula right then made her feel like she'd had mimosas with the pancakes instead of coffee. She was nearly positive that one could not get drunk off one bite of Eli's pancakes.

"You're moving out then?" Marlee asked again, the hope of before eroding away.

Scotty deeply exhaled through his nose. "I figured I'd take off for a little bit. We'll both get our bearings before any more big decisions are made."

Decisions like who got the house?

Eli made a noise that sounded like a half growl.

"You mean you don't want to be in town when people start calling," Marlee confirmed. He would leave that to her. Of course, he would. She'd always handled things like that.

Scotty pinched the bridge of his nose. "I figured I'd give you some space. I know this"—he gestured between them and to her friends—"wasn't expected."

"So…not moving out." You didn't live with someone for a decade and not know how they handled things. Scotty wouldn't move out. Scotty would continue to rely on her parents. Scotty wouldn't understand that there was something wrong with that.

"Of course, I'm not moving, this is my home. We went over this earlier on the patio."

"Where are you goin'?" Eli asked like that was the most important question. "Is it a trip?"

"Yeah, Scotty, where *are* you going?" Kellie moved in to flank Marlee on the right. Sadie was on her left. Becca right behind. And Eli? A vein in his forehead pulsed in a way that probably wasn't super healthy.

"We're all so curious," Becca said over a mouthful of bacon. Scotty hated it when people talked with their mouth full. Total pet peeve.

"Leelee." Scotty tilted his head toward his office-turned-bedroom. "A minute."

"Don't do it, Marlee." Sadie linked her arm with Marlee's. "He can say, right here, where he's going."

Scotty looked between all of them and then at Lothario, who currently ignored him and, instead, eyeballed Eli's shoe. "Your parents offered me their condo in St. Lucia."

Another knife pierced her heart. "You mean the one where we were going to spend our honeymoon?"

He pinched his lips together. "It's not like that."

"That's a little cliché, Scotty." Becca had swallowed the bacon. "Even for you."

Scotty opened his mouth to reply. Then he shut it without a word coming out.

"By 'offered,' you mean you asked them if you could stay there?" It wasn't like Marlee didn't know how Scotty worked. And she knew her parents even better. Scotty had gone to their place, told them he'd broken it off, and asked if he could use their condo. They'd said yes, so he'd grabbed a venti caramel latte from Starbucks, drank it on the café patio, and then returned home in time for the impromptu pancake party.

"Leelee, I know you're upset, but this isn't supposed to—"

"I think you should probably go," Eli said before Scotty could get the rest out.

"Who are you?" Scotty asked, his forehead scrunching. "Exactly?"

Eli stalked toward him, spatula at the ready. "I'm the caterer. We met when you picked out hand salads and carrot tarts."

Marlee could tell the instant Scotty remembered. He'd been a bit of a pill the day they'd picked out the hors d'oeuvres. Marlee had insisted he come along, take some part in the wedding planning. He hadn't wanted to. She'd assumed he just preferred his time on the golf course, but she was now pretty sure it was because he had known the wedding wouldn't happen.

"And you're here because…?" Scotty asked, drawing out the last word.

"Because I invited him." Marlee stepped forward. "And you're being rude, so you should go." Her words came out breathier than she wanted them to.

Lothario let out a bark.

"This isn't how I wanted us to be." Scotty backed up, palms toward Marlee. "I'll just grab my suitcase and get out of here."

His suitcase. His suitcase for their honeymoon. Their honeymoon to start their marriage. Their marriage that would have existed because he'd proposed. He'd proposed because he loved her more. She didn't move, only vaguely aware that her friends were all there, Scotty was there, and Lothario was barking his little head off.

His alert bark. It took only a moment for her to realize she had been holding her breath. No, not holding it. Her chest had gone tight. A vise around her lungs and throat. She wasn't pulling air like she should. Her exhale sounded like her esophagus had sprung a leak.

Dammit.

She tried harder to pull a breath.

"Marlee?" Sadie shook her. "Where's your inhaler?"

Lothario was going bananas.

She pushed against her chest.

"The cabinet with the plates," she tried to say.

The closest inhaler was in the cabinet. She struggled to say it again, but Scotty grabbed the red tube and held it to Marlee's lips like he'd done a thousand times before. She inhaled at the exact moment he pressed the cannister, an orchestrated dance she'd have to start doing on her own. She grabbed the container from him, gripping it tight in her palm. "I've got it."

Scotty let go, and for the first time since he'd broken it off, Marlee realized that once upon a time she'd loved him. And he'd always said he loved her more. And there was a time when it wasn't on autopilot. He'd said it and they'd both believed it.

"Why did you say I was the best thing that ever happened

to you?" And now she was crying again. Tears trailed down her cheeks.

He didn't answer. Only shook his head.

This was the last time, the very last time, she'd ever cry over him. He didn't deserve her tears. She wiped them away with the back of her hand.

"Sadie, you'll watch her? Make sure it doesn't happen again? She'll probably need another puff in a minute and then her steroid treatment tonight." Scotty's voice was rougher than usual.

Scotty didn't need to brief them. Marlee could manage this on her own.

"We've got this," Eli replied. Sometime in the middle of everything, he'd picked up Lothario and held him in his grip.

"Then I'll just…" Scotty shook his head and moved to the office, closing the door behind him.

"So… Vegas?" Sadie linked her arm tighter with Marlee's.

Marlee nodded.

Yes, Vegas was sounding better and better.

Chapter Four

WHEN ELI HAD WOKEN up that morning, he'd expected to spend the day prepping the four-course meal for Marlee's wedding. Nowhere, in any of the many recesses of his brain, had he even considered that he'd end the day with his jean-clad ass on a leather bench seat of a hot-pink Lincoln stretch limousine, a crystal champagne flute in his hand, purple lights flashing over his head, and a chihuahua with his leg in a cast passed out on his sneakers. All while they cruised the Vegas Strip and his baby sister chattered away with her three best friends about all the shit he did not need to know.

"Whatever happened to that guy with the goatee?" Becca asked Sadie.

She flinched and shook her head. "It was a no go."

"'cause he had that whole foot thing she wasn't into," Kellie said as though Eli wasn't sitting there and they weren't discussing his little sister.

He shivered at the thought of Sadie and a guy with a goatee or *any* kind of foot thing.

"I'm right here, ladies." Eli pointed to his chest.

"Jump right on in anytime." Kellie leaned over the space

between their bench seats and faux whispered in his personal space, "You're just one of the girls this weekend."

And wasn't that fun?

"When did that happen with Goatee Guy? I thought you two were trying to make it work?" Marlee was in her element with her girlfriends, all thoughts of Scotty clearly pushed aside for the trip.

But Eli had been there during her asthma attack, had a first-row seat to Scotty jumping right in to help her, and the look in Marlee's eyes when it registered that what they had was ending. All the declarations from before breakfast about her being over him dissolved like an antacid in a tall glass of bubbly. Marlee had put on a good front, recovered from the slip quickly, Eli gave her that. But he could see Scotty's damage. And he was pretty sure Scotty saw it, too. Not that he felt bad for the guy—but he'd looked like Lothario must've when the bike tire got him.

Eli tossed back the exceptionally expensive champagne in his glass.

He shouldn't have crashed the girls' weekend. But at the same time, he didn't want to end up on a twelve-hour emergency drive to bail them out of trouble when the call came in. Sadie might be a successful attorney these days, Kellie an accountant, Becca a—what the hell did Becca do for work?— but when the four of them all got together, they had a history of not making the best choices.

Case in point? Three years ago, they'd all decided to go zip-lining for their semiannual meet-up and not one of them had considered filling the gas tank before heading up to Idaho Springs. The whole batch of them got stuck on the side of the mountain, and he'd been the one on call to bring Marlee's Jaguar F-Pace a fresh tank of gasoline. Or—and he still had no idea how this one even happened—two years ago when Marlee and Kellie had managed to handcuff themselves together using Kellie's then cop-boyfriend's work-issued handcuffs. Becca had swallowed the key, for reasons still unknown. Eli had ended up sawing off the bracelets with a hacksaw.

Yep, these girls in Sin City required on-site supervision.

Also, the four of them hadn't given him any choice in his attendance. Marlee had booked his ticket before he'd given the A-OK.

Marlee leaned over and refilled his glass of bubbly. "Don't you look reflective."

"Thinking of all the times I've had to bail out your asses over the years." Thank fuck they only got together twice a year. Well, three times this year since Marlee had the whole wedding shindig going on.

"You love us." Marlee maneuvered herself to sit next to him.

Even though Marlee was from old money in Denver, her parents had believed attending public school for a few years would be good for her. Show her that it's not all about a bank account. That's how she'd met her friends. They'd spent their teenage years getting into trouble together, and he'd bet her parents rethought that stance on public school more than once throughout those years. But by that time, it'd been too late.

"What would you do without us keeping you on your toes?" Marlee asked.

"I would read a book, Mar." He took the most masculine sip of fizzy booze that he could manage. "Maybe take up golf."

She flinched. Golf was Scotty's game.

Shit.

"I would've hated the golf, so you saved me from that." He tried for recovery.

"At least there's good champagne." She held up the cloth napkin–wrapped bottle, little rivulets of condensation soaking the black label underneath her manicured thumb.

Eli really would've preferred a beer. Or a couple fingers of whiskey. But Marlee didn't skimp, and he was personally affronted by anyone who would let good *Dom Pérignon* go to waste.

His phone buzzed beside him.

Jase.

Eli glanced over the message. His buddy Jase had an engagement party coming up next week. Since his fiancée was out with her girls, Jase wanted to know if Eli could hang out at their other buddy's—Brek's—bar that night. Yes, Eli wanted to. He sagged in the seat, tilted his head toward the ceiling of the car, and stared at the purple lights above. He'd made his Vegas bed when he shoved his duffle bag into the overhead compartment and sat his ass in one of the first-class seats Marlee had splurged on for all of them.

He tossed back the rest of his champagne and held it out to Marlee for a refill.

She didn't hesitate.

"You know what we should do?" Sadie asked. "We should play the game we made up that time in Cabo. Remember?"

"The dare game." Becca squealed. "I forgot about that. Let's do it."

"This game sounds like it's going to end with one, or all, of us making regrettable decisions." Eli balanced the flute of champagne on his knee.

"Of course, it will." Becca topped off her champagne. "That's the point. Marlee needs to loosen up after the day she's had."

"And we literally packed up all of her possessions in less than two hours," Kellie chimed in. "So, I think, we all need a bit of fun."

"That wasn't *all* of my possessions," Marlee said with a huff.

"Enough of them that we deserve some unwind time," Kellie amended.

"Okay, so"—Marlee flashed a pair of jazz hands—"I've

been thinking. Since Scotty is out of the picture, I need to get my life back together. Step one, come to Vegas."

"Step two, play the dare game." Becca lifted her cup.

"What's step three?" Eli asked, more than a little afraid of the answer.

"Step three is to be determined." Marlee nodded like she was totally in charge of her life.

Becca poured more champagne, listing a bit to the right. "I like getting Marlee's life back together. We should get her life back together every few months."

"Who's going to go first?" Sadie's gaze shifted between all of them, landing on Eli. "Boys first."

"I don't even know how to play the game." And he would bet he was better off for it.

Becca's cheeks were already a tad drunk-flushed. "It's easy. You just dare one of us to do something. Then we do it."

Well, that was a stupid game.

"It's like truth or dare, but no truth questions." Marlee leaned in, poking him with her elbow. "Unless you want truth questions instead. It's been awhile since we played. We can make new rules."

"I dare any of you?" Eli asked. "Anything I want?"

"And when that person is done, they dare someone else." Becca dug through the limo's minibar.

This game might actually work out okay if he played it right. "I dare all of you to leave me at the hotel with a six-pack of beer and free cable while you spend the next few hours at the spa." The Broncos were playing. He could still catch the game. And the girls could have their fun at a spa—they'd spent a large portion of the flight detailing all they wanted to get done there. Win. Win. Win. And no one had to hit the craps table.

"No." Marlee dropped the bottle of champagne in the silver bucket beside the minibar. "Since I'm the jilted bride, I reserve the right to veto any and all dares."

"It's true," Sadie said over a sip of Dom. "I think we wrote that in the rules when we first played."

"You"—Eli pointed a finger at her—"lie."

"Maybe, but we haven't added the truth portion of the game." Sadie shrugged.

"New rule. Since Eli's dare was rejected by Marlee, he has to answer a question." Becca was having way too much fun making up rules to a nonexistent game.

"I have one." Sadie winked at him. "What's your beef with relationships?"

They were going to play all their cards right up front then.

"I don't have any beef with relationships." Question answered. Onward.

"That's not true. You have to tell the truth." Sadie shook her head slowly.

"You have to tell the truth or we all get a question," Becca said, a bundle of cheer and made-up rules.

"I'll go next," Kellie said. "Why aren't you ever in relationships if you don't have any *beef* with them?"

"I already answered my question." He poured himself another glass. Looked like he'd need it. "No more questions."

"We all get a question," Marlee announced. "Marlee's trip, Marlee's rules."

"I don't like this game." Eli leveled a glare at his sister, hoping maybe blood would run thicker than champagne and she would take his side on this.

"Don't look at me, bud." Sadie pinched her lips into a thin smile. She was enjoying this way too much.

Marlee rolled her eyes and made a sour face. "There has to be some benefit to all the crap that happened today."

They wanted to know why he didn't do the commitment thing? He didn't do relationships because he didn't do long term. He didn't do long term because he didn't want anyone to rely on him. He'd done that dance and had the permanent bruises stomped onto his feet to prove it. He didn't have any desire for a repeat. Things worked out better when it was just number one and number one alone. He did what he wanted. Came and went when he wanted. And no one was there to tell him he should do things differently.

With four pairs of eyes trained on him, he decided to go with the easiest dodge he could find. "I've just never met anyone worth the effort."

Partially true. Not a lie. But also not the entire truth.

"Okay, my question next," Marlee announced. "If you had to shag one of us, which one would it be and why? Sadie is excluded from the scenario, for obvious reasons."

Eli met Marlee's gaze, a fire sparking in her eyes. It may have only been a question, but it sure as hell felt like a dare. "All of you. Can't pick just one, it wouldn't be fair."

Sadie snorted.

"Eli is the worst at this game," Becca huffed. "New rule, let's move on."

Let's move on was a rule? How was that a rule?

"I'll go next. Since he picked me to shag." Kellie rubbed her hands together like she was about to have a lot of fun with this one.

"I picked all of you." Eli leaned back against the leather seat as they pulled up to the Bellagio, the champagne bubbling through his bloodstream.

"But we know you meant me." Kellie leaned forward to pat his leg. "I'm going to dare Marlee."

Kellie didn't get further than that before the limo reached the bell station.

A bellman opened the door to let them escape the confines of the dare-ridden limousine. And not a moment too soon.

"Ms. Medford?" he asked.

"That's me." Marlee lifted a sleepy Lothario, tucking him in her handbag. His head stuck out over the top as she slid from the vehicle. "I'm the perpetual Ms. Medford."

"Welcome to the Bellagio." The bellman held his hand out to help her steady herself on those insane platform heels. "The penthouse is ready for you and your guests."

Marlee had reserved the penthouse for them?

Of course, she had. She was Marlee.

"Kellie?" Marlee asked once they were all out of the limo and headed inside the marble lobby. "Let's get this party started." She turned to her friend. "Present your dare."

Those were usually famous last words, but he was there to ensure, this time, they wouldn't be.

Kellie held up her cell phone. "It's almost amateur hour at the strip joint near Fremont Street."

"I'm not hearing a dare in that." Marlee blinked with an innocence he knew was utter bullshit.

Kellie cleared her throat. "I dare you take a turn on the pole."

"Fun." Marlee did a shoulder lift and sauntered toward the concierge.

Well. Fuck.

Chapter Five

MARLEE NEVER WOULD'VE THOUGHT DANCING with a pole could be so freeing. And yet, she was having the best time with her girlfriends—and Eli. Of course, Lothario was there, too. Given the amount they'd had to drink, the dog was the official designated sober one.

They'd moved on to the next jaunt of their evening of fun, and it involved tattoos.

The tattoo parlor near the strip joint Kellie had discovered specialized in both permanent and henna tats. Also, adult toys and an impressive variety of condoms, it seemed. Who freaking knew there were so many kinds of protection? After the girls had all had a turn on the pole, Becca's dare landed them right there in the tattoo shop.

"It says if you use a little lemon juice and salt, it'll come right off." Marlee searched through the Google app on her phone to find out how Eli might remove the henna facial tattoo before it wore down on its own after approximately four weeks.

Not that he'd asked her to look it up for him, but she'd seen the expression on the un-inked half of his face when he looked into the mirror after the tattoo artist was done. Red henna ink made its way across one side of his forehead, along his jaw, and down his chin in a tribal pattern.

That expression? The one on Eli's face when he saw the handiwork in the mirror? Yeah, not a look of joy.

Then again, Eli rarely had a look of joy. He was a man with a practiced look of indifference. Like, if he were a bouncer, he would have always had his bouncer face on. You either knew exactly where you stood with Eli or had no idea at all.

She thumbed through the other ideas the Internet presented for henna removal. "You can also try rubbing alcohol, but that's hell on your pores, so avoid that."

When she'd been a teenager, she'd had a bout of acne that the prescription stuff wasn't touching, so she'd tried rubbing alcohol. It'd stripped the hell out of her skin. She'd sworn never to do that again. Always go straight for the laser treatments. Don't mess with the creams.

"No rubbing alcohol, got it." Eli spun the display rack of condoms so that the plastic packages rattled together. He chugged a swig from the beer bottle in his other hand. "I'll save the alcohol for my liver."

On their way to the tattoo parlor, they'd hit up one of the convenience stores to keep the alcohol flowing, hence the beer in Eli's fist and the vodka shooters tucked in Marlee's cleavage. Everyone was getting matching real tattoos—a little heart right below one of their ankle bones. Everyone but Eli, who had said no to the real deal and ended up with the regrettable henna covering half of his face instead.

The whole thing was Becca's dare, but the heart was Marlee's idea. The henna facial tattoo was Sadie's.

The heart tattoo meant a lot to Marlee. The official third step of Marlee's new life plan. If there was anything she'd learned in the past twenty-four hours, it was that she couldn't rely on a man for happily ever after. There was no great love story for her, but her friends would always be there for her.

They were her happily ever after. They would have to be her great love story.

"We'll save the rubbing alcohol as a last resort." Marlee tucked the phone in her bra. "The pores on your face are actually really delicate."

"My pores are delicate?" Eli leaned against the counter. Taunting. Sexy.

Blah. No.

Finding Eli sexy had no place in getting her life back in order. Besides, nothing about Eli was delicate, and she absolutely couldn't think of him as sexy, even if he was. Her hormones were just all jacked up from the jilting. This was simply a touch of the cliché best-friend's-brother infatuation.

The fact that the face ink was ridiculously hot on Eli was merely a universal truth. Undisputable. It had nothing to do with Marlee's desire to rebel. Not. A. Thing.

Marlee shook off the inventory of his hotness scale.

"Not just *your* pores are delicate, everyone's are," she said. There, that sounded normal. Not like she'd been checking him out...or thinking about how he was there, and she was there, and he was standing right next to a whole tower of safe sex, and she had vodka in her bra, and that sounded like a lot of fun.

"Your ankle okay?" Eli glanced pointedly toward the new heart.

Marlee's ankle was the first to go under the needle, and the little tattoo hurt like a sonofabitch. She wouldn't be getting another anytime soon. Scotty didn't believe in tattoos. Which was—Marlee was certain—the catalyst for Becca's dare. Marlee enjoyed looking at tats. She had been an art major in college and completed a whole paper on tattoos as artwork. That paper hadn't been hard to write—she loved studying all the different types of ink and the process of creating something that a person would wear forever.

"It hurts a little, but not too bad now." Marlee stood,

leaving Lothario lounging in his doggie bag, and moved next to Eli. "It means a lot that everyone's doing this. Not just the tattoos, but the weekend. I feel like I've been so out of touch with the world."

"You girls know how to have a party." Eli slung his arm around her shoulder, tucking her into his side.

"You sure you don't want a heart tattoo?" Marlee looked up at him, her hand resting against his firm pectoral muscles. He wasn't against tattoos. He already had a whole sleeve of tats. She'd seen him in his chef's jacket with the sleeves rolled up during their tasting.

Whoever had done Eli's was an exceptional artist. What started at the wrist as a tree trunk branched into a mosaic of skin graffiti that could've easily graced the cover of *Inked* magazine or won one of those television tattoo competitions.

"I'm sure. You girls should just enjoy your tats." Eli smiled down at her.

She wasn't ashamed to say that his approval made her want to lick all the ink on his arms. It just did. Fact of nature.

"I'm glad you're here." Marlee pulled a little glass bottle of vodka from her cleavage and took a sip.

Eli raised his eyebrows.

"Want some?" She offered the bottle to him.

He set his beer aside, wrapped his lips around the shooter, and tilted it onto his tongue. Her own lips went dry, and her salivary glands kicked into overdrive.

The static buzz she'd been feeling around him intensified. She could've sworn he was going to kiss her. Lean in. Press his mouth to hers. And she bet he tasted amazing.

"Check it out, this one makes your dick look like a tuxedo." Eli broke free of the moment, passed her the vodka, and grabbed one of the condoms on the rack next to her, holding up the package.

With the moment effectively fractured, she re-capped the

shooter, tucked it back in her cleavage, and sauntered to the other side of the display.

"That's better than the SpongeBob one." Marlee held up the offending condom. "I'm just saying that if your penis is dressed like a cartoon character, it's not getting anywhere near my pineapple under the sea," she continued.

Eli started whistling the *SpongeBob SquarePants* theme song.

"Don't let my brother anywhere near your pineapple." Sadie emerged from the curtain separating the front area from the tattoo table in the back.

"No one is getting near my pineapple for a very long time," Marlee assured. Not that anyone had been under the sea for a while—not since what seemed like forever ago when Scotty decreed they should push pause on that portion of their relationship so their wedding night would be even more special.

"But when they do, they should be wearing a tuxedo." Sadie grabbed the tuxedo condom from Eli and tossed it to Marlee. "My treat. I'll have them add it to the bill."

Marlee held up the plastic-wrapped condom. "You're always so thoughtful."

"I am, aren't I?" Sadie replied, her head tilted to the side.

Marlee tucked the condom in her bra, next to her phone.

"How much shit can you fit in there?" Eli asked, staring at her chest. He wasn't staring inappropriately, more like he was genuinely asking the question.

"There's not that much," Marlee said. "It's easier than carting around a second purse."

"Because your first purse is reserved for the dog," Eli confirmed.

Well, yes. She pressed her eyebrows together and nodded at him.

"Eli, are you sure you don't want to reconsider a real tattoo?" Sadie tilted her ankle to admire the fresh little heart tat.

"Eli already has his tattoo," Eli replied, gesturing to his face.

"That hardly counts." Sadie dropped beside Lothario on the imitation leather sofa. "Don't you want something permanent to remember your first girls' trip?"

"Not particularly." Eli was acting all aloof. "But I will take a SpongeBob condom. You never know when a lucky lady may be in the mood for cartoon sex."

Eli acted like he didn't have a care in the world, but Marlee knew him better than that. He pushed people away, sure. The first inkling that someone needed him, though? He was right there. Case in point? Marlee's house that morning. Second case in point? This trip.

"Eli won't need the tattoo. He'll always have the memories, won't you, Eli?" Marlee asked.

"Memories and approximately four weeks of a face tattoo." He lifted his beer to her.

Becca emerged from the curtain next. "Okay, so we've done the dancing and the tattoos. The dare game has been fun, but I think it's time to say goodbye."

"Agreed," Eli mumbled.

"For our next game, we'll all hang out at the Luxor and try to pick up members of the Blue Man Group. First one to get laid with a blue dick wins." She followed her declaration of the game with a dance move fitting of the pole.

"Marlee has to get him to wear a tuxedo condom when she gets her Blue Man," Sadie added. "It's a rule."

"You know how black is slimming and white kinda makes us all look fat?" Becca asked.

"I so do," Marlee replied. It was one of the hardest parts of New York's Fashion Week.

"What do you suppose the blue paint does to their dicks?" Becca dropped to the couch on the other side of Sadie. "Lengthen or…?"

"Absolutely no more booze for you." Eli grabbed a bottle

of water from the plastic grocery sack he'd snagged at the convenience store. He popped off the lid like it was a beer bottle and handed it to her. "Drink that."

"Aye, Cap'n Eli." Becca saluted him and then spilled a solid quarter of the water down the front of her silk blouse.

"I just had the best idea." Sadie stopped stroking Lothario's head and pointed between Eli and Marlee. "You two should get married."

Say what? Marlee's blood pressure rose, and she did her best to ignore what her best friend had just said and focused instead on the idea that blue paint might possibly make a penis look smaller.

"Why would this be the best idea?" Eli asked as calm as though he were ordering a Corona at the swim-up Bellagio bar.

He grabbed another bottle of water and handed it to Sadie.

She took it. "Not really married, just the motions. To prove to both of you that it's not scary."

"I never said I was scared of marriage," Marlee said quickly. "I'm all for it. Was ready to do it this weekend. Not feeling like I need to prove that again."

With her luck, she'd get to the altar and then get left again. No, thank you.

"Great, then it's just Eli with marriage issues," Sadie said, all sugar and honey.

Eli glared at her, his forehead all scrunched up. "I don't have marriage issues."

"We all know you do. But hear me out, it's like therapy." Sadie started talking with her hands like she was in the court-room and Eli was on the interrogation stand.

"I can assure you, this is not like therapy," Eli practically growled.

"Objection, Your Honor," Becca said with a giggle. "Eli didn't wait for the question."

"I'll allow it," Marlee said, electing herself to the judge position in this new game of *Taunt the Eli*.

"For fuck's sake." He closed his eyes and inhaled deeply.

Marlee wasn't going to marry him. He didn't have anything to worry about.

"Isn't there a kind of therapy where you force people to do the things that make them uncomfortable?" Sadie asked Becca.

"There is immersion therapy, but I'm pretty sure this wouldn't fall into that category. But"—Becca paused dramatically—"it would be fun to watch."

"That's the truth," Kellie added.

"Do I get a say at all in this?" Marlee asked. "As the self-appointed judge, I feel like I should get a say."

"You're not really getting married. Just the motions," Sadie said.

Oh, like she'd done for the past year? She knew all about that.

"You know what? I'll get the tattoo." Eli released a deep sigh.

"What?" Becca tilted her ear toward Eli. "I didn't hear that. What did you say?"

Eli ran a hand over his face. "I do this and then we drop the Blue Man game. We sure as fuck drop the Eli-gets-married game. We just go back to the hotel and think about the things we've done. The things we've seen. Because even though I did my best not to, I saw the start of what you did to that poor pole back there, Sadie. And I'll never be the same."

Marlee smiled like she was reliving the show. Sadie had rocked it. That's what she'd done. And they'd all kept their clothes on, so it wasn't *that* bad.

"Here's what I propose." Becca stuck her finger in the air like she'd had ten too many of her own cleavage shots. "You get that heart tat."

Marlee tried to understand her. Wasn't that what they'd just decided?

"On my arm," Eli clarified.

"On your penis for all I care." Becca wobbled a tad.

Eli flinched.

"Then we'll put a pin in the idea of the Blue Man orgy until after another round of drinks," she finished, pausing while they all stared at her.

"Done," Eli said.

All right then, Eli was going to get inked after all.

Chapter Six
NEARLY MIDNIGHT

"I CAN'T BELIEVE THEY CRASHED." Marlee's friends had all passed out while they binge-watched the new *Gilmore Girls*—Marlee's favorite. Despite Becca's insistence that they head over to the Luxor, the pit stop at their penthouse had turned out to be just what they needed—her friends, not her. She was still ready to play. They were definitely not.

Kellie snored softly from where she'd stretched out on the floor, Lothario under her arm.

"They were pretty drunk." Eli stretched on the sofa, his body long enough for his toes to touch one end while his head rested on the opposite pillowed armrest.

"Then why aren't we?" Marlee asked. This wasn't fair at all. She was practically sober. And it's not like she hadn't given it her best effort.

Eli winked at her. The dimples in his cheeks, which she rarely saw, peeked from beside his lips. "Because we are the responsible ones."

That was unacceptable. Marlee stood, dropping her blanket to the floor.

"C'mon." She grabbed her phone and little wallet, shoving them in her bra.

"Mar?" Eli's eyes grew bigger.

She mimicked his expression. "Eli?"

"It's late." He didn't stand.

"It's, like, midnight. We cannot be those people who are in bed, in Vegas, by midnight."

"You mean like these people?" He gestured around the room. "Aren't they your people?"

"Totally not the point." She scrawled a note next to the phone. *Went out with Eli. Be back later.*

"You're going out with or without me, aren't you?" He ran a hand over his henna-tattooed face.

She lifted her eyebrows in response. "I think I'm going to go figure out what step four is in my life plan."

"Shit." He tossed his feet over the side of the couch and snagged Lothario. "Let's go, then."

THE RED BRICKS making up the wall outside of the one-story motel were more than a little wobbly. Marlee would bet if she pushed on them with her fingertip, they'd ripple. She tried it.

They didn't ripple.

She tried again.

Nope, still just a brick wall.

"Are you trying to push over the motel?" Eli asked, his voice rough. It had to be almost dawn. But then again, what the heck did she know?

"Maybe you should try?" she asked, leaning her shoulder blades onto the brick exterior of whatever this place was. It'd come with the marriage package Eli had purchased for her. They'd done the pretend wedding, proving to each other over green twist ties that neither of them had any issues with a wedding.

There had been enough lemon martinis to make the

edges of the world fuzzy and wrap her in a cocoon of lemon-flavored bliss. *Gah*, when was the last time she'd been this lit? Had this much fun?

She glanced over her shoulder at Eli, Lothario sleeping in the pink bag slung over his shoulder.

Motel key in hand, Eli stalked past her to open the door. He let her pass.

They'd chosen the palm paradise suite.

"It's amazing," she whispered.

Palm leaves were painted on the walls, and there were hanging vines draped throughout the room. The door clicked behind Eli. He set Lothario's bag on the floor.

And then he looked at her like he'd done at the tattoo parlor. Like he wanted to kiss her. And okay, maybe she was off her game, but a guy didn't get that flicker in his eyes for just anyone.

She was going to do it. Kiss him. Make sure she still had it.

Step five, kiss Eli (and enjoy it).

Before he could say anything, she stood on her tiptoes and lightly pressed her lips to his. Testing. Seeing if that's what he wanted.

He kissed her back.

Oh boy, did he kiss her back.

His tongue slid along the seam of her lips, his arms wrapped around her, and holy hell, her toes were actually curling. But this wasn't that kind of kiss. Not for long, anyway. This was the kind of kiss she hadn't had in years. The kind lit by pure desire and exploration. The kind that meant nothing and everything, because in that moment, it was both.

She melted into his embrace and let him do what he wanted to her. Tonight was all about nothing. And it was about everything. It was about Eli.

Mostly, though…it was about her.

He ran his hand down her back to the base of her spine.

She pressed against him, his very defined erection pressing against her belly.

She smiled into his kiss.

Yeah, she still had it.

Had it at that very moment, as a matter of fact.

Eli massaged her ass, pulling her against him, encouraging her to take whatever she wanted.

She wanted it all.

Pulling his shirt from his waistband, she helped him get it over his head. Then she did the same to hers, only breaking the kiss long enough to pull the fabric across her face, before going right back to devouring him.

She unhooked her bra, and he tossed it over his shoulder.

They were skin to skin. Her chest pressed against his pecs. His mouth against hers. The insanity of her life melted at her feet, melted because of him.

It was him. Maybe it'd always been him. Maybe it should've always been him. But right now? The past didn't count. It didn't matter. The future didn't matter, either. There was only now.

She pulled him backward with her, falling onto the bed with his body on top of hers. And the dance then started again—mouth to mouth, hands everywhere. He shoved her skirt up around her waist, and her panties were gone.

Neither of them spoke. The only sounds were that of two people who had had enough of the world and were taking solace in what their bodies could provide.

A release.

Two people who were, for the first time in forever, enjoying the act of sex for what it was. Not for what it should be. Or what it once was. But just letting it...be.

His hand found her heat while his mouth never left her own.

She dropped her head onto the pillow, her eyes rolling

backward as he massaged circles with his thumb—bringing her to the edge and letting her feel everything he felt.

His drunken gaze caught hers, his eyes dilated a tad too much, his breathing just a bit too shallow—just like hers. There was no henna tattoo. There was no broken engagement. There was no Las Vegas.

There was him.

There was her.

There was no condom.

Shit.

She pushed at his shoulders. "Condom."

"I prefer to be called Eli." He went back to kissing her.

Gah, no, he didn't get it. "We need a condom. It's in my bra."

He pulled back, his lips swollen and red from kissing. Her lipstick was smeared across his mouth.

She wiped at it with the pad of her thumb.

"We need a condom," she repeated.

His expression turned confused, and then, like a rubber band snapping back into itself, some memory seemed to fall into place. He lifted off of her, standing from the bed.

And that was that. Rejected twice in one day. She was just butter on a roll.

She pinched her eyes closed. If he left now, she'd fall apart. Disintegrate on the spot. There was no twelve-step life plan that could help her recover from the rejection.

But no. No, she wouldn't fall apart. After everything life had thrown at her, she'd kept it together. She wouldn't fall apart now.

Peeling open her eyelids, she followed his movements across the cheap motel room to her bra. He held up the tuxedo condom like he'd bet on red and the roulette ball just fell into the crimson slot. He started back toward the bed, a silly grin she'd never expected pasted on his lips. He paused and grabbed his wallet, pulling another condom from inside.

"Are we planning to have a big night tonight, Mr. Howard?" She giggled.

He crawled back over her on the bed, depositing the two condoms on the pillow. "I am, Mrs. H."

Her heart seemed to get warm at the sort-of endearment.

Then, Eli Howard did something she never would've expected. He chuckled and nuzzled her neck, right where her pulse kicked in the veins underneath her skin. His body was warm, they were both drunk, and his hands were exploring the skin along her ribcage up to her breasts.

She pulled his lips to hers. "No time for slow."

"Aye, captain." He shucked off his pants and she got a solid look at Eli naked.

Eli was impressive with clothes on. Without them? She shivered, spreading her thighs in invitation.

He handled the tuxedo condom and, dressed in his formal best, he drove home—hitting all the right spots and lighting her up like a firecracker.

If this was being married, then she could get used to it.

Married to Eli. She smiled to herself. Wasn't that the best joke ever?

Chapter Seven
THE DAY AFTER

THE PROBLEM with waking up married is that you're married. Wedded bliss. Or in the case of Eli, the biggest clusterfuck of his life.

He swallowed down an aspirin and glanced across the king-size hotel bed to where his new wife slept. Marlee was a helluva lot of Vegas fun, evidenced by the state of their motel room and his likely inability to walk.

He was a Las Vegas idiot with spotty memory and a wife.

A wife.

Sonofabitch.

A thin sheet covered him. She had the no-tell-motel-grade comforter burritoed around herself. Their clothes were… Well, they weren't on their bodies, that was for certain. He lifted the sheet to be sure, and no, he hadn't brought his pajamas to this sleepover.

He glanced at Lothario curled up in his own love nest made of Eli's shoes.

Eli's extremities went numb, and his lungs let out a breath seemingly on their own accord while he flipped through the mental film of the night before. There'd been a dare, there'd been a jilted bride, there'd been the caterer—that would be him—and there'd been twist-tie wedding rings and a ceremony.

He got the heart tattoo. They went back to the penthouse and the other girls passed out. He and Marlee got to talking. They had drinks. They decided to take Sadie up on her dare and go through the motions of a wedding ceremony for the photos. Just for the photos. Because wouldn't it be so funny?

Then they'd signed the papers because they were both too drunk to think straight.

Then there was the afterparty that was only between the two of them.

He was screwed tighter than the cap on a bottle of Two-Buck Chuck from Trader Joe's.

A screwed man with two choices. One, figure out a way to rewind time and rethink his choices from the night before. Or two, wake up Marlee so they could get to work on the annulment that needed to happen. Preferably before anyone else found out what they'd done.

The bridal suite—and he used that term ever so loosely—had come with the discount just-off-the-Vegas-Strip wedding package they'd purchased in a fit of drunken dare. In their mutual alcohol-induced stupors, he and Marlee had opted for the palm paradise room after they'd been married by a man in a Liberace costume. Eli hadn't known who Liberace was before the wedding. Why they'd chosen to stay at this place instead of in Marlee's suite at the Bellagio, only drunk Eli could say. And he wasn't around anymore.

Responsible Eli was now in control.

And he was married. The green twist tie Marlee had stuck on his left finger said so. He grabbed the stack of papers from the nightstand where he'd tossed them at some point the night before, searching out the marriage license. He said a prayer that they hadn't both signed it and his rusty memory was wrong.

Nope. The God of Vegas Marriages hadn't come through

for him. Two signatures graced the dotted lines. Two signatures that looked remarkably sober given their state the night before.

He groaned. They'd both signed it. They weren't supposed to sign it. They were supposed to pretend to sign it. Under no circumstances were they supposed to use their real names.

Then again, they weren't supposed to have had marital relations, either. His reflection in the gold-framed mirror on the ceiling over the mattress taunted him, so he turned away. That wasn't much better. The walls were painted with an overgrowth of palm leaves. A one-dimensional toucan gave him the side-eye from over the dresser and a stuffed monkey swung from a vine over the television. Marlee's bra was draped beside him, where he had tossed it the night before.

The Marlee he'd known from their teenage years was not the same woman who turned out to be a wildcat in paradise. That Marlee was reserved and polite. His wife? Well, she wasn't reserved, that was for sure.

"Eli?" Marlee asked with a just-woke-up confused twinge in her voice.

He turned to her, adjusting the sheet to cover his lower half. "Hey."

She peeled open her eyelids and stared at him. "Tell me this is a dream."

They'd gotten a license. They'd hit up some chapel off the Strip. This was not a joke. This was not a drill. This sucker was the real deal.

"Not a dream, Mar." Running a hand over his face, he was about eighteen hours past a five o'clock shadow. About six hours into his marriage with Marlee. And a solid thirty minutes before the aspirin kicked in.

"Shit." She pressed her fingertips to her eyelids.

Yep. He agreed with that sentiment. *Never*, he'd sworn he would *never* get married.

"My parents are going to kill me." Marlee rolled off the bed and landed on the floor with a *thunk.*

He leaned over the edge of the bed. She was fine. Dazed, but fine. He shook the bottle of aspirin and handed it to her. Drunk Eli was a bastard, but at least he remembered to get the aspirin.

Even in a mess of blankets on a motel floor, Marlee looked amazing. She might've had the same hangover as he did, but she didn't look it. Just the same Marlee he'd always known. The blanket slipped, exposing the edge of her breast. Marlee didn't have the fake breasts that one might expect on a socialite with her kind of money. Nope. They were all hers. Heavy in his palm, her brown nipples pert and ready for his mouth.

He knew this from firsthand experience.

"Your parents won't find out," he said, pretty certain they could tuck this away and no one would ever know.

The night before, he and Marlee had stumbled down the sidewalk to this room, laughing hysterically about what they'd done. They laughed about how pissed her ex-fiancé would be when he found out she'd gotten married without him and how funny her parents would find it.

Last night? Drunk last night? It was funny.

Today? Sober today? It was not funny.

"Mom and Dad are going to find out." Marlee shuffled to the sink, poured a glass of water, and took two aspirin. "They find out everything."

"Please don't tell your parents," Eli said. Marlee's parents were more than slightly overbearing. They were also wealthy beyond belief. And they were not going to be happy that Marlee had gotten married to the caterer in charge of the food for the wedding that never happened.

"I have to tell my parents." The comforter stayed wrapped around her body while Marlee rounded up her clothes. "They'll figure it out when we show up together married."

Every time she said the *m*-word, he swore a vein in his head erupted in a small aneurysm. "We're not going to stay… the way we are."

"We can't just not be married. Divorce takes time." The comforter slipped and she quickly pulled it up.

"Stop saying that."

"Divorce?"

"The *m*-word." Did he have to spell it out?

She pulled her bra from the vine over the television. "Married?"

For fuck's sake. "Stop."

She blinked hard at him. "What do you want to call it?"

"Let's just call it the mistake."

"Okay, we can't just not be mistaked. Divorce takes time."

There would be no divorce. There was no need for a divorce in a…mistake…that should have never happened.

"We are going to call Sadie and we're going to get this *thing* annulled." Not that he knew much, but he was pretty sure getting married while drunk in Vegas counted toward the qualifications for annulment. His attorney sister would be able to say for sure.

"Say it, Eli." Marlee leveled her gaze at him. "Marriage."

"No."

"Marriage," she said again.

If she kept at it, he'd be dead. Dead from multiple aneurysms. "I'm not saying it."

"Marriage." That time she drew it out, letting it melt on her tongue like the lemon drop martinis she'd drunk the night before.

He threw his arm over his eyes.

"Your sister was right. You do have an issue with marriage."

"Seriously, stop."

She stopped. They stayed silent for a moment, the only sound the ticking of his watch on the... Where the hell was it?

He pinched his lips together. He wasn't against the institution of marriage. He *was* against putting himself in a position to put everyone else's needs before his own. He'd been there, done that, bought the T-shirt, and lost the scholarship to study with culinary geniuses in Europe and the chance to open his own restaurant. He'd ended up at the local culinary academy and opened a catering company instead—cheaper tuition and overhead he could handle.

But he did still have dreams of his restaurant, and nothing was going to get in the way this time. According to his buddy Dean, the financial planner, he was about a year away from having the funds to open Eats Grille in LoDo—Denver's trendy neighborhood and *the* place for up-and-coming chefs.

"You okay?" He moved his arm from his eyes so he could see her.

She rubbed at her eyelids with the pads of her fingertips. "I'm fine. You?"

Eli finally answered her question. "I'm mistaked."

"Yeah." Marlee pulled her thin white dress over her head, letting it fall down her body like a waterfall of cotton. "Me, too."

And she was now mistaked to the wrong man. "Marlee..."

"You realize this is going to hit the paper in Denver? There's no way they're not going to cover it." Marlee sat beside him on the bed, scooting closer to examine the marriage license in his hand.

"We'll fix this." No one had to know. Just him, and Marlee, and Sadie.

He'd never had anything but brotherly feelings toward Marlee. She was his kid sister's best friend. But with her hand pressed against his and her perfume in the air, he was feeling things for her he'd never expected. Wires were getting crossed between his heart and his groin, and that was unacceptable. She slipped her hand onto his thigh and left it there like it wasn't heating his blood and making him question the benefit of an immediate annulment before they could take advantage of the only good part of being husband and wife.

He lifted Marlee's hand and held it in his own, giving it a squeeze. It was meant to be comforting and not show how he'd moved it because he'd been worried that if she drifted just a few inches to the right…well…they might have a repeat of their three a.m. acrobatics.

Marlee snuggled deeper into the pillows. "Eli?"

"Yeah?"

"I'm glad you're not being a dick about this."

"Why would I be a dick about this?"

She gave him a look. "You know why."

"You mean 'cause you're loaded?" he asked.

"I mean because for a guy who has sworn off marriage, you're handling this"—she held up her own twist-tied finger—"remarkably well."

"And I'll continue handling it well if you'll stop saying that word." He reached for his cell phone. "Where's Sadie?"

"Where did we leave her?"

He racked his brain. That must've been right around the blackout portion of his evening. "The penthouse with Becca and Kellie." He snagged his cell phone and pulled up his sister's number, putting her on speaker.

After three rings, she answered, "Please tell me Marlee is with you."

Marlee and Sadie were tighter than the twist tie on his ring finger. Of course, she was worried.

"She's with me." No doubt. After last night? She was definitely with him.

"You guys didn't have sex, did you?" Sadie always did

have that sixth sense about things. And she didn't sound happy about what had gone down.

Marlee didn't answer, she just side-eyed Eli with a what-the-hell-do-I-say expression.

"I'll take my fifth amendment privilege on that question," Eli finally said.

"I'm fine," Marlee said from beside him. "Your brother is very attentive."

"Seriously? Things I never needed to know. Ever." Sadie made a gagging noise in the back of her throat.

Eli leaned closer to the phone. "We need legal help today."

That got Sadie's attention. "Where are you?" She switched from little sister to attorney Sadie in an instant. "Are you in jail?"

"Chill. We're in a hotel room." Eli slid his glance to Marlee.

"We took you up on that dare," Marlee said into the phone.

The line went silent.

"So we're going to need some help getting an annulment pushed through," Eli finished for Marlee.

More silence.

"Sadie?"

She coughed. "Marlee?"

He handed his cell phone to Marlee.

"Hey." Her arm brushed Eli's.

"Take me off speaker," Sadie demanded.

Marlee did as directed and held his phone to her ear.

"No," she replied to whatever his sister had asked. "Yes." Now, she bit at her lip. "No prenup." She glanced at Eli in apology. "It wasn't like we planned it."

"Phone?" Eli held out his hand.

Marlee returned it. He pushed the speaker button.

"Sadie? It's me. I'm not an ass. I'm not going to take any

of Marlee's money. I don't want her house. I just want this to have never happened."

There was clicking of keyboard keys in the background. Sadie never went anywhere without her work laptop. "You can go to the courthouse first thing Monday with the rest of the weekend oopsies. But I've got to be home by noon Monday, so you two are going to be on your own. Looks simple: you file, show up in front of the judge, and this never happened."

Which was exactly what he wanted.

Chapter Eight
MONDAY MORNING

"OH MY GOD. Oh my God. Oh my God," Marlee whispered under her breath.

"Mar." Eli reached for her hand and squeezed. "Chill."

Oh crap, his tie was crooked. Marlee reached for it, adjusting his collar until it was nearly straight.

He cleared his throat, pushing her hands down from the blue silk necktie and lacing his fingers with hers.

"I'm not done," she whispered. Sadie had instructed them both to come dressed in their best. That meant a suit for Eli— along with a microdermabrasion treatment that removed most of the henna—and a cleavage-covering blouse with slacks for Marlee. Eli clearly wasn't happy about the suit, and even less excited about the hours he'd spent at the spa, but he'd followed Sadie's instructions.

Except his tie was crooked.

And looking his best didn't involve an off-kilter tie. Not after the emergency trip to Neiman-Marcus for a blouse that matched that exact shade of JC Penney cobalt. They couldn't ruin it now with something as easy to fix as crooked silk. Marlee unlaced their hands and tugged at the cloth.

"All rise," the bailiff said. "The honorable Judge Milburn presiding."

Crap. Marlee finished with a pat-and-smooth. Eli gently pushed her hands aside.

She turned just as the judge entered the courtroom. Before them now stood a seventy-something woman with salt-and-pepper hair wearing a judge robe that made Marlee's palms start to sweat.

The courtrooms, the judges, the bench thingy, the "all rise"—they did a number on Marlee ever since she, Sadie, Kellie, and Becca had had a tad too much fun at that hockey game when they were twenty and had gotten arrested for indecent exposure. For the record, they were totally covered. Painted torsos, just like the guys next to them who *hadn't* gotten arrested. Unlike the guys next to them, they even had pasties covering the important bits. Still, the officer didn't think that was enough. Her parents had hired an attorney and used all their country club connections to get Marlee and her friends off the hook. The judge let them go, but the raised blood pressure, the sweaty palms, and the inability to speak without hesitating whenever she got near a courthouse had all remained.

So, no, a courtroom had no place in her get-my-life-together plan.

Judge Milburn smiled and, huh, maybe she wasn't so bad. Definitely a grandmother type. The sugary sweet kind of grandmother with laugh lines and kind eyes. Yes, not so bad. This would be easy.

Marlee released Eli's hand and wiped her hands against her slacks.

"Please be seated." This judge was already nicer than the last one. Yes, that guy had ended up letting them all off with a warning, but he hadn't been kind about it. There was no "please" back then. "Mr. and Mrs. Howard," Judge Milburn began, "we'll make this as simple as possible. I understand you're here today for an annulment?"

"Yes," Eli said, scooching forward to speak into the microphone on the desk.

"Yes." Marlee stumbled over the word, knocking against the microphone so it made that unpleasant squealing sound.

She folded her hands in her lap.

It was Monday morning. She should've been in Denver delivering coffee to her friends, not in a Vegas courtroom knocking over microphones.

Eli's hand found hers and gave it a squeeze. Not removing his hand, he must have somehow realized she needed the support.

"I understand you were both inebriated at the time of the marriage?" the judge asked.

Eli flinched at the word "marriage."

"Yes, Your Honor," Marlee said without even a squeak.

"And how long have you two known each other?" The judge continued with her questioning, jotting notes as she spoke.

"For forever," Marlee answered with only a half stumble over the last word.

"Since we were teenagers, Your Honor," Eli said without any issue.

"And how long had you been planning to get married?" she asked without moving her gaze from her notepad.

"About two years," Marlee answered without thinking.

Crap.

Judge Milburn looked up, eyebrows raised.

Eli gaped at Marlee, his eyes wide.

Marlee swallowed the dryness in her throat. "May I clarify?"

"Please do." Judge Milburn nodded.

"I mean I've been wedding planning for about eighteen months. But then we were here, and we had too much to drink, and this"—Marlee gestured between her and Eli, whacking his chest in the process—"just happened."

"I see." The judge made more notes. Marlee could practically feel the ink scratches on that notepad in her bones. "To clarify, you've known each other since you were teenagers?"

"Yes, Your Honor," Eli answered.

"Yes." Marlee confirmed on a cough. Seriously, was there no water in the Las Vegas courthouse? It was the desert, for goodness sake.

"And you spent around eighteen months planning the wedding?"

"Not me. I didn't plan a wedding." Eli shook his head quickly.

"Mrs. Howard, you spent about eighteen months planning the wedding?" The judge glanced at Marlee over her bifocals.

"Ms. Medford, not Mrs. Howard," Marlee corrected. It seemed like an important note to make in annulment proceedings. "And yes, but not for this wedding. Not here in Las Vegas. This one just—"

"Your Honor." Eli kept his attention on the judge. "I think—"

The judge held up her hand and ticked her head to the side. There was now a dash of siracha in her cinnamon sugar demeanor. "Mr. Medford—"

"Mr. Howard," Eli corrected.

The judge licked her top lip and gestured to Marlee. "I'd like to hear what else Ms. Medford was going to say about the marriage."

Eli flinched again at the word.

"Nothing else. That was it." Marlee wished the rolling chair would open up and swallow her whole. "But you might want to note on your pad to use a different word. Eli doesn't care for that one."

"Shit," Eli said under his breath just loud enough for Marlee to catch.

"Which word?" Judge Milburn asked.

"'Marriage.' It makes him itchy." Well, it did. He had hives creeping up past his collar line.

"Mar," he nearly growled the word.

"Well, it bugs you. She should know so she'll stop using it." Marlee turned her attention back to the judge. "He prefers to call what happened 'mistaked.'"

Eli ran both hands over his face, stopping at his mouth.

Marlee resisted the urge to do the same. This wasn't happening. They just needed a do-over.

"Your Honor, may I start over?" Marlee asked.

"No, we've done that once. I think we've come too far this time." The judge set her pen down with a great deal of intention. Apparently, she didn't need to take any more notes.

"Why do you want this annulment, Ms. Medford?" the judge asked.

Marlee glanced at Eli. He was staring at the ceiling, his chest rising and falling too quickly.

"No need to consult with Mr. Howard," the judge assured. "I just want to hear your reasons."

Okay, well, Marlee could explain them. There were lots of reasons why the wedding shouldn't have happened. She just needed to get herself together and be succinct, starting with—

"Because my parents are going to be so mad." That was probably not where she should've started. And yet, the chair wasn't swallowing her yet, so she just kept talking. "See…it's just…they spent all the money on the other wedding, and then we got tattoos and I danced with a pole, and then Eli and I got so drunk, and then this happened, and we just need to make it so that it didn't happen." There it was, a reasonable version of all the whys.

The judge nodded and continued to make her notes. "The other wedding was to happen on what date?"

"Saturday." Marlee paused, the flush of embarrassment from Scotty's dismissal a fresh wound added to the current annulment proceedings.

"Mr. Howard, what is the reason you want this annulment?" Judge McJudgey was apparently done with questioning Marlee. Thank God.

"Because the wedding was a mistake." Eli pulled at his tie and it went totally to the side.

"You're all crooked," Marlee whispered, reaching to adjust his tie again.

His Adam's apple bobbed as she made the fix.

"Sorry," Marlee mumbled, abruptly stopping her attempt at straightening. She threaded her fingers together and vowed to not say another word.

"Mr. Howard, do you care for Ms. Medford?" the judge asked.

"Of course, I do," he said.

He did? That was so sweet. "You do?" Marlee asked. "Really?"

The glance he tossed her way had a touch of the look drunken Eli had melted her with on their wedding night.

"Yeah, Mar. I think we covered that on our wedding night." He caught himself when the words left his mouth.

Marlee shifted her gaze to the judge. "He just means—"

"I know what he means, Ms. Medford." McJudgey pursed her mouth into a very unflattering line. "Mr. Howard, are you and Ms. Medford both over the age of eighteen?"

"Yes." He was fisting his hands so hard his knuckles were turning white.

"And you're not related by blood?" the judge asked.

"No, Your Honor." The hives were creeping up to his jawline. He'd probably need one of Marlee's emergency Benadryl soon.

"Ms. Medford, do you concur with Mr. Howard's statements?" McJudgey asked.

Marlee squirmed under the direct questioning. What? Oh, right. Not related. And not under eighteen. "Yes…Your Honor."

"And did you both, at the time of the marriage, understand what was happening?" She glanced between them.

"Yes." Eli slumped against his chair.

The judge glanced to Marlee. "Ms. Medford?"

"Yes." Marlee tried to sound confident, but all the Barbizon training in the world hadn't prepared her for this moment.

"Did anyone force either of you to enter into this union?" McJudgey picked up the pen and started scribbling some notes once more.

"No," Eli said first.

"No," Marlee echoed. A dare probably didn't count as forcing. However, it was worth a try. "Actually…"

"Yes, Ms. Medford?"

"Does a dare count as forcing someone to get married?" The no-cleavage blouse was starting to get really warm.

Eli wasn't breathing. Marlee reached for her inhaler, but he took a thin breath before she even got the first button of her blouse undone in order to reach for the inhaler tucked in her bra.

"What would the consequence of the dare have been had you not done it?" McJudgey asked, glaring at Eli as though he'd been the one to issue the dare.

"No consequences. My sister and Marlee's friends dared us. All in good fun."

"They were my bridal party." Marlee heard herself say. *Shut up. Shut up.* Technically, the dare was issued so much earlier in the night that it really didn't count. "We just wanted the pictures," Marlee whispered.

"So there were no consequences to this dare?" McJudgey continued with the questioning.

"No, Your Honor," Eli spoke clearly, not even looking Marlee's way.

Marlee was wrecking this. No more talking, just yes and no. "No."

"Neither of you are married to anyone else?"

Close, but, "No," Marlee answered.

"No." Eli pulled at his tie again, totally wrecking it.

"I think I have all the information I need." The judge leaned forward, elbows on her desk. "Do you know how many couples I see here in my courtroom every Monday morning?"

Marlee's heart started pressing against her lungs in a way she'd never known was possible. She shook her head.

"No, Your Honor," Eli said. The red flush creeping up his cheeks countered the smooth words.

"I've been a Las Vegas judge for thirty years, and every Monday morning, it's the same thing. The weekend revelers show up looking to erase the past." There was no sugar anymore. Just a whole lot of snap. "I, for one, am sick of it. Two weeks from retirement, and this is what I spend my time doing." She stood.

"All rise," the bailiff said a touch too late.

"We just need the annulment," Marlee whispered into the microphone.

The judge wasn't done yet.

"I don't know what your story is, and I don't care. You don't meet the grounds of annulment in the State of Nevada, so I wish you all the luck on your divorce." After a smack of the gavel, she shuffled from the room.

"Fu-u-uck," Eli said under his breath. The red was now absent as he'd gone pale.

Marlee opened her mouth. Closed it. Opened it. "I'm not even sure what happened in here."

The one thing she was sure of? They were still married. Mistaked.

It didn't matter what they called it, because this was the real deal.

Chapter Nine
LATER THAT DAY

"I'LL COME with you when you explain things to your parents." Eli lifted Marlee's last suitcase into her SUV.

"No." If there was one thing Marlee was sure of, it was that this was not the time for Eli to meet her parents. She'd prefer that they liked her best friend's brother, not hate him on sight because of a mutual bad decision that would soon result in divorce. "It's best if I just do this alone."

Marlee had finally turned her phone on at the Las Vegas airport and it immediately went bananas. The *Denver Post* had run a story of her wedding in the online social section. *What Happened in Vegas? Who is Marlee's Mystery Groom?*

That's what the headline read. So far, they didn't have Eli's name. But that was only temporary. They both knew that.

After a momentary bout of heart palpitations, she had shut the thing off. The idea of turning it on made the pit in her stomach turn to acid.

She had to deal with all the calls.

All the questions.

Scotty.

Wasn't it just her luck that the weekend she got married in

Vegas was the same weekend one of Denver's first round draft picks got arrested after trashing a hotel room at The Wynn? And wasn't it just her luck that the *Denver Post* reporter sent to cover that story caught her leaving the annulment hearing? And wasn't it just her luck that he then started nosing around in her personal business?

Every possible scenario of facing her parents had played through her brain. She decided going with the truth was her best bet—just lay it all out there for them.

A jumbo jet scraped through the Denver sky over the parking garage. Becca and Kellie had flown straight home from Vegas, leaving Marlee and Eli with the uncomfortable silence that followed them on to the plane back to Colorado.

Neither had said much after the disaster in the courtroom. He'd called Sadie immediately, and she was already working on the divorce paperwork. Once everything was filed, there would be a ninety-day period before the divorce became final.

One crisis at a time. There was no over or under, so the only way to come out on the other side of this mess was straight through. She'd laid out the steps in her mind, and step one was checking into the hotel. Step two was spilling the news to her parents before a nosy reporter at the *Post* did it for her. Step three was finding a new job—since she was in no way ever working with Scotty again.

Step four was figuring out what she could do to build up some good juju. She'd already missed her Monday morning coffee delivery to Bert. She'd need to come up with something else.

"Okay." Eli shoved his hands into the pockets of his jeans, his thumbs sticking out over the sides.

"So." Marlee unlocked her driver's side door.

"Do you want my number?" Eli asked. "In case you need anything?"

"I have it." Marlee held up her hot-pink, rhinestoned case.

"That's my work number. I don't usually answer it outside of business hours. You'll need my personal line." He shifted on his sneakered feet.

"Sure." Marlee fidgeted with the power button, finally pressing it so the phone turned on.

It immediately started pinging and pinging and pinging with unread message after unread message. She flinched at each one as if she were Eli and every ping was a recording of the word *marriage* instead of *piiiiing*.

She didn't look at the screen. That would be step five in her plan.

Instead, she handed her phone to him so he could add the number. "I'll be at the Four Seasons. And you have my number."

First things first, take her time checking in, getting settled, and hanging up her clothes in the closet.

Eli tapped his information into her contacts.

"All set." He gave her phone back.

"Okay." She stared at it. Two hundred and seventy-five new text messages flashed back at her.

She swallowed the dry feeling in her throat.

Time to face life. Whatever that meant, now that Scotty wasn't part of it.

This was it. Yes, the weekend had sucked donkey balls, but she hadn't been alone during any of it. Her friends had seen to that.

Eli pulled open her door for her, and she slipped onto the seat. "Eli, I'm really sorry."

"This whole thing isn't your fault." He started to close the door but paused. "I'm sorry, too."

She fussed with the edge of her shirt. "And about the thing that happened after we got married—"

"You don't need to go there." He squeezed her shoulder —the bare part exposed by the peekaboo sleeve. "It happened. It was great. Now, we move forward."

"It was great, wasn't it?" Her gaze cemented on his.

He nodded, not letting go of her shoulder. "And it must never happen again."

"Agreed." Yes, they'd been drunk. But they weren't quite at the sign-the-wrong-name-on-the-license drunk. Deep down, she knew they both had understood what was happening.

And that was the part that made the hair on her arms stand tall.

It had been great. He had been great.

"Now, let's never speak of it again," he said, continuing to hold her gaze.

"Agreed." A smile toyed with the corners of her mouth.

The thing she'd never fully realized about Eli before was that he had this way of giving his full attention when he was talking to someone. Not that he talked often, but when he did, he gave his full focus. Scotty was always doing ten different things. With Eli? When he talked to her? He made it clear she was the only thing that mattered.

He had to know that he mattered to her, too.

She slid from the seat and hugged him like a lifeline.

He hugged her back.

A totally platonic move, but it was quite possibly one of the most intimate moments of her life.

"Okay." She sighed heavily.

"Okay." He trailed a fingertip over her cheek.

She climbed back into her car. He waited while she backed out of the parking space. She gave a little wave and then moved onward to the exit. Lothario barked from his spot on the passenger seat.

"Me, too," she whispered. "I'm going to miss him, too."

And she would. He had played a huge role in the healing that needed to take place post-Scotty. Now, she was on her own. Her life was hers to figure out. She turned on the stereo and let Adele's soul music fill the air along I-70 toward downtown.

If her life was a movie, this would be where the montage of her getting herself together would start. A blank canvas scared the hell out of her. But a blank canvas was hope. Was anything she wanted it to be. She was ready for this, for what came next.

She pulled up to the valet stand. Adele's music continued to play in her head even as she stepped from the car, even as she pushed through the rotating doors, even as she sauntered to check-in.

"Marlee Medford, here to check in." She passed over her American Express.

"Welcome to the Four Seasons, Ms. Medford." The desk clerk clicked away on the registration computer.

He frowned.

More clicking.

An abundance of frowning.

Pressure began to form at Marlee's temples. He continued frowning. Frowning and clicking.

"It seems that your card has been declined." The desk clerk slid her American Express back to her side of the counter. He had no poker face, the confusion as clear as the lines on his forehead. "I'm sorry."

"No, that's not possible." Marlee pushed it back toward him. "Could you please try again?"

"Of course." He did his clicking thing as he glanced at the card, then at the screen, then back at the card.

"I'm so sorry." The desk clerk pushed it back to her. "Perhaps a different form of payment?"

Marlee pulled her emergency backup Visa from her bra. This couldn't be happening. Her cards were all tied into her trust. Her stomach clenched around a volleyball-sized knot of realization. Her trust was managed by her parents—terms set down when her grandmother passed away when Marlee was eight. She didn't get control until she turned thirty-five, and that was still years away.

Her grandmother had wanted Marlee to be old enough to really understand money management before she got control. Marlee had always thought that wasn't a big deal. Until now.

Her mouth went dry.

"I'm sorry, Ms. Medford." The desk clerk handed that plastic card back as well. "Would you care to use our house phone to call the credit card company?"

"No," Marlee sighed. "I'll contact them." She held up her cell.

But she didn't need to call. Her parents had to know what had happened in Vegas.

She'd been cut off.

SO STEP two was now step one and that was fine. Perfect, actually.

Marlee pulled into the U-shaped brick driveway that led to her parents' front door. She strode to the massive red door and pushed it open. "Mom? Dad?"

She set Lothario on the floor. He loved coming to visit his Mimi and PopPop.

Marlee'd always had visions of her and Scotty's kids doing the same whenever they would have eventually had them. Another sting to her heart and a not-going-to-happen dream.

"Oh, thank goodness." Her mother scurried down the marble staircase to Marlee. "You're here." She wrapped Marlee in an Elizabeth Arden–scented hug. "We've been so worried."

Her mom was more casual than a lot of their society friends. Still, casual for her mom meant a nice pair of pressed slacks and a matching blouse. Tonight, the set was pastel blue and accompanied by a set of pearl earrings and her standard string of Jackie O–inspired pearls.

"Marlee." Her dad emerged from the hallway leading to the kitchen. He hugged her as well. His starched button-up shirt and slacks would've been formal for most, but these were his lounging clothes. The ones he wore around the house. At work, it was always a full suit and tie. "You haven't answered our calls."

They must've been genuinely concerned, since neither of them gave a second glance to Lothario, who was clearly feeling the sting of that rejection given the look on his little chihuahua face.

"Is that why you turned off my credit cards?" Marlee appreciated their concern—really, she did. She also wished they would have given her the time and space to come on her own.

"We had multiple reasons for that." Her mom worried at her bottom lip. "We think you and Scotty made a mistake. This is one of those times a little communication can go a long way. Come, let's talk in the kitchen."

All the communication in the world wasn't going to fix what was broken between Marlee and Scotty. Her parents flanked her as they crossed their arms behind her and scooted her forward down the hall. Lothario thumped behind them.

It was Italian night in the house. If she had to guess, her dad had made his famous saltimbocca. One of her favorite meals. Chicken breast that practically melted in the mouth with parmesan and mozzarella and prosciutto de parma. Absolutely divine.

At least, if she had to face their reasons for cutting her off, she'd be well fed.

Her dad loved to cook and took every opportunity he could to practice his kitchen skills. Most of the time, they had an on-staff chef because he worked so much, but cooking was one of his favorite things. Some men took up golf—like Scotty

—but her dad loved to cook. He and Eli would probably get along famously if they gave each other a shot.

Marlee hadn't gotten the culinary gene, given her propensity to burn anything that came within ten feet of the stove. Microwave popcorn, she could handle. Toast in the toaster, a pretty safe bet. Anything else? Yeah, no.

They rounded the Grecian column marking the kitchen entrance.

Scotty sat at a barstool noshing away on prosciutto and chicken.

Marlee's stomach seemed to lurch to the left, her appetite totally gone. He was supposed to be on a beach somewhere far, far from here.

"No." Marlee started to step backward. "This is not going to happen. Ever."

"We asked Scotty to come back so you two can work through whatever this thing is that's gone wrong," her father said.

Scotty dabbed at the right side of his mouth with a white linen napkin. He looked her over head to toe.

"He told you he was going to break up with me, and you didn't mention it." Marlee pulled away from her parents. "He broke off the wedding, and you sent him to the tropics."

"I never thought he'd actually be stupid enough to go through with it." Dad glared daggers at Scotty.

Scotty flinched.

"Blowing off steam before a wedding is one thing," her mother said. "This is something else."

"This is called a breakup." Marlee glanced up to where her mom stood on her left.

"Leelee." Her nickname was rough against Scotty's vocal cords.

He said nothing more, which was perfect. There wasn't anything more to say.

"The whole family just needs to talk." Her dad reached for her and gave her a side squeeze.

That was all great, but Scotty wasn't technically family. Given his recent decision to cancel the wedding, he'd never be part of the family.

She waited for the sinking feeling to come back—the sadness of years lost, of kids that would never burst through the door of their grandparents' house... An abandoned future. It didn't come. Instead, she wished Eli was with her. If anything, to make Scotty squirm. More because instinct told her he'd have her back.

"If this is a family meeting, I'll ask, why is Scotty here?" she asked.

Scotty grimaced. "There's no need to be mean."

He was totally right. He didn't deserve any emotion from her. Not even anger.

"This is complicated." Her mom started fixing a plate. Marlee knew it was for her. "But we thought the two of you might be able to talk through some of the unpleasantness if we all got together. Everyone just needs to be open to the conversation. Set the anger aside."

"I'm not angry." Marlee took the offered plate, picked up a fork, and cut into the tender chicken with the side of it—all while standing. She refused to sit near Scotty. Yes, it seemed petty. Really, she didn't want to have to smell his scent, relive their memories. Not yet, anyway. Would she get there? Yes. She'd get there. No doubt about it. However, that wasn't today.

"You got married." Scotty folded the napkin, creasing it between his middle and index finger. "It's all over the Internet."

"Scotty," her dad said quietly. "We aren't discussing that part yet."

Marlee couldn't get a good read on Scotty. He didn't seem

sad. She'd thought he might be a little sad, but he just seemed indifferent. Like it didn't matter.

Like she didn't matter, and that made her heart ache.

"Yes, I got married. And?" Marlee said with a strong dose of annoyance. Her inner attitude was apparently on the scene. Scotty never got doses of Marlee's attitude. No one did, really. "You didn't want to do it, so someone else did."

Which wasn't entirely the truth, but also not entirely a lie. It was what she and her besties called a try—part truth, part lie.

"You're acting ridiculous." Scotty moved with precision, setting his knife and fork beside his plate.

"Really, Scotty, you're being very unhelpful." Her mother gave Scotty a look that could boil ice water.

"I'm being ridiculous?" Marlee asked, ignoring her parents. "You called off our wedding with less than two days to go. Shouldn't you be on our honeymoon?"

"I was just boarding the plane when my phone started ringing. We had to call in a special public relations team to handle the questions. You know better than anyone what kind of damage something like this can do to the organization. We could lose sponsors. A little heads-up would've been good."

That's what he was worried about? Losing his precious sponsors? "And you came back, because?"

"Leelee." He looked at her like she was the one being utterly impossible. "You got married." There was a touch of sadness in those words now.

The sadness jerked at the strings around her heart. She vowed to clip them when it came to Scotty. He had no business tugging on them anymore.

"Mom?" Marlee decided to go straight to the one ally she was sure to have. "I got married. It wasn't planned. Sadie is handling the divorce. Is that why you and Dad shut off my credit cards?"

Her mom made a slightly strangled noise. "We worried you wouldn't come home until we forced our hand."

"I was coming straight over as soon as I got settled at the hotel."

"Who is it?" Scotty asked. "Who's the guy?"

Marlee pressed her eyes closed. "It's really none of your business."

"Who is he, Marlee?" her mom asked.

Now, her mother? Her mother would insist on an answer.

"His name is Eli. Eli Howard. Sadie's brother," Marlee said, attempting to make it sound totally normal.

"The caterer?" Scotty asked.

Marlee ignored him.

"You should stay here." Her mom fussed with a plate she was fixing for Marlee's dad. "The hotel will be so lonely. We think here is a better choice."

"You married our caterer?" Scotty's voice pitched higher.

"Scotty." Her dad shook his head. "Stay here, Marlee."

"Or at the house," Scotty added. "You can stay with me at the house."

"Someplace this Eli Howard doesn't bother you." Her dad took the plate and sat at the barstool across from Scotty. They were all comfortable in the kitchen. It's where the family gathered unless the event was formal.

What he meant was so Eli Howard didn't bother her trust fund.

"You're worried he's in it for my money?" she asked.

"You have to be careful with your money, Marlee." Her dad shoved his hands on his hips, exasperated.

"I trust Eli," Marlee said. "Totally trust him. He's not going to take my money."

"C'mon, you understand how people work." Scotty wiped at his mouth. "He married you *because* you have a lot of money. We froze your accounts to protect your assets." Scotty stood as though he was going to step toward her, reason with her.

She officially clipped those heartstrings. "You don't have any say over my accounts."

Her grandmother had assigned her parents as trustees, not Scotty.

"Scotty isn't involved in the finances," her father said. "Your mother and I made the decision."

They didn't know Eli. Didn't know who he really was. Eli had never cared that she had money. "Eli married me because we got drunk. Now we're dealing with it. We've already started the divorce papers."

"Once the divorce goes through, we'll turn everything back on," her mother said.

"If Scotty is at our house, then I won't be. And if Scotty is here, then I won't be. And if Scotty's at the office, then I won't be." Marlee glanced from her parents to Scotty. "I'll find somewhere else."

It's not like she pulled a paycheck from the family business. She'd never needed one. Now, it seemed, she needed one.

"Your mother and I know you're upset." Her dad bowed his head, speaking to the counter. "We know you're hurt. Good decisions don't happen when a person is hurting, so we will be there for you through this. When the divorce is final, we'll open your accounts again. Until then, we don't want this Eli to have access to all your funds or cause further hurt. So you'll stay here with us, and we'll support you through this."

Marlee stared at him like he'd suddenly grown a mole in the center of his forehead. "You're serious."

"We're very serious." Her mom laid a hand against her dad's back. "We want to be sure you're okay."

"I move in here and you give me some kind of allowance or something?" Marlee's heart beat faster. Her frustration with the judge in Vegas had nothing on her frustration with her parents. "And that's supposed to protect me from Eli? The one person who has consistently been there for me since Scotty scraped me off?"

"Leelee—"

"It's best this way. And it's just for now," her mom said softly.

"No." Marlee picked up Lothario, turned toward the hallway, and made her way to the front door. Her chest heaved. Her eyes got hot. Unshed tears stung her eyelids.

None of them followed her. They didn't think they'd need to. She was a trust-fund baby and they'd cut the cord. A spoiled little rich girl with no money wouldn't survive in the world without them. Her only hope was to crawl back down that hall and beg for money.

She wouldn't do that.

She had a degree. She had friends. She had…Eli.

With Lothario still snuggled in her purse, she climbed into her SUV and did the one thing she never thought she'd do.

She called her husband.

Chapter Ten

ELI NEEDED A SERIOUS REWIND. Rewind and reboot. Go back, start over, change the outcome.

He scrubbed his palm over his face.

"Your family is being a bag of dicks, Mar. You're welcome to stay with me," he said into the phone.

"Thank you, Eli. Really," she replied, the muffled sound of her mouth close to the phone.

"See you in a few." He ended the call, already headed to the coin-operated washer at the end of the building to toss in his spare set of sheets. Marlee would take his bed. He'd pull out the sofa for himself. Scotty could suck it.

He thought he could tell Marlee what to do after he broke her to fucking pieces? It took all Eli had in him not to hop in his Jeep and rearrange the guy's nose into his eyebrows. He'd already broken her heart, wasn't that enough? Did he have to turn her parents against her, too?

He shot a text to Sadie, letting her know they could really use this divorce.

The response he got was less than helpful.

Divorces take time. Should have something in the next day or so for you to sign.

He'd barely set the washer on permanent press and got back to the apartment before the timer on the oven started flipping out. He hurried to the kitchen to make it shut up. Careful not to burn the shit out of his hands, he used a kitchen towel to pull out the ceramic dish of enchiladas.

He hoped Marlee was into Mexican food.

Not that he was trying to impress her. He didn't have any reason to impress anyone. If he were trying to impress her, he wouldn't be using month-old frozen enchiladas he'd tossed in the deep freezer after the Miller wedding.

No, he wasn't trying to impress Marlee. The fact that he hoped she liked his food was purely an ego thing. Not a husband thing.

He gulped at the thought.

He needed to get used to the word.

"Husband." He let it slide over his vocal cords. That wasn't so bad.

"Marriage," he said it, but he also practically choked on it. Nope. Not there yet.

For the briefest of moments, he considered tossing a heap of margaritas in the blender, but he and Marlee didn't make good decisions when alcohol was involved. Instead, he figured they'd have iced tea. Iced tea was safe. Iced tea was not margaritas.

Which sucked.

His phone rang. He snagged it. Shit. His mom. He hadn't called her.

"Mom," he said into the receiver. "Hi."

There was a pause. He knew she was there, he could hear her breathing.

"I got a funny call today from Sadie," she finally said. He just bet she did. "About my son's wedding," she continued. "I said she must be mistaken, because my son wouldn't get married without telling his mother."

"I literally just got back to town, swear I was stopping by

to tell you in person." He'd planned on doing that until Marlee had called. "It's not what you think it is."

"Then I hope you'll tell me what it is?"

"It was a mistake, and Sadie is handling the divorce." Not once did he have to use the *m*-word. Go him.

The soft knock on the front door had him moving there.

"Look, Marlee's staying with me for a little bit. Long story, but I'll fill you in once I get her settled."

"Eli?" his mother asked. He could hear the smile in her voice.

"Yeah?" He hustled to open the door.

"Maybe hold off on the divorce," she said, then the line went dead.

He paused. Took three deep breaths. Smoothed his hair. Demanded his heart stop tripping over each beat.

Then he opened the door.

"Hey." He reached for her suitcase but paused because she'd been crying.

That asshole, Scotty, had made her cry. Again.

Eli never wanted to break a nose so badly in his life.

"Thank you." Marlee followed Eli and her suitcase inside. She set Lothario's purse on the floor to let him roam. He went straight for Eli's shoes. Because of course, he did. "Thank you for letting us stay with you."

Her eyes were puffy as shit from crying, but her words were strong. She wasn't looking for his strength, she just needed to know someone had her back. So he focused on what he could do—lay it all out there.

"Well, first of all, we're in this bind together, so it makes sense we work through it as a team. And second, you're my friend and you're practically my family, so of course, you can stay. And third, my mother will disown me if I get mistaked to someone and then don't let them crash at my place when their ex utterly screws them over."

Marlee stepped into the living room. Never had anyone

ever looked more out of place than socialite Marlee in his living space. Not that his apartment wasn't kept up. Sadie had helped him pick out his furniture, so it all matched. His mother insisted on deep cleaning the place twice a month—even though he offered to hire someone. This just ticked her off, so he quit mentioning it. At least her attention made it so the place didn't reek of bachelorhood. But even if the apartment wasn't a dump, Marlee was a puzzle piece that didn't fit. No, she looked like she belonged at Tiffany's. Not waiting for clean sheets and month-old frozen enchiladas.

"It isn't just Scotty. Mom and Dad think you're after my trust fund. I know that's not true." She rubbed at her forehead with the heel of her palm. "But I know them. I know what they're thinking. They think I'll be back tomorrow with my tail tucked between my legs like Lothario after his accident. I refuse. If I have to sell my clothes and buy a plane ticket to couch surf at Sadie's, then that's what I'll do. I'm going to get a job—and not one that they control. And then I'm going to start my new self-sufficient life."

Preach it. That's how he lived, and it was the only way to go.

"Speaking of Sadie, I texted her. She'll hurry through the paperwork." He lifted Marlee's suitcase, carrying it to his bedroom. "Should have something to sign in the next day or so."

"Then the ninety-day purgatory begins." Her footsteps were soft behind him. "You know the media is going to figure out that you're the one I married."

He knew. He'd been bracing for it. He nodded.

"I'm sorry, Eli," she whispered.

"Wasn't just you who stood in front of Liberace and said 'I do.'" He lifted a shoulder. "Maybe it'll bring in new clients? Who knows."

She nodded. Hopefully, something good would come of this for one of them.

"Aw, when did you take this?" she asked.

He paused. Turned.

She was looking at the family picture his mom had hung in the hallway. Last Thanksgiving when everyone was together, she'd had a professional photographer come and take the photo. His mom, dad, Eli, and his four sisters. The girls all moved away after college; he'd been the only one who stayed put. They all got degrees and worked in offices all over the country. "Last year. Everyone came home for Thanksgiving."

"I haven't seen Nicole in forever. Sadie said she doesn't make it back much." Marlee stepped closer to him.

"She's busy changing the world." And he was proud of her. She *had* made it to Europe. Studied foreign relations and now worked in some government office she couldn't talk about.

"I figured you can set up shop in my bedroom." He tilted his head toward the room.

Marlee raised her eyebrows.

That sounded wrong. "I mean, I'm moving out so you can have the real bed. I'll sleep on the sofa. It pulls out." Unlike him. He gulped and kept his eyes forward, unwilling to risk her reaction to his screwup. They'd already agreed they weren't having a repeat of their wedding night. And he was definitely not having sex with the woman he was married to —a woman who would be staying with him for the foreseeable future.

That thought made him start to sweat.

He liked his private space. Liked being able to do what he wanted, whenever he wanted.

His feet slowed the tiniest bit as they moved to his bedroom. Marlee's bedroom. He hadn't even moved his stuff back in since Sadie had slept there.

"I can get a dog bed for Lothario if you don't like him

sleeping on the bed. And help yourself to anything in the kitchen."

Marlee still hadn't spoken. She was behind him though. The whispered *swish* of her feet on his carpet as she moved behind him was a giveaway.

He turned and caught her staring.

"Are you always this nervous when you have a girl sleep over?" She solidly squared him up.

"I don't have sleepovers." Not the kind she meant.

Yes, he'd had hookups. But he either went to their place or he fed them well and they went on their way afterward. No, he didn't have sleepovers.

"Never?" she asked, genuine curiosity in her word.

He shook his head. "Nope."

"Huh." She ran her tongue over her teeth.

"What does that mean?"

"What?"

"The 'huh.'"

"Nothing. It literally means nothing."

"There's a lot of not nothing in that 'huh.'"

"Are you always this weird when you're not drunk?" She followed him into the room.

He set her suitcase on the desk. "I'm not being weird."

She held up her thumb and pointer finger. "A little bit."

"You should be nice because I made enchiladas," he grumped.

"My favorite." She unzipped her suitcase and rummaged through. "So Vegas with me was your first sleepover?"

"What we did was hardly a sleepover."

"It was totally a sleepover." She raised her eyelashes, batting them in his direction.

"This is a ridiculous argument." He shoved his hands in his pockets for lack of a better reaction.

"Do you mind if I take a second before dinner? I haven't even had my post-airplane shower." Marlee was already working on unloading her bag all over his unmade bed, totally oblivious to the fact she was laying her lace panties right where he usually put his head.

He pulled his gaze away from the clothing she was spreading around like butter on a bagel.

A second. She needed a second. He could give her a second. A minute even. Fifteen of them. Fuck, an hour, if that's what it took. "For sure."

"Eli?" she asked.

He was already nearly out the door. "Yeah."

"Stop being weird. This doesn't have to be weird. It's just you and me rooming it up for a bit while our divorce goes through. There's literally nothing weird about that."

Uh-huh. If that's what she said.

"And I just want you to know that once I have money again"—she kept talking. He kept standing there like the weirdo she'd turned him into—"I'll pay you back for all of this." She fluttered her hand around the room.

He tapped two fingertips on the edge of the doorjamb. "You don't owe me anything."

"You don't owe me anything, either."

"You're family. And not just because we signed a paper with our real names. You're family, and family is there for each other." Even when they want to ignore the rest of the world.

She held his gaze, not speaking. Just looked at him like he meant something more.

Ever since the night they'd spent together, she had a way of glancing at him like she was doing just then, and it made him almost want to forget all about his commitment to perpetual bachelorhood.

His blood started to heat. His jeans started to get tight in the crotch. She dabbed at her bottom lip with the tip of her tongue.

"Eli?" she asked.

"Yeah?"

"Thank you," she said it in a way he knew she meant it.

"Anytime, Mar." He headed back toward the kitchen.

Enchiladas.

He should get lost in a paper plate of corn tortillas and sauce. Tortillas and sauce were safer than a room full of Marlee, which was pretty damn dangerous, given that he'd just signed up for a life full of Marlee for the next ninety days.

MARLEE'S PHONE pinged with a new group message.

> Becca: Married and now you're moving in together?

> Kellie: Moved in. She's there, so she's already moved in.

> Becca: Damn, this is all happening so fast.

> Sadie: You should get him to loosen up while you wait for the divorce. De-Eli him a bit.

> Marlee: Do you think that's even possible?

> Kellie: De-Eli-ing him could be fun. And involve more tuxedos.

> Becca: Not the polyester kind.

> Marlee: We agreed we're not doing that again.

> Sadie: Let's talk about something that isn't my brother naked? Pls. & Thx.

> Marlee: Miss you guys. I'll be on De-Eli duty.

Sadie: If anyone can do it, you can.

Marlee was good with goals, and right then, her goal was to get Eli to loosen up. She'd make it step whatever-she-was-on in her get-her-life-back-together plan. He was strung tighter than Scotty that time the airline accidentally sent his prized golf clubs to Phoenix instead of Ft. Lauderdale. But she should also add the immediate need for cash, a divorce, and clothing to her goals list.

She only had two suitcases of clothes. The rest of her boxes were stacked in her garage, held hostage by Scotty. All she had to do was wait until he went golfing the next day. Then she'd go get the rest of her stuff.

Now, where she would put it? That was a totally different question.

Towel-drying her hair, she padded down the hallway to the kitchen-living-dining combo. Eli's place had an open floor plan—one big room with a hallway that led to the bedroom and bath. He was sprawled on the sofa, staring at a football game on the television, a pillow snuggled against his chest.

She was good with goals. He was already super loose, and she hadn't even spoken. She hung a left into the kitchen. He hadn't eaten. The tray of enchiladas was untouched.

"You could've eaten without me." She used a fork to get an enchilada onto her plate, the cheese leaving a long trail between plate and tray.

"Mar." Eli was behind her. Like *right* behind her.

When did he get there?

"Yes, Eli?" She licked a stray string of cheese from her thumb.

He stared at the place she'd licked. "That's not how you plate dinner."

What? Her plate had dinner in the center. What else was she supposed to do?

Eli made a c'mere motion with his fingers. She handed over the paper plate.

Taking his time, he smoothed the cheese so it didn't all flop down one side. Then, he added sliced black olives, a dollop of sour cream, and finished with a dusting of some kind of white stuff.

"What's that?" she asked.

"Cotija. Now, it's ready to eat." He slipped the plate back into her waiting hand.

She started to say something about how he was an artist, but she stopped herself. He was a professional, and he probably didn't think of himself like that.

"I always thought you'd open a restaurant," she said instead. "I mean, catering is great, but I figured you'd have a whole chain and be on one of those cooking shows."

"Television? No. Restaurant? Yes." He winked at her.

"Serious?" she asked. "When?"

"Catering pays the bills. Lower overhead, all that. I've been saving for a while."

The way his gaze went a bit listless as he spoke told her it'd been more than just a while.

"I can't believe you had time to make all this. I barely had time to get rejected by the Four Seasons, American Express, and my parents." She stabbed a fork into her tortilla and chicken, raising it to her lips.

"Don't be too impressed. I keep a stash in the freezer for times when I'm too tired to start from scratch."

Lothario thumped his three-good-legged way into the kitchen.

Marlee sampled the forkful of goodness. Holy crap. If this is what Eli kept in his freezer, she was using hers wrong all these years. She let the tastes meld together on her tongue, closed her eyes, and experienced the flavors. "This is amazing."

She opened her eyes to find Eli staring at her, his lips parted.

He wasn't moving.

"Sorry." She licked at her lips. "I got carried away. Should we sit?"

"Yeah." Eli seemed to shake off whatever had caught his attention. Plate in hand, he headed to the coffee table and sofa.

Sure, he didn't have a kitchen table. And they ate off paper plates. None of that mattered when he could cook up a masterpiece like this.

Plate in his lap, he dug in.

Marlee shifted and balanced her plate on her knees. "I need a job."

"You're not going back to the office?" he asked.

She shook her head. "I think distance from Scotty and my parents might be best until the divorce goes through. They know my weaknesses. They'll figure out a way to get me to do what they want." They always did.

But not this time.

"I can ask around. Brek could probably use another wait-ress over at the bar," Eli suggested.

"What about you?" she asked. "Do you have any need for an art history major with minor event planning experience and a super cute dog?"

"When you put it like that, how could I possibly say no?" he replied. "But I'm all staffed up right now."

"You think Brek's waitresses make good tips?" She could waitress. It could be fun. She'd get to chat with people and hang out where there was live music.

He slid his gaze over her. Slowly. Like he was savoring a bite of a culinary masterpiece. Something flickered in his eyes. "I can probably come up with something in the kitchen."

"You just said you don't need me."

"I can always find something." He shrugged.

"Are you just jealous that I might get tips from handsome guys?" Could he possibly be jealous? She was pretty sure that was the flicker.

His cheeks got red when she mentioned being jealous.

He was so cute when he got all weird and jealous.

"I don't get jealous," he said on a huff.

If she hadn't seen the little glimmer of jealousy, she would have believed that. Eli was the epitome of a lone wolf. He just didn't realize that he had a full pack of family backing him up at all times.

"That wasn't an answer to my original question. Do you think I could make good tips at the bar?" she asked.

He bristled. "Yeah, Mar, I think the tips would be good."

"I should try for that then." She focused on her plate. It was either that or the television—but football was on—or Eli, and he was prickly as all heck.

"Seriously, Mar. I can find something for you to do in the kitchen."

"Health insurance, vacation time, all that?" she asked around a bite of cheesy goodness.

He scowled. "What did I get myself into with you?"

She nudged him with her elbow. "I'm messing with you. If there's something I can help out with, that'd be awesome. At least until I can find something more permanent."

"The dog's gonna have to stay in the office. He can't be in the kitchen." Eli acted surly toward Lothario, but Marlee knew deep down he had a soft spot for the dog. She'd caught him *not* glaring at Lothario more than once. He even petted him a time or two. "You can't have a dog in the kitchen. Health codes and all that," he said.

"Fair enough." Lothario wouldn't like to be where everyone was walking anyway. He had a solid fear of being stepped on. "This is going to be great. And maybe I can waitress, too. Extra money is extra money." Not even a day and she had a sort-of job with her sort-of husband, which was fantastic until they could get that real divorce.

Chapter Eleven

ELI NEEDED a night out with his buddies. A night without a reminder that he was in a marriage, waiting on a divorce. They'd only been back one day, but he wasn't used to having others in his space. He'd specifically arranged his schedule when Sadie had stayed with him so he was at work most of the time.

That morning, he'd gone with Marlee while she distributed a dozen cups of Starbucks to a crew of homeless folks who met her at the corner by the drive-thru. This was apparently a ritual of hers a few days a week.

That was the morning. Then, they'd spent the day together at the kitchen, picked up the boxes from her house, and that led to where they were now. Home. His home.

Lothario sat on the floor by Eli's feet while he shaved. He whined and tilted his head like Eli should say something.

"I see your mom dressed you in your blingy collar tonight." She had a whole slew of collars for the mutt. Tonight's was a rhinestone number that matched the rhinestones on Marlee's socks. Yes, Marlee had rhinestoned socks. And she coordinated them with her dog.

Lothario shook his whole body in response.

Which was exactly the response Eli would have had if he'd been forced to wear a rhinestoned collar that matched Marlee's socks.

"Just tell her no next time," Eli said. "Tell her you are your own man and you'll pick out your own collar."

Lothario huffed, walked in a circle, and plopped down on the top of Eli's foot.

"Make yourself at home." He rubbed the shaving foam between his hands. "Just don't get sexy with my foot while I'm shaving. I don't want to cut myself."

Lothario rolled onto his back, tongue lolling to the side.

He had made himself right at home in Eli's apartment. Lothario had officially started a relationship with each pair of Eli's shoes. He'd also taken to following Eli around instead of Marlee.

"I don't have asthma, kid," he'd said more than once.

Lothario didn't care. Eli was his new infatuation.

Which was funny, since his mom was Eli's new infatuation.

What kind of woman wore rhinestoned socks to deliver coffee to the homeless? And it wasn't like she volunteered with a charity—she knew these guys, genuinely cared about them. And they cared about her, too, it seemed.

What was Eli supposed to do with that?

Hence his need to step away for a bit. Distance meant clarity. Clarity was good. He rubbed the foam over his cheeks.

Lothario just lay there, watching Eli like he was a showgirl on one of those poles Marlee had danced on.

"Just because I said you can hang out with me doesn't mean you can look at me like that. I'm not your entertainment." Eli pressed the razor against his jawline.

Lothario snuggled against Eli's foot in response.

"I'm more than a pair of feet, little dude. Get to know me, you'll see."

"What are your plans tonight, cowboy?" Marlee propped

herself against the doorjamb while Eli finished shaving. He startled at her voice but didn't cut himself. He glanced at her reflection in the mirror.

"My buddy's engagement party." His buddy, Jase, was getting married to his fiancée, Heather. On purpose.

At least when Eli did it, it was a total accident. One by one, his buddies were falling into the pit of marital bliss.

They'd string him up by his nuts when they found out he'd already hit the neon-lit altar and had the live-in wife to prove it.

"Lothario wants to come, but I told him he needs to do his job and make sure you can breathe. He defiled my workout shoes in retaliation."

"I promise I will buy you an entirely new wardrobe of shoes once I have money again." Marlee made an X over her heart with the tip of her index finger. "Cross my heart."

He grinned.

"Look what Sadie had someone drop off." She held up an envelope and pulled out a stack of papers.

"Are those what I think they are?" he asked. Not that he was in a hurry to divorce Marlee, but getting his life back in some semblance of order was a good thing.

"Divorce papers ready to sign." She smiled brightly.

Too bright.

One could crack a tooth on the intensity of that smile.

His heart did a little dip as she clicked a pen in her hand, flipped through the papers, held the packet up against the wall, and signed at the yellow flags. There was only a brief pause and a slight frown as she scrawled her signature on the last line.

"All done." She set the papers on the counter, placing the pen on top. "Your turn."

He stopped shaving for a moment to scribble his own signature on the correct lines, not allowing himself to feel anything other than relief that things were moving forward.

"Should we have champagne or something to celebrate?" She fidgeted with the edge of the paper.

"I think we should have drinks because it sounds fun, not because we're getting a divorce." He tried to catch her gaze, but she focused on shoving the papers back in the envelope.

"I'll get these filed." She still wouldn't meet his eyes.

He tilted her chin up with his index finger so their eyes finally met.

"You okay?" he asked.

"Fine. You?" She bit her lower lip.

"Fine."

"Good." She quickly nodded and held the envelope against her chest.

"Good."

Now who was being weird?

The scent of burnt metal tickled his nose. "Are you cooking something?"

"Dammit." Marlee turned, bolting toward the kitchen.

He let out a sigh. "Little dude, it's a good thing I like her."

He hadn't had a roommate since he'd moved into his own place after culinary school. Not that they couldn't coexist in the space together. They could. They did. She was just *there*. And when she was there, he found himself attracted to her. Their little tumble in the sheets had flipped some kind of switch in him, and his dick wanted to come out and play some more, specifically with her.

Which was a recipe for disaster because they were in the middle of a divorce. Sex had no business in their divorce. Just like feelings had no business in their marriage. And he was starting to worry he had some of those for her, too.

Shaving cream still on half his face, he followed the scent of burning cookware to the kitchen.

She was filling a super expensive copper-core pot he'd never seen before under the tap—she must've grabbed it when they got her stuff earlier that day.

Steam and smoke billowed from it.

"What were you cooking?" He pushed open the window over the sink.

"I was getting the pot ready to make pasta. I figured I could handle spaghetti. It's just sauce and noodles." She coughed against the steam.

"How do you get a pot ready to make pasta?" He grabbed a towel, fanning the smoke toward the open window.

"I put it on the burner to get it hot. Then I was going to add water and put in the noodles." She looked at him like this was a totally normal way to make pasta.

He'd roll with it. Different people had different ways of cooking. Some did it the right way. Some did it this way. "What stage were you at?"

"The getting-the-pot-hot stage." She turned to set the pot back on the burner. "I got distracted."

"So you literally managed to burn nothing?" Which was a helluva lot better than burning the actual noodles.

"I told you I'm no good in the kitchen." She huffed.

Yes, she told him she couldn't cook. He didn't realize she meant she literally *couldn't* cook.

Maybe he should find something for her to do in the office instead of having her help in the kitchen at work.

"Can I help you get the water boiling?" he asked. "We'll just start over. Go back to the beginning."

"That would be awesome, chef." She shoved her hands against her hips.

His staff called him chef. It'd never made his nerves tingle before. Not like when Marlee said it. He moved to turn the stove on for her. His arm brushed hers as he flicked the knob. The nerve endings all over his body stood on end. Wired. Wanting.

A blob of shaving foam dropped from his face into the water.

"Shit." He wiped at his unshaven cheek, smearing the foam all over his palm.

Marlee looked at him, pressing her lips together.

"Don't say it."

"Say what?" The laugh started in her chest, bubbling up.

"That I managed to ruin boiling the water."

"I won't say that, then." Marlee looked like she was making an attempt to stop laughing. A failed attempt. But an attempt nonetheless.

She grabbed the kitchen towel from the counter to wipe off his cheek. He stood there like a total dip and let her do it. Because it felt nice. Marlee touching him felt nice.

He closed his eyes, breathing her in.

"So an engagement party, huh?" she asked.

What? Oh, Jase's party. Right. He nodded.

"Tuesday is kind of an odd night for an engagement party. That seems more of a Friday or Saturday night kind of soiree."

"The bar's slow on Tuesday, so it works better for Brek. The rest of us work a lot of weddings and weekend events, so weekdays are usually best."

"That sounds fun." She cocked her head to the side like Lothario had done earlier.

He waited for her to say something.

She didn't say anything.

She smiled.

He smiled.

Everyone was smiling. No one was talking.

"Aren't you going to ask me what my plans are tonight?" she finally asked.

He raised his eyebrows in what he figured was a clear invitation for her to spill whatever was on her mind.

She didn't spill.

"What are you up to?" he asked, mostly so he didn't go back to that mental place of wanting her touching him. He busied himself by dumping the ruined water, rinsing the pot, and filling it again.

"I'm glad you asked." She hopped up on the counter next to the stove. "I have no plans tonight."

That was hard to believe. Marlee had a social calendar that rivaled any of the Hiltons or those housewives on cable.

He set the pot on the stovetop. "That's not like you."

"Nope." Marlee nudged the box of spaghetti pasta back and forth with the tip of her finger. "But apparently, now that I can't pay for everything, my local friends are all *busy*." She made air quotes with her fingers around the word.

"They're shitty friends." He dumped a few tablespoons of salt into the water.

"I know that now." She thinned her lips. "I didn't know that before. So until Sadie files that paperwork to get my money back and my *friends* come around, or I convince Sadie or Becca or Kellie to move back, it looks like I'm on my own." She continued toying with the pasta box. "Tonight, I'll just Skype with Sadie, Becca, and Kellie…or something."

Eli could be dense. He knew this. He worked hard not to be. But… Did Marlee want to come to the engagement party?

He hadn't asked because, well, why would he? They weren't a couple. But they were friends. And they were currently still married.

She flipped through her phone like it held an invitation to whatever shindig her not-really-friends were hosting and it had her name engraved on it.

"You wanna come?" he asked gently. "You should come. Velma's excellent in the kitchen, so the grub should be good."

Better than the burnt nothing they were making at his place.

"Yes," Marlee said way too quickly. She jumped off the counter. "I want to come. What's the dress code?"

Uh. "Clothes?"

"What are you wearing?" She looked him over top to bottom. His nerves started to tingle at the blatant inspection.

Uh. "This?"

Jeans and a T-shirt. It was Brek and Velma's pad, not a formal event.

"Jeans to an engagement party?" Marlee asked, her eyebrows dropping together while she stared at his...jeans.

Uh. "Yeah?"

"Okay. I'll make it work." She kissed him on his clean-shaven cheek, her lips pressing against the newly smooth skin in a move that was supposed to be totally platonic. But her lips on his cheek made him want to turn his head toward her mouth so he could kiss her like he really wanted. So he could run his tongue along hers. Press his body into hers so she melted against him like pasta sauce on a plate of noodles.

He didn't. He just stared into the air like a putz who'd just agreed to go on a date with his wife.

THEY WERE LATE. Eli didn't do late.

Marlee had taken quite a bit of time to get herself ready for the party. He couldn't argue with the results. The dress she'd pulled out of one of the many boxes littering his apartment hugged every curve on her body. She was always pretty. Beautiful, really. But that blue dress? That blue dress made Marlee look like she belonged on the arm of a guy with a Ferrari and all access to red-carpet events. Not a caterer with a Jeep Cherokee.

The elevator opened at the hallway to Brek and Velma's apartment. "You'll like 'em. They're good people," he assured.

"They're your people, which means I'll probably love them." Marlee stopped texting his sister and linked her free arm through his. Her other arm held Lothario in the purse.

While Eli was getting used to a roommate and to her touching him, he was not used to the way his blood heated whenever she did it. The way just that little movement made him want more. It made him want all of her. The touches. The smiles. Everything.

And that was unacceptable.

He was already responsible for the role he played in epically screwing up her life. He was willing to step up. But he couldn't make himself responsible for her happiness. He did better alone, and it was best he remember that.

With Marlee on one arm and a bottle of wine in the other, he somehow also managed to carry the set of copper mixing bowls he'd bought for Heather and Jase's kitchen. Heather baked kickass cookies, and she had her own commercial kitchen to do it in. She'd appreciate them. Jase? Eh.

"Brek and Velma are hosting. Heather and Jase are getting married. Claire and Dean will be here, too." Marlee looked up at him for confirmation. She'd been practicing their names the whole way from the liquor store.

He nodded. "Yep."

"You were friends with the guys in high school."

"Yep."

"Like Becca, Sadie, and me."

"Yep."

"Without all the drama we caused."

"Eh." He wouldn't go quite that far. Brek, Dean, and Jase had caused a load of drama. Eli was too busy at home to take part.

"And you're disappointed because you usually bring food." She bobbed her head as she spoke to herself. It was cute.

He might've mentioned once or twice how bringing food was his thing.

The stop at the liquor store for a bottle of wine had taken

a bit longer than usual since Marlee's tastes ran toward the five-hundred-dollar bottles they kept in the special case and his Visa was more a middle-of-the-road kind of card. They'd finally settled on a respectable Cab Sav that didn't require a salesperson to pull it from a locked cabinet.

Bringing a bottle of red was okay. But it also made him tug at the collar of the button-down shirt Marlee had insisted —with an abundance of enthusiasm—worked better with her dress. He was a chef. He brought food to these things. However, he hadn't had a chance since they'd just gotten back, and he had a new roommate—two if he counted Lothario—and he was hustling to fill the gaps in his catering schedule for the months ahead, and he'd just signed divorce papers.

He paused at the door to their apartment, gently disentangling his arm from Marlee's so he could turn the handle.

"Do we just walk in?" Marlee asked.

His buddy Brek lived there with his wife, Velma, and their kid, Lily. These were his best friends. The ones who knew him, supported him, and had his back. Marlee had her crew —Sadie, Becca, Kellie. He had his—Brek, Jase, Dean. And their wives. Well, Heather and Jase weren't hitched yet. Hence the engagement party. Point being, none of them knocked anymore when they visited each other.

"Yup." Eli turned the handle, pushing the door in.

He held the door so Marlee could pass through, swallowing the lump of holy-shit-I-brought-my-wife-to-meet-my-friends lodged in his trachea.

His friends were already there, scattered around the kitchen island. Velma and Brek's place was a fancy-ass—that was Brek's description—apartment overlooking Washington Park. Velma had decked the place out in white furniture. Brek had added a ridiculous painting of a pigeon dressed like he was from the 1800s—blue jacket, white ascot, and a look like he was supremely unhappy to be gracing the mantle.

All conversation stopped when Marlee and Eli stepped through the doorway. Six sets of eyes focused intently on the two of them.

His hand seemed to be a magnet to Marlee's waist. Walking into a room of people she didn't know must be hard, but he had her back and he wanted her to know. She turned to him, the little smile at the corner of her lips making him feel ten feet tall.

He met her smile with one of his own.

"Sorry I couldn't cook for this. Just got back to town." He handed the bottle to Velma.

"Where'd you take off to?" Brek asked, always way too curious for his own good.

Eli grunted because he didn't want to deal with explanations at that specific moment. Let him get settled. Let him say hello. Then they could deal with it. What he wanted, right then, was a beer.

He beelined for the minibar Brek had set up by the sink. He had it stocked. What else could Eli expect from the owner of Denver's newest nightspot? The place was a dive, but Brek had quickly made it the go-to spot in Denver if you wanted to hear a good band. He used to manage Dimefront, the current *it* band, so his connections in the music industry practically made Eli's boeuf bourguignon look like a box of processed macaroni-and-cheese product.

"Are you going to introduce us to your date?" Dean asked from behind him.

Eli started to grunt a reply to that, but Marlee had it covered.

"Oh, I'm not his date," Marlee answered. "We're not dating. And I'm Marlee."

Eli clocked the moment Dean placed her. Of course, it would've been Dean. He followed sports like a Denver super fan. He was also one of Denver's best financial gurus, so he knew the comings and goings of Denver's elite families.

"Marlee Medford?" Dean asked. He sounded surprised. Like he knew her. But of course, he knew her. Knew of her, at least. Her parents were practically Denver royalty. Princess Marlee. Anyone who followed sports knew her.

"That's me." Marlee was clearly in her element. She loved people. People loved her. These were his people. And he was happy to share them with Marlee. She needed people.

Dean squinted in her direction. "I thought I just read in the paper that you—"

"Don't go there." Eli shook his head, his focus on the brown bottle of unopened beer in his palm. Any talk of her ex was forbidden that night. They were there to celebrate the upcoming marriage of his buddy Jase. Not dissect his wife's failed engagement.

"If you're not his date…that makes you…?" Velma's last word hung in the air like a bomb for Jase to diffuse.

Yeah, Jase used to diffuse bombs for the government.

Marlee glanced at Eli with the question in her eyes, *What do you want me to say?* These were his friends. She wasn't going to fuck anything up for him.

He'd do that all on his own. "She's my wife."

Marlee's eyes went all soft, like she was eating his lemon meringue and it was the perfect balance of tart and air and crème. Yes, he'd used the word wife and hadn't had a stroke. It's not like he'd used the *m*-word.

"Fucking hell, I lost the motherfucking goddamned bet," Brek said under his breath, low enough his wife probably couldn't hear.

"*You* got married?" Jase choked on whatever he was chewing. Heather pounded on his back.

"We did." Marlee stared at the artistic pigeon print over the fireplace, her forehead scrunched together.

"*When* did you get married?" Jase asked on a wheeze.

That's when he saw it. Marlee got her groove back. She smiled that smile that could drop a man to his knees begging for her touch. "I think we're going to need hard alcohol for this story." She glanced at Eli and winked. "Actually, I think that's what got us into this mess."

"Can we start over?" Dean's wife, Claire, asked. "I'm Claire. This is my husband, Dean. Brek. Velma. Heather. Jase. And you're Marlee. And you got married to Eli?"

The way Claire said it was like it was just part of the introductions.

"Oh, he doesn't like that word," Marlee said quickly. "The *m*-word."

Actually, he'd been doing much better with it lately. Not the concept, but the word didn't elicit cold sweats anymore.

"Married?" Velma asked.

"Shhh." Marlee shook her head. "It makes Eli twitchy."

"I'm fine." Eli took a pull of his beer. "You can say it."

"Can you say it?" Marlee asked, the dare as clear as the sparkle in her eyes.

"I don't need to say it. It happened. We're here. There's nothing to say." And that's all he had to say about that.

"He can't say it." Marlee shrugged toward Velma.

He strode toward her. "Mar, I can totally say it."

"Then say it," she said all sing-song like.

She stared up at him. Her chin tilted to the side.

He held her eyes. No one said anything. And it really didn't matter. They were in a room full of his friends, but it was only him and Marlee.

"Married." He ground his incisors together. "See, I can say it."

Her face did the soft thing that went straight to his gut. "I knew you had it in you."

She leaned forward, and swear to fuck, he thought she was going to kiss him. His lips parted like they were ready for whatever she wanted to plant on them. And he would've liked it. Fuck it all, he would've liked it. Instead, she patted his cheek and smiled that dreamy smile of hers.

He didn't even care that there was a room full of friends watching their exchange.

"He calls her Mar," Heather not-so-quietly whispered.

Now? Now he cared.

Shit.

With the moment broken, he stepped back. Lifted his Coors to his lips like a Rocky Mountain armor.

"This is the best." Claire leaned forward, chin in palms, her elbows on the counter.

Jase recovered from his choking episode. "You two keep doing what you're doing. Epic shit going down right here."

Eli couldn't get his tongue to move. There was so much he wanted to say. To Marlee. To his friends. But like always, his tongue seemed to be adhered to the top of his mouth with high-grade peanut butter.

"Don't get too excited," Marlee said with a solid look toward Eli that made his knees turn to plum-flavored jam. "We're in the middle of the divorce."

He grunted in reply. What else was he supposed to say?

"It's all very amicable," Marlee assured. "He's even letting Lothario and me stay with him while things get finalized."

Now it was Brek's turn to choke on a chip. "She lives with you?"

Of course, she did. He wasn't an asshole. "Yep."

"Who's Lothario?" Claire asked.

Marlee lifted him from her purse. "This is Lothario."

She held up the little guy.

"Sweet fuck," Brek said.

Velma glared at him.

"I think cussing is allowed in this situation," Brek said, defending his word choice.

Dean moved to pour himself a few fingers of whiskey from Brek's stash. He paused near Eli.

"You got new ink," Dean said. He pointed to the heart on Eli's arm.

"We both did." Marlee turned her ankle to display her matching heart. "We were drunk." She pulled a you-know-how-it-goes face.

Dean played by all the rules, though. He'd never get inked and married in Vegas.

"You know what I think?" Velma asked. "I think that you guys should go start the grill and we'll stay here and get to know Marlee."

"And Lothario," Heather added.

"We're grilling?" Eli asked. And suddenly, the world looked better. Shinier. Give him a cut of meat and a cooking surface and he could make magic. Magic that didn't involve any conversation about marriage. He knew the word. Knew what he'd done. He was dealing with it all on an hourly basis.

Brek grabbed a stunning tray of beef tenderloin roast from the fridge. All laid out and ready for Eli to escape into cooking. He looked at Marlee.

He wouldn't leave her if she wasn't good, wasn't okay with being left alone with the wives and fiancée of his best friends.

"Go do your thing," she said. A blessing that would get him out of the awkwardness and into his element.

"That's mine." Eli took the tray from Brek, heading toward the grill on the balcony.

He had a load of explaining to do to his friends. And a cut of meat to cook.

Thank God for meat and friends.

MARLEE COULD TELL these ladies were the real deal. Like Becca, Kellie, and Sadie…they were authentic. Looking back, her so-called Denver friends hadn't been warm in the beginning. Not until they learned what she had to offer. Namely, money.

Heather had a fun vibe to her that Marlee knew could get them both in trouble—the kind of trouble they'd have a heck of a lot of fun doing. Heather's long brown hair was pulled tight into a ponytail. She was a jeans and T-shirt kind of girl with wicked cute pink ballet flats.

Claire had dark hair and a body that Marlee would kill for. Not that she'd actually work out to get a body like that—way too much effort would be involved in that project. But she could appreciate it on someone else. Claire was not a jeans and T-shirt girl. She was the cute dress and strappy sandal girl. And probably sweater dress girl when it got chilly.

And Velma? Velma had blonde hair and a warmth that Marlee hoped would stay genuine. Velma was super pretty. She had curves and she rocked them. Her dress wasn't as casual as Claire's, but it wasn't a full business suit either.

She'd slipped off to the bathroom after Eli headed for the grill. She wanted to check her lipstick, and she wanted to check in with the girls.

> Marlee: I'm making new friends. Eli's friends.

Sadie: ...

Becca: How goes the de-Eli-ing?

> Marlee: Good. He's grilling a roast. Happy.

Sadie: I can't believe he took u tonight! That's amazing.

> Marlee: Divorce papers, new friends & a breakthrough. Yay me!

Kellie: I hope you enjoy Eli's meat! 😊

Becca: Leave it to Kel to go there.

Sadie: Can we not? He's my b-r-o-t-h-e-r. Insert vomit emoji.

Becca: Sadie is voice-texting again.

Sadie: Damn it. It's supposed to actually put
the emoji.

Marlee: GTG

She tucked the phone away and headed back to the
kitchen, settling on a barstool next to Claire and Lothario.

"You married Eli?" Heather asked. "And he just went
along with it?"

"That doesn't sound like something Eli would just go
along with." Claire reached to pet Lothario. He immediately
nuzzled her hand. Marlee kept her eye on him in case he got
any dirty ideas.

"We screwed up. That's all," Marlee said.

"I have literally never known Eli to screw up." Velma
multitasked, somehow managing to fix a salad and potatoes
and prep dessert all at once. "Frankly, I think a good screwup
is just what he needs." She paled. "I didn't mean that like
you're a screwup. I mean—"

"She didn't mean how that sounded." Claire giggled.
"She means Eli needs his life shaken up."

Marlee chuckled. She liked these ladies. They were kind,
and they probably didn't expect her to pay for everything. "I
totally agree. I hadn't had a chance to hang out with him for
a while."

What with all the wedding planning and the like. And the
fact she only really got to see him when Sadie came to town.

"Can I help with that?" Marlee asked as Velma worked.

Not that she'd be much help in the kitchen, but she could
certainly do something to help out.

"Nope." Velma flashed her a smile. "I've got it."

"You two met in Vegas then?" Claire asked. Lothario had
made himself at home in her lap.

"Oh no. I've known Eli since we were teenagers. His sister
is my best friend." Better just explain it all at once so they
understood that what happened didn't mean anything perma-

nent. "I was supposed to get married, but my fiancé decided not to go through with it at the last minute. My friends decided to get me out of town for the weekend. Eli came along with us on the wedding-didn't-happen Vegas trip. And then this happened." She flicked her hair over her shoulder. Eli hadn't appreciated the amount of time it had taken her to blow it out. But the results were worth it. "It wasn't planned. Hence the divorce."

"And now you're living with him?" Velma confirmed.

Marlee wiped a line of condensation from the side of her glass. "Things kind of went south for me when we got back."

Velma stilled mid-salad-toss. "The Medford account."

Marlee paused. Eli had said Velma worked with Dean in finance.

"You probably work on my parents' accounts." Marlee lifted Lothario onto her lap. "It's okay. It's not a secret. They cut me off because I made a bad choice and got married. That's why Eli is letting me stay with him."

Velma and Claire shared a look that held a whole lot of conversation without any words.

"Don't worry," Marlee added. "I'm not taking advantage or anything. He said it was okay and I promised to pay him back once this whole thing is over."

"That's not what we were thinking," Claire said. "We're all actually really excited that Eli brought someone around."

"He's never brought anyone before?" Marlee asked. That didn't seem right. Eli was a great guy. He deserved to be happy. Not that one had to be in a relationship to be happy. Eli just didn't seem like a guy that should be alone all the time.

Sure, he acted like he preferred it. She didn't buy the act. How many times had she noticed him texting his sisters? His mom? His dad? Calling Sadie?

"I guess our next party will be a wedding shower for you and Eli," Velma said.

Velma was just being nice, Marlee was confident in that. But the idea of having anything truly wedding related was a big fat kick in the gut. She'd done all that once and now she had a load of gifts to box up and return.

"No wedding shower. That's probably inappropriate with the divorce and all."

"You're not really going to divorce him, are you?" Heather grimaced. "I mean, he's Eli. You can't divorce Eli."

Well, he was Eli. But… "I kind of have to. Since we're not actually a couple."

"But you could be." Heather grinned huge. "I think you should be."

Marlee let her mind wander to that place where maybe she and Eli could work. He was easy to be with. Excellent in bed. Always there for her. She'd expected her life with Eli to last a few months and then she'd go back to a new version of what she'd done before. But life with Eli could be wonderfully comfortable.

Blah. No. No way was she ready for that.

"My fiancé just dumped me after ten years together. There's got to be some kind of period of mourning or something I need to adhere to before I start dating again. And shouldn't I have a rebound guy? I don't want my rebound guy to be my best friend's brother. That would make things so awkward."

Unlike marrying him…

"Maybe we could help you find a rebound guy so that you can be with Eli?" Claire asked. "We love projects. Especially projects that end with Eli not being so grumpy all the time."

Eli wasn't grumpy. Eli was just misunderstood. Marlee opened her mouth to say just that—

"There will be no hooking Eli's wife up with a rebound guy," Jase said from behind Marlee. "If you need a project, I have a wall that needs paint."

Jase wandered into the kitchen, moving behind Heather

to nuzzle her neck before he grabbed a couple of beers off the counter.

"Shoo," Heather said. "This is girl stuff."

"What's girl stuff?" Brek asked, coming inside and taking one of the beer bottles from Jase.

"Trying to find Marlee a hookup so she can be with Eli." Jase gave Heather a clear don't-you-dare look.

"Well, that's the worst idea I've heard in a while." Brek popped the bottle cap off his beer.

"Which is why we're going to do it." Claire shrugged.

"Don't you worry you'll piss off the beast by finding his wife someone else?" Jase asked, standing behind Heather with his arms around her.

Marlee glanced away, her throat suddenly filled with cotton. She missed that feeling. The feeling of a man behind her. A man who wanted to touch her.

"Finding her someone else will ensure that the two of them end up together," Claire said like it was really a thing.

"Who ends up together?" Eli stomped into the kitchen.

"You two." Jase pointed between them with the end of his beer bottle.

"For fuck's sake," Eli said under his breath.

"They're coming up with this themselves," Marlee assured. "We're in the middle of a very amicable divorce. I don't want to do anything to compromise that."

And the idea of hooking up with anyone made Marlee's skin start to itch. Well, not Eli. That hookup was actually pretty fun.

"Well, at least come out with us next week?" Velma asked. "I get another night off from mom duty."

Marlee perked up. She missed having lots of plans. She needed plans. "That sounds really fun."

"Great." Claire clapped her hands quietly. "And we'll only try to set you up with the cute ones."

"And only if you want to," Heather added.

Well, that was…great.

Eli caught Marlee's gaze. She shook her head slightly.

He sighed and headed back to the patio.

"Excuse me for a minute." Marlee followed him to where Dean stood watching the grill.

"Hi. It's Dean?" Marlee asked.

"Yup." He smiled an easy smile.

"I'm still learning names." Marlee moved beside Eli as he checked the roast. "Do you mind giving Eli and me a second?"

Dean did a quick take between the two of them. "Yup."

Clearly sensing Eli's tension, Dean hurried inside, pulling the door closed behind him.

Marlee leaned against the railing overlooking Washington Park. "You know I'm not going to see anyone while we're still married, right?"

He looked straight ahead, no emotion in his features. She couldn't help but notice how his jaw clenched and his grip on the railing made his knuckles go white. "You can do what you want to do."

She squeezed his arm. "Well, I know *that*. But you've been great to me and I don't want you to think I'd just go off with someone else."

"Mar." He caught her gaze, pinned it with his. "I don't have any claim on you."

Her heart clenched.

No, no, he didn't.

But yes, yes, he did.

"Do you want to see anyone else while we wait for the divorce?" she asked, hoping like crazy he didn't want to date while they were married. But she didn't have a claim on him, either. The sensitive skin along her arms prickled at the idea of him with someone else. Which made no sense.

He pressed his palm against his neck, bunching the muscles of his triceps. "No. I guess not."

She let out a breath. "So we'll just not. It doesn't mean anything. We're just trying to not be awkward about the situation we're in."

"That's all it is?" His Adam's apple bobbed in his throat.

Was that all this was? She was still supposed to be mourning her relationship with Scotty, not having a conversation like this with Eli.

The air seemed to snap between them, waiting for her answer.

"It's all it should be, right?" she asked. "I should take some time to figure out my life. I mean, you don't want me to work for you forever. I need to find something permanent. And a place to live."

"Ninety days and you get your old life back," he pointed out.

"Looks like it." She shook her head, refusing to go back to a numb reality that included attending dinner parties with "friends" who only cared about her American Express and working at a job where she didn't even get a paycheck. These months would be about Marlee finding her footing in a life that she designed herself.

The thing about Eli was that he took a lot of time to think before he spoke. Sometimes, he took a lot of time and then never said anything. It's who he was. Had been ever since Marlee first met him. He didn't use words unless they were words that meant something. Important words.

He cleared his throat. "In all the time I've known you, and it's been a long time, you've never been without a guy on your hook. If that's what you need, I don't want to stop you."

That's what he thought? She needed a guy? Always needed a man?

No.

Had she always been with someone? She went back through the years before Scotty. There had only been small patches where she wasn't dating someone...all the way back to seventh grade and her first "official" boyfriend. Huh. She'd never realized that before.

She bounced on her toes, doing her best to be cheery. No one wanted deep thoughts at an engagement party. She certainly didn't need to be evaluating her entire romantic history here. "Then that's all the more reason I should take this time and learn to just be me."

"You think you can do that?" he asked, clearly not buying it.

When she was a teenager, Eli always saw right through her bullshit. Apparently, that hadn't changed.

"Of course." She kicked off from the railing. "And you know what?"

"I bet you're gonna tell me." He opened the grill cover, poked at the roast with a pair of tongs.

"In all that time, you've never been with anyone. Maybe it's you we should be setting up." She said it, but the idea of Eli with anyone made her heart feel funny. Not good funny. Ache funny. "A little project for my new friends and me?"

"Don't even think about it." He pulled her against his side like she was a kid sister.

Except being so close to him made her not feel one bit like his sister.

She laid her head against his shoulder. "I like you, Eli."

"I like you, too, Mar." He tilted his head against the crown of hers, planting a soft kiss there.

Okay. So they weren't seeing other people. They were married. And she was not getting a brotherly vibe from him. That didn't necessarily *mean* anything.

"I'm glad we're getting a divorce so we can spend time together." She glanced up to catch him staring at her.

He chuckled. "Me, too."

Disentangling herself from his hug, she bounced her way over to watch the traffic by the park. "And I'm glad I'm not trying to cook spaghetti back at your place."

That got her a bark of a laugh. "Me, too, Mar. Me, too."

This would be the best divorce in the history of all divorces.

Her cell buzzed. She didn't dare chance a glance to see who was calling. It kept buzzing. Finally, she yanked it out, not answering and not recognizing the number calling.

"Maybe you should get that?" Eli asked when the phone continued to buzz at them.

"Hello," Marlee said.

"Marlee?" a voice she vaguely recognized asked in return. "This is Constance. From the *Denver Post.*"

Marlee stilled. She knew Constance. Not well, but she'd met her a few times. They'd had lunch once to discuss sponsoring one of the team events. She was nice enough. Super serious about her job, which Marlee could understand and admire. Except when the job was to spill Marlee's dirty laundry all over the Mile High City.

"I don't have a comment," Marlee said before Constance could continue.

Eli raised his eyebrows in her direction.

"On anything," she added quickly.

"I'm just calling to confirm that Eli Howard is the man you married in Vegas," Constance continued.

"Please, don't go there with this. Please," Marlee said.

"We got the name from Scott Bishop," Constance continued, her voice quieter. Like she was letting Marlee know so it didn't blindside her.

Still, it totally blindsided her.

Marlee's blood seemed to stop pumping. As if she didn't already have a load of reasons to dislike her ex, he was still piling them on.

"Still no comment." Marlee held firm.

"Who is it?" Eli asked.

"It's the paper," she mouthed back.

Eli slipped the phone from her ear while Constance continued speaking.

He held Marlee's cell to his own ear. "She said no comment."

His expression went dark. Scary dark. Then he pushed the end button and handed the phone back to her.

"They know it's you," she said, tucking her phone away.

"Yep." He stared at the grill.

"I'm sorry, Eli," she said. And she was. Really sorry her circumstances were about to take over more than his bedroom and some closet space.

"Not your fault, Mar," he said.

Then he did the quiet thing again. She didn't try to fill the space with words. This time, she just let things be.

Chapter Twelve
TEN WEEKS UNTIL THE DIVORCE
BECOMES FINAL

WORKING in a kitchen was not super fun. Working in a kitchen actually pretty much sucked. And not just because she was Marlee and kitchens were kind of her nemesis, either. Eli might be all quiet and thoughtful in his daily life, but in his kitchen? He was all about barking orders and demanding precision. If he hadn't been directing his barking toward her a good part of the time, she probably would've found it sexy. A guy who knew what he was doing directing a staff who knew exactly what they were doing? Yeah, hot. And then there was Marlee, who had no idea what she was doing, which made the barking of the orders run like a cheese grater over her skin. Yes, she'd mastered the use of a grater and could now shred cheddar so it looked like it came in one of the bags from the grocery store. This was a skill she never thought she'd take pride in.

She'd never known there was a wrong way to grate cheese. Turned out, there was. There was also an incorrect way to wash the pots and pans. And a wrong way to stir the soup. And a wrong way to use words, too. The staff were all, "Yes, chef," and "behind," and "hot plate." Marlee had learned the first day not to call him Eli in the kitchen when the staff all looked at her like she'd violated the cardinal rule of kitchening.

Eli hadn't seemed to care, but she didn't like the not-so-nice looks. She picked up the "chef" thing pretty quickly. Then *Eli* had looked at her funny, but he didn't correct her. And given that he corrected everything, she figured that meant it was what she was supposed to do. Working in a kitchen was crazy.

She tossed another batch of slivered almonds over yet another tray of chicken breasts. Eli had an assembly line going and her only job was to almond the chicken. Chicken that looked freaking amazing all nestled in a tray of cream sauce. Her stomach rumbled. Starving was a distinct possibility if she didn't get something to eat soon.

That's the one thing she hadn't expected from working in a kitchen—she was hungry all the time.

And to top it all off, even though what Eli paid her seemed totally fair, by the time his bookkeeper got done taking out all the money for the government, there wasn't nearly as much as Marlee had thought there'd be.

When she'd asked Eli about it, he had explained some blah-blah about taxes and benefits.

She tried to understand, but the bottom line was the same —her paycheck was pitiful.

"Less almonds." Eli stopped behind her. "Spread them out more."

Less almonds? She was literally putting on the exact number of almonds he'd shown her, in the exact same spots.

"Yes, chef," she said instead of saying what she really wanted to say about him micromanaging the almonds. She didn't glance at him, because if she did, two things would happen. One, she would tell him to lay off because the almonds were exactly as he'd shown her. And two, if she looked his way, she'd get all tongue-tied because he was in his chef's jacket with the sleeves rolled up to his elbows and his hair was wrapped in a bandana thing that made her stutter and want to beg him for a Vegas repeat every time he wore it. Which was stupid, because she didn't really like him when he wore it.

Her stomach growled again, the lightheaded, haven't-eaten feeling making her sway just a tad. Three more trays and she'd be done screwing up his almonds. She flicked each slivered almond individually now, ensuring each one landed with an appropriate amount of space between it and the others. It was like painting. Art. If she thought of it as almond art, she didn't want to strangle Eli quite so badly.

"Mar?" he asked.

She tossed the last almond on her current casserole masterpiece. "Yes, chef?"

He didn't say anything. Dammit. She hated when he did this. She was going to have to look at him.

"Marlee." Man, he never used her full name. She pursed her lips. What had she messed up this time? The almonds were going exactly where he'd asked.

She flicked one last almond sliver in defiance and braced herself for the hit of sexy Chef Eli.

Sexy Chef Eli wasn't barky, his eyebrows were all furrowed. "You feeling okay?"

Food was a necessity. She shouldn't have skipped breakfast, but she got up late and it was Monday and that meant she had a corner coffee delivery for Bert and his friends. And with her weird work schedule, her body clock was all wonky. The last week had been crazy busy with events every day. Staying up way late and getting up again early for the next round.

"Marlee." Now, he was barky again.

She gave an internal eye roll. "Yes, chef?"

"You didn't answer my question." He stalked closer, pressing the back of his hand to her forehead.

She batted it away. "I'm fine. Starving, that's all."

Using the inside of her elbow, she brushed a stray hair that had fallen from the side of her hairnet.

No touching of the hair with fingers when in the kitchen. Eli'd made that clear on her first kitchen day.

"I'll go grab something when we're done with these," she said.

Jase kept Lothario at the flower shop next door while Marlee was in the kitchen. Lothario loved it there. Customers lavished him with attention, and he wasn't stuffed in Eli's office. Once she finished these, she would grab the sandwich she'd made that morning—she hadn't burned the peanut butter and jelly—and go hang out with her dog for a while.

"You've been doing your inhalers and stuff?" Eli asked, like he had been the one managing her asthma for all these years.

Of course, she'd been doing her inhalers and "stuff."

"Yeah," she replied.

Eli stared at her for a moment. She stared back, making it a point to exaggerate the motion. He might be the chef, and he might be her husband, but he was also being super weird.

His sneakers squeaked against the sealed cement floor as he turned, grabbed a take-out box, and dished up a heaping mound of chicken divan. He didn't take time to carefully put the slivered almonds on top like Marlee had been doing. Like he *told* her to do. Nope, he got away with just slopping a handful on top.

Marlee glared at his back and went back to flicking the almonds.

At least they didn't have to serve at this event. This was a drop and go, and then she could sleep for three days. After that, she'd have a girls' night with Velma, Heather, and Claire. Then she'd come back and muddle through again.

"Eat." He pushed the open tray toward her, a fork sticking out the top.

She raised her eyebrows at him. Yes, she was starving. No,

he did not get to boss her around. Even when the bossing was something she'd actually want to do.

"Please," he said softer.

Fine. She'd eat. But only because she was really hungry. She reached for the tray. The room went a little wobbly, like when she couldn't breathe and the dizzy spells started. But she could breathe just fine.

Tired and hungry and working her butt off. It's times like this she missed money.

Not enough to go live with her parents or—God help her —Scotty until the divorce was final. But enough to wish she had some green bills in her wallet beyond the ones with an Andrew Jackson.

"Stool." Eli was all barky again. He should just go hang out with Lothario and they could bark together and hump things.

Ack. No.

Visions of Eli in those positions were strictly off-limits. Especially barky Eli in his bandana and chef's jacket.

Marlee started to move to go grab the stool Eli wanted. He touched her arm before she even got a step away. "Not you. The stool's *for* you."

Oh, well, that was kind of sweet.

Mark, his sous-chef that day, handed over the stool.

Eli gently guided Marlee to sit, like he hadn't been grouching at her about almonds three minutes earlier. Before she could reach for the fork, he had a slice of chicken speared at the end of it, waiting at her lips. She slid her gaze to him. Totally ridiculous. He was being totally ridiculous.

Still, Eli in his chef gear feeding her? She opened her mouth, closed her eyes, and bit into the chicken as soft as butter with creamy sauce, almonds, and asparagus. There was definitely a visceral response going on inside of her to this food. If it was true that she could burn anything—and oh boy, it was—then it was just as true that Eli could cook anything. She didn't moan, but damn, she came close.

"You're absolved." She wiped at the edge of her mouth with her fingertips, making a mental note that she was no longer scrubbed in and would need to re-scrub in so Eli didn't lose his mind.

"Absolved of what?" His eyebrows furrowed.

Eli didn't seem to even notice she'd wiped her lips with her fingers. Sexy, concerned Chef Eli was someone she could get used to, especially when he fed her. He held a napkin out to her—okay, apparently, he'd noticed.

She dabbed the paper against her lips.

"For bossing me around with the almonds." She took the fork from him, practically Hoovering the chicken. "You can boss me around all you want if I get to eat this."

With her blood sugar stabilizing, the dizziness began to subside.

"Grab us a water," he said to one of the other staff. A lot of the bark was missing this time.

He passed the bottle of water to her. She uncapped it, taking a long drink.

"Can I talk to you in the office?" he asked.

Shit.

"Is it 'cause I brought up the almonds?" she asked, her mouth still full.

"Mar." He jerked his head toward the glass partitions of the small room in the back that he used as an office. "Alone?"

"It's because I screwed them up, isn't it?" And this is what it was like to get fired. Damn.

She grabbed the rest of the boxed chicken—if he was going to let her go, she was totally taking the chicken.

He strode to the office. She followed, still noshing on the chicken, the water bottle capped and tucked in the pocket of her black apron. *Eats*, the name of his catering company, embroidered on the front.

Her heels tapped against the floor. *Fired. Fired. Fired*, they seemed to echo.

Yes, she wore her heels because they matched the T-shirt with his logo. The one he made all of his workers wear when they were in the kitchen.

"It's fine if it's not working out, but I can't eventually pay you rent if you don't keep paying me." Also, she couldn't buy gas. Or coffee for Bert and his friends. Or Lothario's special dog food. Or pretty much anything else.

Eli closed the door, which was kind of funny given that the office was totally glass and everyone could see in anyway.

"You need to take a day off. You're working way too hard." He sat on the edge of his desk, his hands gripping the dark wood on both sides of his thighs. He kept the office as organized as the kitchen—everything in its place at all times.

Marlee perched in the chair next to his desk, setting the box of chicken on the tabletop so she could finish. "I'm not working harder than you."

"You almost passed out." At least barky Eli was gone. She liked this Eli much better. Still in his sexy clothes, without the edge.

She chewed a bite. Swallowed. Studied how he'd just chucked a bunch of nuts at the plate. He was wrong. She hadn't almost passed out. The dizzy had just gotten to her. Now that she had eaten, she'd be better. Unless he got grumpy about almonds again.

"I did not almost pass out. I just don't get to taste the food while I work like you do." Not that she held it against him, but she noted all those individual spoon calories and, frankly, envied them.

He pressed his palm against the back of his neck, triceps bunching through the polyester of his chef jacket. "I think you're pushing yourself too hard. Let's just go back. Start over."

"So are you firing me or sending me home with pay and I

come back tomorrow?" She gestured at him with the tines of the fork.

"Take tomorrow off." He crossed his arms. "And take the rest of the day today so you can get some rest."

"But you're still paying me?" Look, she didn't mean to be pushy, but her tank was on empty and she'd spent all her money on Bert's coffee and Lothario's vet bill to remove his cast. At least he didn't thump around on three legs anymore.

"Yeah." He nodded.

"Perfect." She stood. "See? You feed me and I'm not even a little dizzy." She did a little bounce to prove her point.

Judging by the way his eyes thinned, he wasn't amused.

"You think you can bring some of this home for dinner?" She lifted the now empty box, ignoring his reaction to her bounce.

The edges of his lips twitched. There it was. He wasn't really mad. He never really was.

"I'll come up with something for dinner," he said.

"Or I can try spaghetti again?" She was pretty sure she knew exactly where she'd gone wrong.

"Don't touch the stove. I'll bring dinner." He opened the door.

She lifted her keys from the cup thingy on his desk.

"And maybe some of those cupcake things?" she asked.

Those looked amazing. All German chocolate goodness that made her wish she could pop on a plane and go to Europe.

"Sure." He had a half smile going on that paired really well with the bandana.

She grabbed the bottle of water, tugged off her apron, and hung it on the hook by his desk. "Bring extra of those."

Now, he was fully smiling. "See you at home."

Home. One word gave her warm fuzzies all over. She decided to revel in it instead of worrying about what would happen when she got money again and had to move out.

She made her way to Jase's flower shop, yanking off the hairnet along the way. Shoving the door open, the perfume of flowers drifted over her as she hurried into the shop.

"Lothario." She opened her arms, dropping to her knees. "My baby."

Lothario scampered straight for her, his paws slipping just a bit on the floor. He licked her cheek.

"Mommy missed you, too," Marlee said.

"Your dog defiled the vase holding a dozen roses earlier," Jase mumbled.

"Did he break it?" *Gah*, someone please tell her he hadn't broken anything. She was fresh out of cash until her next paycheck.

Heck, there wasn't even any change for Eli's coin-operated washing machine. The fact that those even existed was a freaking travesty. Who had to put in quarters to run a load of whites? *That* should be free.

"No, he just needed some privacy." Jase stood back from a floral arrangement the size of the ones Marlee's mom kept in the foyer. Marlee used to love looking at the flowers that changed every other day. Now? Now, she realized that the kind of money her parents spent each week on flowers alone would pay for a decent apartment downtown for her and Lothario.

Not that she'd spoken much to her parents since they cut her off. A few check-in texts here and there, and consistently avoiding their dinner invitations, lunch invitations, brunch invitations. Why did she need to go eat with them when she had her own personal chef?

"That's a bad doggy," Marlee said, but Lothario knew she didn't mean it. He was who he was, and everyone would just have to learn to accept that about him. As long as he didn't hurt himself or break vases in the process.

"How are you, Marlee?" Aspen, her wedding planner,

stood by a rack of vases. Marlee had been so intent on Lothario that she hadn't even seen her there.

She hadn't seen Aspen since everything fell apart.

"Hey." Marlee scooped the dog in her arms and stood. "I'm good."

Aspen had been amazing in the not-getting-married madness, handling the mess. She was also Brek's sister, and she worked in an office on the same street as Jase, Eli, and Heather. Denver was like that—everyone was connected in some way.

"Is this your newest?" Marlee peeked into the stroller at the tiny baby sleeping there.

"It is." Aspen shifted the stroller just a little so Marlee could get a better look.

Sleeping babies were Marlee's kryptonite. Her ovaries did a little let's-have-one jig. Marlee immediately told them to be quiet.

"Thank you again." Marlee looked away from the sleeping baby to Aspen. "For everything you did after…you know."

"It's my job." Aspen shrugged. "And you've thanked me enough. We're good."

Marlee could've hugged her. "Thanks."

"And I'm out, Jase." Aspen waved to Jase. "See you around, Marlee."

"See you around," Marlee whispered back.

She sauntered over to Jase and his flowers. "You need about four more lilies on the left and it'll be perfect."

He slid his gaze to her.

She raised her eyebrows in her best *what?* expression. When it came to art—especially flowers—she was like a savant. After the office flowers would get delivered each week, she'd made it her own personal job to fix the arrangements. No, it had nothing to do with the company events she helped plan, but yes, it was necessary. It was also number one hundred and sixty-five on the list of things she did that drove Scotty nuts. Which, she'd always assumed, was why he didn't buy her flowers.

"You wanna show me?" Jase asked.

She set Lothario on the ground, grabbed the lilies, snipped off the ends so they'd get a nice drink of water in the Oasis floral foam, and with the precision of someone who couldn't afford to pay for them if she screwed them up, poked them precisely where they'd look best. She didn't need to step back for the full effect to know the arrangement was now complete.

"What do you think of that one?" He jerked his chin toward a bouquet of white roses and succulents in a bamboo-inspired vase.

"Do you have anything that looks ropey? Or like a vine?" She scanned the tabletop, not coming up with anything that would work. Most of the time, flowers looked best when their symmetry was precise. But with the way the succulents tilted, a few ropey vines would be perfect for balance.

"Ropey?" he asked, eyebrows raised.

"Something that looks like a rope?" she replied, eyebrows also raised.

"Let's check the back." Jase headed toward a walk-in cooler.

The cold air blew against her skin as she inventoried the selection. She snagged a few fig branches from one of his oversized white buckets. "This'll work."

She moved back to the table, twisting the vine so it would bend at the precise angle she needed and maneuvering it through the roses so it'd hold. "There."

"That's decent." Jase turned the vase so he could see from the other side.

"It's not decent. It's perfect." Marlee stood by that asser-tion. "It's like a painting, but with flowers."

Jase turned the vase again. "Do you know anything about flowers?"

"I know which ones I like." Marlee shrugged. "And I rearrange them when I see them at the office. Used to see them at the office," she amended.

"How much is Eli paying you?" Jase asked. "My assistant left. I've been doing everything myself for the past few weeks."

"Eli isn't paying me very much. But I pretty much screw up everything over there and mooch off his food and sleep in his bed." She shrugged.

Jase tilted his head to the right just a tad.

"I mean, he's not sleeping in the bed with me," Marlee assured. "But he could." Not that he would. Or that she wanted it. "He just takes the couch because of the divorce." And now she was going to shut up.

Jase crossed his arms. "I'll pay you double whatever he's paying."

Well, that was better than fussing with almonds and ruining soup, but—"What's the job, exactly?"

"Helping me out in the shop, arranging flowers, manning the cash register, talking to customers—"

"I love talking to people." She really did. No one really chatted in the kitchen. Everyone stayed focused on the food. Which, you know, as someone who ate food, she appreciated that they kept their focus where it should be. But as someone who also liked to chitchat, it was annoying as hell that no one talked.

He smiled huge. "And some deliveries."

"I can do deliveries. I have a driver's license and every-thing." And his van probably had plenty of gas. "Do I have to pay the tax things?"

Because those really were a pain in the tush.

Jase smirked. "Well, yeah. It's sort of the law."

"Do I have to pay a lot of them?" she asked.

He leveled a stare at her, clearly trying to figure her out. "I'll pay you triple."

"There's still taxes. I don't like paying those."

"Marlee, I can't negotiate out the taxes, but there will be more money when you get your check from *me* versus when you get your check from *Eli*."

Well, that worked, too. "Deal."

She'd once mentioned to her dad that she'd thought about becoming a florist.

He'd informed her it wasn't an appropriate position for someone of her pedigree. Now, it would be what kept Lothario fed, which made it all the more fitting.

"When can you start?" Jase held out his hand.

She shook it. "Uh, now? Eli sent me home early because I didn't eat lunch and I screwed up his almonds."

Jase's eyebrows scrunched together. "Did you get lunch or should I call something in?"

Nope, she was good. "Eli fed me before he sent me home."

Now, he could relax knowing that she would not be tripping over everything in his kitchen or screwing up his jobs.

"Marlee, I have about ten arrangements to finish this afternoon. If you help me, I'll never make you do anything with almonds," Jase promised.

"Then you think you can stop me?" Because truth was, she would arrange flowers for free. Well, she would've before she didn't have any money. Now, she'd need to charge. But only because Lothario liked special only-available-online food. He was struggling through the kibble she was able to afford, but he didn't have to whine for her to know he preferred the other. "But Eli may need my help with some of his events since he's been planning on me being there." She didn't want to leave him high and dry, but he was going to be over the moon that she wasn't all up in his face all the time. "So I'll have to work out some kind of a schedule."

"Fair enough." Jase pulled a binder from beside the cash register. "This is where I keep the special orders. I also make a list every Monday of the stock we'll want to keep in the shop that week."

Marlee rubbed her hands together. "Gimme."

ELI HAD BEEN WORKING Marlee too hard. Hell, he was exhausted, and he was used to the late hours and early mornings. He'd been busting his butt to keep shaving off the days until he could afford to open his new restaurant. But thanks to his new wife, he'd just landed a fundraising gala. If it went well, he could likely shave ten months off Dean's timetable with all the extra gigs that would follow.

As soon as he came out as her mystery groom, the call came in from the committee chair for the Consolidated Means gala. Their caterer had bailed, and Marlee had talked her into hiring Eli.

Usually, after a marathon couple of weeks, he'd head up to the mountains with a tent and no cell service. Now that Marlee was staying with him, he'd find something to do closer to home after the big gala. He just hoped like hell that the business following the event would make it all worth it.

With a large brown bag of leftovers tucked under his arm, he paused at the edge of the parking lot. Marlee's Jag was still parked right next to his Jeep. She hadn't gone home to rest.

His stomach dropped.

Not that he had any right to tell her what to do or where to go, but she'd looked so wiped earlier. He didn't want to be responsible for that.

She was either at Jase's flower shop or Heather's cookie shop. He'd start with Jase. It was closer anyway, and since Jase was his buddy and it wasn't totally out of the ordinary for him to stop in after work for a beer, it wouldn't look like he was tracking down his soon-to-be ex-wife.

Turning back toward the sidewalk, he practically jogged to Jase's door. Not because he was worried about Marlee. Only because he wanted to see his buddy.

The cowbell on the door clunked as he pushed it open. Eighties hair band music blared from the speakers—Van Halen this time—and Marlee was fussing with an arrangement of tulips, one of The Flower Pot's aprons hugging her waist.

Marlee was not resting.

Lothario was hanging out next to her on Jase's flower-arranging station in the middle of the store. Lothario saw him first. Barked. Jumped off the counter and bounded toward Eli. Eli's feet, anyway.

Marlee turned. "Eli. Hey."

"Mar." He strode to the counter.

"Oh, is that for me?" Her eyes danced.

Yeah, it was all for her. Dinner, and he'd put aside a dozen cupcakes just for her. He nodded.

"Why aren't you resting?" he asked as carefully as he could, because he really had no business asking her about anything she did.

"I am." She held up the bouquet. "See?"

"This isn't resting. This is working for Jase."

"Yeah. So he kind of hired me. But congratulations to you, you don't have to worry about your almonds anymore." She grinned like this was a good thing.

His gut clenched. She was quitting? He liked her in his kitchen. Maybe he liked her there too much.

"Don't worry, though, I told Jase I needed to finish out the events you've got me scheduled for."

"Mar, you don't have to work somewhere else." Eli shifted his foot from where Lothario was loving up on it.

"Yes, she does." Jase lugged out a couple buckets of various blooms. "Because your wife is like a floral genius."

"Ex-wife," she corrected.

"Wife, because the divorce isn't final," Eli corrected her correction. Why? He had no fucking idea. She just wasn't his ex. What was she? He had no real idea. But she wasn't his ex-anything. Not yet.

She and Jase both looked at him oddly.

"And I really am good with flowers," she continued. "And he's paying me extra so I don't have to worry about the taxes."

"That is not entirely the case, but we'll roll with it." Jase set the flower buckets beside her. "I can see that you are not happy about sharing Marlee. But watch her. She's amazing."

Yes, Eli knew how amazing she was. And he didn't want to share that. Jase may be one of his best friends, but he wasn't sharing Marlee.

"She's tired, Jase. She's supposed to be taking the afternoon to rest so she doesn't collapse." Fuck, she'd almost passed out in front of him. He couldn't forgive himself for pushing her so hard.

"I'm not going to collapse. This is like rest for me." Marlee grabbed a vase from the center of the work counter. "But if you brought me cupcakes, I'm ready for a break."

"You can call it a day." Jase opened the paper sack, rifling through the food Eli had put aside for Marlee. "Are there really cupcakes in here?"

"They're not for you." Eli practically growled at his friend. "Unless Marlee wants to share."

Now, Marlee was looking at him odd again. He was going to get a complex.

"Are *you* okay?" she asked. "All this talk of me passing out —which didn't happen, I might add—and now you look like you're about to eat Jase."

"He can't eat me. He knows I can take him." Jase

continued rifling through the sack, finally pulling out the tray of cupcakes. "Sweet fuck, these look amazing."

Marlee cracked open the plastic cupcake box. "I have been waiting all day for this."

She pulled off the wrapper and sank her teeth into the cake and icing. He could watch her eat all day. Funny thing about chefs, they loved watching people eat their creations. Eli was no different. It's a high like he never got anywhere else. But when Marlee sank her teeth into his food? It was like she was sinking herself into his soul.

He was becoming a Marlee addict.

And that was unacceptable.

Chapter Thirteen

NINE WEEKS UNTIL THE DIVORCE IS FINALIZED

THE FIRST TIME Marlee had taken Bert a cup of coffee, it'd been an accident. She'd unintentionally ordered a vanilla latte instead of a caramel latte, so she'd had an extra. Bert had been flying a sign on the corner and she'd offered the extra to him. He'd been so thrilled she swore she'd keep doing it. There was something about making him happy that made her happy. It was, after all, just a cup of coffee. Then his friends had started showing up, and she'd brought them coffee, too. Yes, she could've donated a boatload of money to a charity—and she did back when she had it—but doing it her way meant she also got to make friends. Got to see that a cup of coffee could make a difference in a person's day.

Delivering flowers was no different. It brought about the same rush.

Kellie: Marlee's too busy for us.

Becca: Because she's married with a job, she's practically a grown up.

Marlee: I love my job.

Sadie: I love that you love your job.

Marlee: I have deliveries. Chat when I'm done?

Becca: We're here.

Marlee: Pocket friends are the best.

Kellie: Go get 'em, girl.

"I'm going to run this batch over to the museum." Marlee boxed up the delivery she'd prepared. Jase's delivery driver, Ethan, was gone that afternoon, so Marlee was on delivery duty. And. She. Loved. It.

Delivering flowers made people happy. Which meant it made her happy. Which meant everyone was happy and she loved her job.

Which sucked, because Eli wasn't thrilled about her job. He didn't say anything. He didn't have to. After a month of living together, it seemed they knew each other better than she and Scotty had after ten years.

He brought her food when she was working, and they still saw each other in the evenings. He was so funny about everything. Half the time, he grumbled and avoided her. The other half, he was bringing her food and checking on her.

"Vait," Jase's grandmother, Babushka, hollered from the back room. "Vait for me."

Jase's grandmother was Russian to the core. Marlee's grandmother had been prim and proper and loved Marlee with all her heart. Jase's grandmother was not prim and proper. With her strong opinions, thick accent, and eccentric style—Marlee had no idea there were that many shades of lime green or that you could get flip-flops in pink or a manicure to match—Babushka was a total kick in the pants. The woman was pushing ninety and made Marlee smile all day long. That wasn't even an exaggeration. Babushka was crazy and awesome, and Marlee loved spending time with her. Well, when Babushka was at the shop. She wasn't always at the shop. She lived at the retirement community up the block, so she spent a lot of time there. Although, she'd been stopping by more frequently as of late.

"You're coming?" Marlee asked.

"Of course, no von gives me great-grandbabies. I have nothing to do. I'm not staying around here to rot." Babushka shuffled to the back exit with Marlee in her wake, lugging the box.

Marlee definitely didn't want to leave her there to rot.

"You'll drive," Babushka said.

Marlee would have to, seeing as how Babushka had no driver's license and Heather had shared the story of Babushka totaling Heather's cookie delivery van in an effort to push Jase and Heather together.

"Lothario, come." Babushka snapped her fingers.

Lothario trotted along beside her.

Eli had officially been replaced as his favorite. And he had yet to hump any part of Babushka or her clothing. Marlee had a theory about that: Lothario and Babushka were kindred spirits of sorts—Babushka had two boyfriends and Lothario had an affinity for Eli's shoes, Scotty's sweaters, and Jase's vases. Lothario and Babushka understood each other on some deep level.

"I'm stealing your grandmother," Marlee yelled to Jase.

"Are you stealing her or is she stealing you?" Jase yelled back.

Er.

"I'm not really sure," Marlee replied.

At that point, it didn't really matter. Did it?

Jase stuck his head out of the cooler. "If you're not back in two hours, I'll sic Eli on you."

Marlee rolled her eyes. "Like that will do any good."

Jase rolled his eyes right back at her. "Have you met your husband?"

"Ex-husband," Marlee corrected.

"Uh-huh." Jase rolled his eyes.

Marlee rolled her eyes right back. "Fine. Two hours, max."

"And if she tries to make you do anything illegal, immoral, or just plain inappropriate, just say no," Jase added.

"Got it." Marlee grabbed the keys to the delivery van.

"Marlee," Jase said her name like it was the most important name in the world. "Just. Say. No."

The way he said it made her whole spine shiver.

Sheesh. Babushka was intense, but Marlee could handle her.

"Jase," Marlee said his name like it had the same amount of importance. "She's like ninety. I got this."

"Shit," Jase muttered. He shook his head. "Take care of her. Don't let her do anything stupid."

What kind of trouble could Babushka possibly get Marlee into? She shook off the idea and hurried out the door, box in hand, to find Babushka and Lothario.

"MAN, WE HAVE A PROBLEM," Jase said from the door of Eli's kitchen.

Eli glanced up from where he folded empanadas—his grandmother's recipe. "Jase."

"Man." Jase marched into the kitchen without even washing his fucking hands. "We. Have. A. Problem."

"Can it wait until after I'm done here?" Eli asked, his focus back on the dough in front of him. The last time Jase had barged in his kitchen to tell him they had a major issue was a week ago when Jase didn't like where Eli had parked his Jeep.

For the record, Eli had been in his allotted spot, Jase had just wanted to use it to load his delivery van.

"It's Marlee." Jase shoved his hands on his hips.

Eli snapped to attention. "What about Marlee?"

"Babushka hijacked her, and I have no idea where they went. Neither are picking up their phones, and Marlee said she'd be back over an hour ago."

Eli let out a breath. He didn't need to freak out. "So they got sidetracked."

"She said two hours." Jase pointed a finger at Eli. "She said two hours and that was three hours and thirty minutes ago."

Still not anything to be flipped out about. Eli would give Marlee a call, she'd answer, all would be good. He set the tray of empanadas aside, washed his hands, grabbed his cell, and dialed Marlee's number.

"Hi, I'm not available right now…" Marlee's voice said through the speaker. Eli pressed the end button. Shit.

"Where were they going?" he asked Jase.

"Officially?" Jase asked, his voice getting high-pitched at the end. "The museum for a delivery."

"That's like thirty minutes away," Eli pointed out. It would take an hour of driving. Add in any stops along the way and they just got distracted. This was Marlee—she liked to hand out free coffee to the homeless and stop in at Neiman Marcus to window shop.

"Unofficially? She's Babushka. Who the hell knows where she's going to abscond with your wife?" Jase's voice got faster and faster toward the end.

"I don't have a wife tracker on her, what do you want me to do?" Eli asked. He wasn't worried yet, but he tilted on the precipice of concern.

"Help me find her." Jase grabbed his own phone from his pocket and started dialing numbers. "I'll call Brek and Dean, we'll get a search party started."

Heather breezed through the door. "Any updates?"

"Not yet." Jase was still fussing with his phone. "I'm calling the guys. We'll start looking by zone."

"Has anyone called the retirement home?" Eli asked. "Where Babushka lives?"

Start at the epicenter and then work outward from there.

Jase and Heather both stared at him a beat.

"On it," Heather said first.

She started dialing numbers, turning her back to them.

"Man, for a dude who got so pissed off that I stole your wife, you're remarkably calm about the fact that she's with Babushka," Jase said.

"Well, you stole her from me. Babushka stole her from you. All's fair when it comes to Marlee," Eli said, a tiny part of him reveling in the knowledge that Jase lost her, too—even if it was only for the afternoon.

"Fuck that." Jase continued texting God-knew-who. "She's the best florist I've ever had. Do you know she has her own clients now? They won't even let me touch their arrangements, it *has* to be Marlee. She can't get stolen by my grandmother, arrested, and tossed into the middle of Babushka's latest bullshit. She'll quit and I'll have to do it all myself again."

"She's at the retirement home," Heather said, clearly relieved.

"What the fuck is she doing there?" Jase scowled.

Being stolen by his Babushka, if Eli had to chance a guess.

"Arts and crafts," Heather added. "They said she's in the arts and crafts room."

"She's supposed to be at work." Jase marched out the door. "Not doing arts and crafts at the senior home."

"Maybe it is work." Eli followed him, locking the door behind them.

Jase harrumphed.

The retirement community was only a block away, so they were hoofing it. Heather hurried to keep up with Jase. Eli lagged behind, enjoying the franticness of Jase about to lose his best floral designer to Babushka and the arts and crafts room of the senior center.

"You"—Jase pointed at him—"are being way too calm about this."

"It's because he doesn't know the damage Babushka can cause." Heather kept her pace up, the retirement community building in sight. "He's only been on the sidelines. Never in the middle."

Eli moved past them, holding the door for Heather. Letting it close before Jase came in.

"The art room is this way." Heather led the way, waving at the front desk lady as they passed.

An old man sat sentry at the door. He'd flipped his walker around, using it as a stool. "Sorry, you can't go in. They're busy."

"Harry, you have to let me through." Heather started to go in straight past him.

Harry stood, wobbling a tad on the way up. "Nope."

The two of them started arguing. Eli took that as an opportunity to slip around Harry and go through the door.

Jase was already in the room, a stunned expression on his face.

"How'd you get in here…?"

A dozen elderly women—and Marlee—were threading together what appeared to be decently large orange silicone penises with some kind of fishing line.

Eli's expression must've mirrored Jase's.

"I'm not even sure what to do with this," he said to no one in particular and everyone all at once.

"Hey, honey." Marlee held one up to Eli, gripping the shaft so the tip pointed toward the ceiling. "It's arts and crafts at the senior center."

"You're supposed to be at work." Jase glowered. "We have customers."

"Looks like she is at work." Eli avoided looking at the way

Marlee held the shaft of the orange penis. His dick was starting to get a little jealous.

"You told me to watch your grandmother and make sure she doesn't get into trouble. This is me doing my job." Marlee clipped off the end of the thick fishing line she'd run through the rubber balls. She handed the dick to the woman on her left. The white-haired woman grabbed hold of the shaft and spun it over her head like a pair of dildo nunchucks.

"These are good." She dropped them into a box at the end of the table.

"Whoa." Heather finally got through Harry at the door. "Why didn't anyone call me?"

"Ven you give me great-grandbabies, I vill tell you things." Babushka didn't use scissors to cut the thread on her own penis nunchucks. She bit it off with her teeth. "Also, you vould have told this one." She shoved her thumb toward Jase.

"Well, now he knows. What are we making?" Heather sat next to Marlee, grabbing a penis by its orange shaft and ignoring the grandbabies comment.

"Tree decorations," Marlee said.

"Marlee tells us vat her fiancé does. Ve vill decorate his trees," Babushka said like this was a totally normal thing to do. "Two days and he calls off the vedding? He is bad man. Bad men get their trees decorated."

"It was all Babushka's idea." Marlee tilted her head toward Jase's grandmother.

"Mar." Eli shook his head. "I really don't want to bail you out of jail today."

"Technically, they're my trees, too. And they can't arrest me for hanging dildos from my own trees. I'm pretty sure there's a law about that."

"Tell me you got legal advice before you jumped in on this." Eli rubbed at the bridge of his nose.

"Sadie said not to get caught." Marlee did the one-shoulder-shrug thing she did right before she made bad decisions.

Pole dancing, marrying him, hanging dildos from her ex's trees. "But she said if we do get caught, they're my trees, so we won't get in trouble. That's why I'm here. I don't want the ladies to go rogue without me. I'm their get-out-of-jail-free card."

"For fuck's sake." Jase sat next to his grandmother. "Don't do this. Can't you go back to that game you ladies play with the flyswatters and the balloons?"

"No." Babushka bopped him on the nose with an orange penis.

Eli had seen some weird shit in his years on this planet. But he'd never, never expected to see Babushka bop his buddy on the nose with a giant orange dick. The laugh bubbled up his throat; he only wished he'd caught it on video.

"Holy crap." Heather's mouth was open wide. "Your grandmother just whacked you with a dildo."

Jase turned pale, then pink. He stood, knocking over the metal folding chair so it collapsed. Stumbling to pick it up—but struggling as it fell open, then closed—Jase finally laid it against the table edge. His chest heaved.

"Eli, looks like you've got this under control. I'm going back to work." Jase beat it to the exit, knocking over another chair in his hurry.

Eli had nothing under control in this situation, but it was fucking funny, so he wasn't going to go back to his empanadas just yet.

"You're still paying me for this," Marlee yelled after Jase. "I'm still at work."

Jase didn't respond.

"He's still paying me," Marlee said to the room, her gaze landing on Eli.

"Of course, he is." Babushka stood to examine the handiwork of her minions. "You are vorking. He pays you for vork."

"Are you going to help?" Marlee asked Eli, grabbing

another set of dildos from the box at the end of the white folding table. She set them out, giving him a pointed glance.

Well, he couldn't let her get arrested on her own, could he? And really, Scotty deserved to have to figure out how to get dildo nunchucks out of his tree.

"Show me how it's done, Mar." He pulled a chair beside her, ready to go full dildo on Scotty's trees.

THERE WAS PROBABLY something in the guidelines of the homeowner's association about tossing fake penises on the trees at her house. Marlee didn't care. Scotty's face when he woke up would make any HOA issues minute.

She punched in her after-hours security code for the gate, pulled her SUV through, and waited for Eli to follow in his Jeep. Right on cue, the night security guard stepped out of the gatehouse.

"Ms. Medford," he said. "Welcome home."

The security guards said the same thing every time she entered the gate. This time, she had to bite her tongue to stop herself from correcting him. This was most definitely not her home.

Her home was now her temporary digs at Eli's.

The temporary part made her throat go thick. So she did what she always did—ignored it and rolled with the life that was handed to her. This was the latest step in her if-life-would-just-go-back-to-normal-that-would-be-fab plan. Who knew which step she was on at this point? She'd stopped counting.

"The Jeep is with me." She glanced into her rearview mirror. Eli was still there. Not that he could've gone anywhere in the short amount of time she'd spoken with the guard. Lately, she found that she checked to ensure he was there more and more. Like he would, *poof*, disappear and she'd be all alone.

Heather sat in the passenger seat of Marlee's SUV with two of Babushka's friends in the backseat. Eli had Babushka and two more with him.

Eli also had the dildo contraband in a box under a black tarp in the backseat.

Marlee pulled down the private tree-lined street toward her old house. She waited for the sadness she'd expected when she'd decided to come back tonight.

There was no heavy feeling tonight, though. She felt light. Happy. Ready to do this thing.

"Are we doing the front or the back?" Heather asked, staring out the window. She'd tried to convince Jase to tag along. Insisted that he had a special skillset that would be helpful. What that skillset was, Marlee wasn't entirely certain.

He declined with colorful language about hard limits and his grandmother whacking him with sex toys.

"We're doing the backyard," Marlee replied. If they did the front, they'd definitely get caught by the night guards. Which meant they were stuck decorating the two aspen trees and the oak tree in the back.

Scotty slept hard. By this time of night, he'd probably downed two Unisom, passed out on the sofa, and wouldn't move until around seven a.m.—if every evening they'd spent together over the past two years was any indication. They only had to cover the security cameras in the back—Babushka had plans for those—and avoid the motion sensors for the light on the back door.

Marlee turned on to the street where she'd lived. The driveway at her house was full, and the street was lined with cars as well.

All the lights were on.

She took a sharp breath.

Either Scotty didn't take his Unisom or he was sleeping through quite the party. Her stomach twisted, bile starting to rise up in her throat. She was pretty sure he hadn't taken the Unisom.

The french fries with dinner were suddenly a horrible idea.

"This isn't possible," she whispered.

Scotty never liked it when she entertained. Hated it when she had too many friends over. Threw a fit when things got too loud or went too late.

"Looks like Scotty isn't asleep," Heather murmured.

No, it didn't look that way. Scotty was having a party.

Marlee's heart fell. She loved parties. Loved having friends over. She itched all over to pop inside, make herself, well…at home…and enjoy the company.

"He's always asleep by now." Marlee crept her car toward their house.

Her Scotty was always asleep, yet here he was, living it up in *her* house. Officially, it was their house, but he was supposed to be mourning the demise of their relationship, not throwing the party he'd never let her have without loads of guilt and a ton of compromise.

Her breath skipped over the pale blue Mercedes parked nearest to the door. Her former friend Brittney's car.

There was Toby's. And Madison's.

Jeffrey's.

Holy shit. They were all here. The ones who had avoided her for weeks.

Numbness settled over her breastbone, down her spine. She wasn't an idiot. She totally understood that they were just putting her off all this time. She totally got that they didn't want to spend time with someone who had no money to pay for things. But having it tossed in her face this way made her really want to throw some orange Halloween dicks at them.

When Marlee had asked Brittney to hang out, Brittney

told her she was in Tahiti for the month. Toby was in Ireland. Jeff worked late every night at his chain of bath salt stores.

Apparently, Brittney and Toby could catch a flight home for Scotty's party. And Jeff didn't need to sell salt scrubs at midnight anymore.

"Are you okay?" Heather asked.

Marlee's recommitment to dildoing the trees was strong. "Fine. The fact that my ex-fiancé dumped me and then took all my friends means nothing."

Heather squeezed Marlee's arm. "You have better friends now."

Deep down, Marlee knew that, but up at the surface? Tonight? Betrayal wasn't a strong enough word.

She drove along the road, parking in front of Mrs. Morris's place. The lights in that house were off. Mrs. Morris had either had her own sleeping pill or she was over at Marlee's house.

Car in park, Marlee swallowed her feelings like a good girl. Eli pulled in behind her and got out of the Jeep. His reflection in her rearview mirror acted as a reassurance that Scotty may have gotten everything that didn't matter when they broke up, but she'd found someone who really did.

The thought made her pause.

Shit.

Was she falling for Eli Howard? She could not be falling for Eli Howard.

Eli who never made commitments. Eli who had divorce papers drawn up and ready within days of their marriage. Eli who would break her heart when their ninety days were up if she wasn't careful.

Her stomach turned over on itself again. She pushed open the car door to step outside.

She couldn't be falling in love with Eli, she hadn't even had a rebound fling yet.

"Marlee?" Heather asked, eyes soft, voice gentle. "Are you okay?"

"Yeah." She was only falling in love with the guy who had the power to totally decimate the remains of her tattered heart.

"She's got man trouble," Dottie announced, extracting herself from the backseat. "I can see it in her eyes."

"Who has man trouble?" Babushka stage-whispered from directly beside Marlee.

Marlee about jumped out of her Christian Louboutin black leather ankle boots. Where the hell had the woman come from?

"No one," Heather whispered back a touch too quickly.

"It's never no von." Babushka pulled a ski mask over her face. "Is it Etta again? I vill talk to her."

They'd all dressed in black. The old women all brought along ski masks, which Marlee found hysterical and frightening at the same time. Frightening because of the fact that they had them already, and it was pretty clear that none of them were skiers, what with the canes and the walkers.

"Do we need ski masks?" Heather asked.

"You should've brought them if you need them," Babushka replied.

"I've got a box of dicks I'd like to unload." Eli strode beside Babushka. "You think we can move this party along?"

"Everybody shush," Heather insisted.

Not that it mattered, *Scotty's* party was in full swing. As long as he and *his* friends didn't go on the back patio, Operation Dicks in Trees could still happen.

"It vill be fine." Babushka patted Marlee's shoulder before she marched up the street to Marlee's old house without waiting for a reply.

"What will be fine?" Eli asked.

"Nothing." Marlee clicked the lock button on the key fob and stuffed it in her bra. She scurried to keep up with

Heather. They'd left Lothario at home this time, not wanting to risk his barking or attack-straddling any of Scotty's sweaters. She unlatched the gate, checking that Scotty's party was of the inside variety.

It was.

The back patio was totally silent. Babushka and Etta made quick work of covering the cameras. Then they motioned for everyone else to come through the gate.

Babushka grabbed a set of nunchucks from Eli's box, swung it over her head, and let it rip. It landed perfectly over one of the top branches of Marlee's favorite aspen tree.

"It's almost like they've done this before," Heather whispered.

Marlee wasn't sure that made her feel better. But it was like her shenanigans with Sadie, Becca, and Kellie, so it felt like coming home. And not because she'd actually lived here for years.

The rest of the elderly women grabbed their own dicks and followed Babushka's lead unloading the decorations. Dottie went to work shoving them in the soft earth where Marlee used to plant flowers in the spring. Instead of mums, snapdragons, and petunias, there were now bright orange penises lining the edge of the walkway.

Funny thing was that the way the orange gleamed in the moonlight? Well, it sort of looked festive—if one squinted and tilted their head to the side.

"I've done some weird shit in my life." Eli came up beside Marlee, the warmth of his body close to hers. "This tops the list."

"I'm pretty sure this is what Sadie, Becca, Kellie, and I will be like when we're old." She leaned against his arm. "I hope so."

"God help us all." He nudged her shoulder with his own.

"I'm not one hundred percent certain, but I think Babushka has ties to the Russian mafia," Marlee whispered.

"I'm nearly one hundred percent certain that you are correct." The edges of his lips twitched.

Marlee. Eli. Moonlight. The whole thing was nearly romantic. Except for the covert mission of the elderly hanging Halloween penises.

Laughter echoed from inside the house, spilling onto the patio. Scotty had their old life, but she had Eli.

For now, at least.

The numbness she'd felt earlier turned to warm embers.

"Scotty's having a party." Marlee glanced at the gray flag-stone on the side of her patio.

"I saw that." Eli swung his arm around her, drawing her against his side.

"My old friends are here." And it shouldn't have bugged her. It really shouldn't have. They were her old friends, not her current friends. Her current friends were fighting for her honor using orange dildos.

Eli pressed a totally platonic kiss on the crown of her head. "Fuck 'em."

She nodded. What he'd said was right. Still, her stomach cramped whenever the laughter started up.

Eli's hand found hers, and he pulled her into the fray with the old women. He handed her an orange penis. "It's almost Halloween. You haven't even hung one decoration. Pretty sure that's not going to work for me."

Marlee took the dick from his hand, swung it over her head, and let go. The orange silicone sailed through the air until it caught on one of the branches of the second aspen tree.

She stared at the orange penis dangling from the tree and swaying in the light breeze. "That was surprisingly freeing."

Eli held another out to her. "The oak tree over there only has a couple."

"*That* oak tree is technically my neighbor's." Marlee took it from his grip. "The other one is mine."

"Their branch is over your fence. Doesn't that make it yours?" Eli whispered.

Sadie would have to clarify that particular law for them if they got caught.

"I think this one's yours." Marlee slid the silicone shaft into his palm.

Eli, the hulk that was Eli, twirled it over his head before letting the makeshift nunchucks go. They flew up, catching the edge of the gutter and hanging there.

"Scotty'll need a ladder to get that one down." Eli gave her a high five, clearly proud of himself.

The funny part of that wasn't that Scotty would need a ladder, the comedy was Scotty actually climbing a ladder. Scotty having to buy or borrow a ladder. Or pay someone to come deal with his new *situation*.

The porch light flicked on, a spotlight on all of them.

The orange dildo crew all froze. Marlee's heart beat faster. Someone had triggered the floodlight.

The old ladies disappeared into the black of night like some kind of secret spies, leaving Heather, Eli, and Marlee bathed in the porch light. Heather dove behind a bush.

Eli pulled Marlee to the edge of the house. She gripped his sleeve, leading him through the night to the other gate.

"Someone triggered the floodlight," Marlee whispered.

"Got that," he whispered back, the rough timbre of his voice scraping against the fine hairs along her neck.

Her heart raced, waiting to see if Scotty would open the door. A lot of the time in the fall, the blowing leaves would set off the floodlight. If she would have been inside, she wouldn't have thought twice about it. But with a full house, someone could easily open the back door to check.

And see everything they'd done.

Dammit.

They needed to be long gone to Dairy Queen for a Blizzard treat before that happened.

Marlee wedged herself against the gate, right near the latch. She pulled Eli next to her. If they got caught, they could run from there.

She held her breath.

Eli held his.

No one opened the door.

The floodlight clicked off, timing out. She still gripped Eli's sleeve. He stood close to her, body to body, not moving away.

She glanced up at him, the whites of his eyes pale in the moonlight. Her index finger pressed against her lips to tell him to be quiet, but she didn't really need to do that. And she didn't really mean to be quiet in the sense of speaking. She meant she was quieting her feelings. The ones he exposed. He seemed to understand that, too.

The night soaked in around them.

There was no party at her ex's, no team of elderly women exacting revenge on her behalf. In that moment, there was only Eli and Marlee. She pressed the length of her body tight against his, hoping like heck he wouldn't pull away.

He didn't move, and his breathing quickened along with her own. They just stood there, the leaves rustling against silicone penises dangling from the trees. Her breasts got heavier, and she stood on her tiptoes, her nipples pressing against his chest through the fabric of their shirts. His firm erection was obvious against her hip.

Neither of them said anything, but his hand went to her waist. She hadn't thought she could get physically closer to him, but he was showing her right there that she could. He made a guttural sound in the back of his throat before his mouth dropped to hers.

This kiss was light to start. Exploring. Erasing any residual numbness and replacing it with heat. Her skin seemed to purr with every stroke of his tongue.

He explored her lips, tongue, the planes of her mouth.

Dipped his tongue against hers. Her blood pounded in her temples, breaths coming quick, fingers gripping his sides.

"Who the fuck hung penises from my fucking trees?" Scotty's voice broke the moment.

Marlee gasped, breaking up the make-out session.

"Son of a bitch." Scotty's words pierced through the night. "There's dog poop on my shoe."

"I think Babushka left a little something extra for him." Eli tucked a strand of hair behind Marlee's ear.

"I'm pretty sure it's legal for me to hang penises from my trees," Marlee whispered. "I'm not sure of the legalities of dog poop."

"We'll just consider that a parting gift from Lothario." Eli used his body to block her from the backyard, but she was already slipping out of the gate and quietly skirting through Mrs. Morris's yard to the street.

His hand gripped in hers, she pulled him behind her, emerging from the greenbelt between the homes to where they'd parked the cars.

Scotty would be calling neighborhood security right about now. The dog poop had probably bought them a solid five minutes. He couldn't stand it when he accidentally stepped in Lothario's poop. He'd always insisted on cleaning it immediately.

She needed to round everyone up so they could all go for ice cream. No way was she going to miss a date with an Oreo Cookie Blizzard with the fudge center to explain the legalities of hanging Halloween decorations in her own trees.

Her feet seemed to stop on their own when the cars came into view.

Everyone was already in them, waiting.

"How'd they all get here first?" Eli asked.

Marlee didn't answer. It didn't matter. All that mattered was that they were all accounted for and it was now time to go, go, go.

She ran to the driver's side of her SUV, pulling open the door and slipping onto the welcoming leather seat.

"I can't believe you had the keys." Heather huffed, but her eyes sparkled with laughter. "Next time, we need to be sure there are two sets of keys."

"So you can leave me?" Marlee turned over the engine, checking in the rearview that Eli was in the Jeep, ready to follow.

"What took you so long?" Etta asked, digging through her purse and emerging with a yellow butterscotch candy.

"They were canoodling." Dottie took the candy Etta offered. "You know, Eli and I canoodled once, too."

Marlee raised her eyebrows in Heather's direction. Not that she didn't believe that Eli had been intimate with other women, but she'd never pegged him as one who scoped out retirement homes for dates.

"It's sort of true," Heather confirmed. "At the senior 'senior' dance. Dottie hijacked him to dance with her."

"We never made it past third base." Dottie shrugged.

Heather dropped her forehead to her palm. "Do you think she properly understands the bases?"

"You didn't get to that stage of the canoodling?" Etta asked, totally serious.

"Close, but no cigar." Dottie scanned the neighborhood through the back window.

Marlee tucked that tidbit aside to ask Eli about it later. Right now? They had ice cream to eat.

Chapter Fourteen

TWO NIGHTS LATER

"LOTHARIO, NO." Marlee scurried after Lothario into the darkened living room. He'd taken her midnight need to use the facilities as an opportunity to bolt to his favorite human. Tonight, that favorite being Eli since Babushka wasn't around. Her dog was a traitor.

Eli lay totally zonked out on the pullout sofa bed, his breaths even. Lothario tossed Marlee a haughty glare before scooting his little butt under the bed, pulling one of Eli's running shoes between his teeth.

She'd gone to bed in her silver silk chemise because it made her feel pretty. It also had a matching sleep mask which she'd pulled up to her forehead. As she dropped to all fours to fish her dog out from under Eli's bed, she wished she'd gone with the cropped cotton pajama pants with little blue flowers and the matching Henley shirt. Then again, Scotty bought her that set, so it was definitely a no.

He hadn't tried to contact her since their tree-decorating event the other night. The only person she'd heard from was her mom, who *really* wanted to take Marlee to coffee. Marlee had replied that she'd be happy to go to coffee once her parents turned her trust fund back on.

Yes, she was a woman on a mission to make it on her own. She still hated that they continued to try to wield their power of money over her head.

Hence the continued stalemate with her mom and dad.

"Lothario," Marlee whispered.

He didn't move.

Eli, however, mumbled something incoherent. She stilled, waiting to ensure he stayed asleep—she didn't want to wake him. Not when things were so weird. Well, weird for her. After the other night when they'd kissed. It was like the kiss had never happened. They'd gotten their ice cream, escaped the clutches of arrest, and didn't speak of it again.

Except her lips still tingled whenever she thought of how his mouth felt against hers. Which was pretty much all the time. Hence the reason she now turned awkward whenever they were in the same room.

"Lothario," she whispered louder, swiping her arm under the bed.

Lothario escaped deeper toward the head of the bed with his love-shoe. Unfortunately, he went to the side closest to the wall. She couldn't fit beside the bed there, so she'd have to climb on the mattress to get to him.

She sat back on her heels. Crud.

Eli grunted and rolled over, pulling the blanket with him and leaving his left side uncovered. His bare left side.

They'd only slept together that one time in Vegas, and neither of them had worn a speck of clothing. But Eli Howard always slept naked? Who knew?

Well, now she knew, and she needed to get her dog and get out of there. Stat.

Carefully, she climbed onto the empty side near the wall, crawling toward Lothario.

She swiped her hand in the air where Lothario had just resided, but he hustled to the other side.

Dammit.

"Mmmm." Eli made a sound deep in the back of his throat.

Marlee stilled. She'd heard that sound before—the last time she'd been in bed with him. In Vegas.

Careful not to move the mattress, she held herself perfectly still. Her breaths came shallow. Her heart raced.

"Mar," he said her name in a hushed whisper, his vocal cords scouring the syllable.

She sat up. He was on the other side of the bed, back to her, his breaths still spaced evenly. The air in her lungs seemed to dip.

"Eli? I'm just getting Lothario and then I'm on my way," she whispered like it was a totally normal thing.

She peered over his shoulder. His eyes were still closed. The blanket covered half of him, and she didn't dare chance a look at the bare corded muscle.

"Mm-hmm." He made another sound she recognized.

This was wrong. He was having a dirty dream and she was right there.

"Marlee." He practically moaned her name.

Okay, enough was enough.

"Eli, you should probably wake up." She shook his shoulder just a little.

Now, what she expected? She expected him to wake up and tell her that she was being a dippy-do for tracking her dog through the living room as he was intent to spend the night with Eli's shoe. She did not expect him to roll into her, pinning her against the bed, his eyes still closed tight.

She didn't expect him to run his nose along her neckline or press his erection against her stomach.

His eyes stayed closed even as he moved his hand to the hem of her nightgown. Still pinned underneath him, she pinched her lips together and held herself still. He was having a really good dream and inviting her to participate. She'd like to participate, of course, but he should probably be aware that she was an active participant. That required him to wake up.

"I like that," he mumbled against her shoulder.

She cleared her throat, ignoring the nerves between her own legs pulsing and begging her to open up and just let things go as they may.

"Eli," she said in her normal voice.

He moaned again, his weight heavy against her, covering her body. For the briefest of moments, she let herself imagine what it would be like to have him inside her again. The safety of him surrounding her, filling her.

"Eli," she said louder. She squirmed against the wet heat pooling at her core. Her body was now the traitor. "Wake up."

She couldn't do this. Not like this.

His eyelids popped open. He had a momentary look of utter confusion. "Mar?"

"Hey." She bit at her lip, did a little finger wave with her right hand.

"Mar." He shot up off her, the air suddenly very empty. He pulled the blanket around himself. "What are you doing?"

"I was getting my dog from under your bed, but then you were having a dream and I tried to wake you up." She sat up, totally averting her eyes from where he lay on the bed. "My bad."

"Your bad?" He rubbed at his eyes with his fingertips.

"I think Lothario is just going to sleep here tonight if you're good with that. I'll go back to bed." She started to scoot past him off the bed, unable to keep her eyes off him.

Eli sat, confusion clearly written on his face. The blanket slid down to his waist.

Yes, she was all in on bedroom activities with him. But now that he was awake? She started to hyperventilate. Lothario barked from under the bed.

164

Where was her inhaler? She needed to get to the one she left on the bookcase.

Before she could move farther, Eli placed both hands on her shoulders, centering her. She looked straight into his gaze, her heartrate dropping to normal levels and her lungs taking air in average breaths.

He ran his thumb over her cheekbone. "Did I hurt you?"

What? "No, why?"

"I was on top and..." His expression was totally soft. "Are you sure I didn't hurt you?"

Her muscles started to relax at the gentleness of his tone. Big, bad Eli Howard was all soft and gooey inside.

She decided to go with honesty. "I was scared."

"Shit." He pulled her against his chest, the top of her head below his chin. "I'm sorry."

"I was scared because I knew I'd enjoy it if we had sex again," she said. "Even asleep, you could never hurt me, Eli. I know that."

It was his turn to go still, his hand cupping the back of her head. His Adam's apple pressed against her cheek as he swallowed hard.

He didn't say anything.

Not exactly the reaction she'd been going for.

"Well?" she asked.

"I'd probably enjoy it, too," he replied.

She pulled back from him. "Probably?"

The edges of his lips quivered with laughter.

Hers followed suit. She fell back on the bed, her forearm covering her eyes, giggling.

He stretched out beside her, the heaviness of the moment gone.

She grabbed a pillow and smacked him square in the face. "Probably?"

He retaliated with his own, missing her head and hitting her shoulder with cloth and down and fluffy fabric.

She couldn't let that stand. Gripping the pillow, she hit him again.

The coordination of what happened next was a little sketchy even as it played out. She laughed. He laughed. She *whomped* him with her pillow. He tickled her along her sides.

"Marlee?" he asked.

"Hmm?"

His expression turned serious. "Definitely. Not probably."

Oh.

"You know what this night is missing?" she asked.

"Lots of things. But what do you think it's missing?"

"Orange dildos." She burst into hysterical laughter at all those old ladies and the orange dildos they'd made for Scotty's trees. Well, they were her trees, too, but since she didn't live there, they were mostly Scotty's.

Then Eli was straddling her, his fingers no longer tickling but pressing gently against her skin. His face only millimeters from hers, their breaths became one between them. "I'm here. You *definitely* don't need an orange anything."

"Probably." She dropped her grip on the pillow, moving her fingertips to his cheek. Exploring the stubble there.

"Definitely," he repeated. "I want to kiss you. I've wanted to kiss you since the other night. Every day since we got back from Vegas."

Oh. Well.

She touched his lips with the tips of her fingers. "Then you should."

He didn't kiss her. No, he moved his hands from her sides, gripping her wrists instead. Holding them above her head, he moved his mouth to hers. Lips to lips, skin to skin, he explored her mouth.

Tonight, he took his time. Tasting. Exploring. Feeling every inch of her mouth.

"I miss you at work," he said between kisses.

"You don't want me there," she assured. "Kitchens and I don't get along."

Like, at all.

"I'm proud of you."

Now *that*, that she didn't expect. "What?"

"You found your calling. You love your work. You've got clients who adore you. Yeah, I'm proud of you."

She sunk her teeth in her lip. "Really?"

No one had ever said that to her before.

"Yeah. But I've been thinking about giving you cooking lessons," he whispered against her cheek.

She pulled back, pressing her eyes into slits. "You really think that's the best use of our time together?"

"Well." He moved his hands down along her torso to the edge of her nightgown. "How do you feel about a lesson right now?"

The nerve endings in her thighs buzzed as he traced circles there with his fingertips.

"I kind of like what we're doing here." She squirmed so his fingers were closer to her sex. "Without the kitchen stuff."

"Trust me?" he asked.

Of course, she did. He was Eli. She trusted him more than anyone else these days. "Yes."

"Let's start with the basics." He pressed little kisses along the edge of her neck. "How to boil water."

She turned her head to kiss his throat. "I know how to boil water."

Little breaths from his mouth played at the sensitive skin under her earlobe.

"Not like I'm about to teach you." The rough timbre of his voice vibrated through the darkness.

Right then, Marlee really wanted Eli to teach her how to cook. Specifically, how to boil water without burning it.

Scooting out from underneath him, she pulled her night-gown over her head and tossed it on the ground beside the bed before shimmying out of her underwear. Without a word, she squirmed back underneath him—back to the same position as before. This time, sans clothes.

Eli chuckled—a husky sound that made the hair on her neck stand on end. He trailed his fingertips along the side of her cheek.

The last time she'd been intimate with Eli, she'd been more than half-drunk. From the vague recesses of her mind, images of him and the way he felt against her, inside her, flashed through her mind. So, on a logical level, she knew he was built in all departments—even the erection department. But totally sober? Him pressed against her thigh?

She couldn't help it, her mouth dropped open.

His hand slipped between her legs. Her body seemed to gravitate toward it, craving the touch right at her core—where she wanted it most. Her heart thrummed, practically purring like a kitten.

Her arms looped around his shoulders. He raised himself over her, his hands still massaging circles on her inner thigh.

She'd seen firsthand in the kitchen how exceptional he was at multitasking. Here? He took it to a whole new level.

"The key is to start the boil slow." His lips were trailing along her neckline, down the slope of her breast, and to her belly button.

"I kind of like fast." She toyed with the black strands of his hair.

The muscles of his shoulders bunched as he laughed. "We'll get there. The boiling point of water takes time. Don't rush it. You rush it, it'll just frustrate you."

He moved his mouth lower down her torso. Slowly.

She could see how not rushing it might frustrate her, too. Still…she'd worked in his kitchen long enough to follow what he said when it came to cooking.

Her skin tingled where his mouth pressed against it, even as his fingers closed in on their target. And when they met it?

She gasped. "Yes, chef."

He groaned. "Fuck."

"I think the water's boiling." She used her hands to tilt his head so his gaze met hers.

He groaned again.

"I think it's time, Eli." Her words were a whisper.

The smile on his lips brushed against the heat of her core, meeting his fingers there. "Only a simmer. We'll get to a full boil soon."

Mouth and hands and pressure and bliss—Eli rubbed and sucked and did his thing. She moaned, fisting her hands into the sheets until he pushed her over the edge of release. She was falling. And Eli was there to catch her.

When she finally came up from bliss, he sat up slowly, a grin on his face that made her insides warm.

Boiling water was pretty damn fun.

He moved from the bed, nearly making her cry. With his erection standing tall, he disappeared to the bedroom. Then he hurried back, a small plastic square in his hand.

"Tell me you have another tuxedo condom," she murmured, the back of her knuckles brushing the pillow over her head as she stretched.

"No such luck." He drew the remarkably normal condom over the length of himself.

Her cheeks heated, the intimacy of what he did so intense. They'd been sharing a home for a month, she'd invaded his life, but watching him prepare himself to take her? For some reason, with Eli, the move sharpened everything to a level far past what she'd ever experienced with just sex.

This wasn't just sex.

Not like before.

This was Eli. They would wake up tomorrow and still live together. Still be married. Still have to get through the rest of the divorce.

Tonight, though? Tonight, he would be inside her.

She spread her thighs to make room for him, took his weight, and breathed his scent of oak and Eli. As she arched her back to meet him, he seated himself inside her warmth.

Like it was the first time for them.

"Eli," she whispered, catching his gaze. He had to know that it was only him in that moment. Only them.

His eyelids fell heavy. The thick cords of his neck pulsed with his restraint. She moved, urging him on. "I'm ready for you."

That was all it took. He snapped.

He pressed inside her, stretching, filling. She moved against him, urging him on. There were no words—there didn't need to be. He set the rhythm and she matched it, meeting each thrust with a tilt of her hips.

The water was at a boil and they were on fire.

Together.

Chapter Fifteen

ELI'D HAD sex with his wife.

He peeled his eyes open, turning toward Marlee. She was still sleeping.

He needed to go back to the night before. Start it over again. Not complicate an already complicated situation. He didn't want to go back, though.

Marlee was a beautiful woman, there was no one in the world who could deny that. Marlee may have lived in a world where women worked out fourteen hours a day to sculpt their bodies into masterpieces, but she didn't have to. Marlee's body was perfect as it was. The curves, the comfort of her wrapped around him. Her breasts heavy and real. Laugh lines starting to etch around the corners of her eyes that many in her world would've Botoxed away. But Marlee didn't. They were part of who she was.

Yes, she was real.

And right then, she was his.

He'd never wanted someone to be his before. Didn't want the responsibility that came with anything long term.

But with Marlee sleeping next to him? His heart tied itself into a confused knot.

He had a full day ahead of him. Food to make for people he didn't know. What he needed to do was roll out of bed, hop in the shower, and get his ass to work. Get as far away from Marlee as he could before she got any further under his skin.

What he was going to do?

Well, he was in bed with Marlee. And she was his wife... for now. So he was going to kiss her. Then they'd see what came next.

A restart of a different kind—not to erase anything, just to relive it.

The tips of her fingers twitched in her sleep. As though she was one of the fairy-tale princesses coming out of slumber that his sisters used to watch on VHS, her eyes fluttered open. She stared vacantly at the ceiling before settling her gaze on him. "Hey, chef."

This was not a fairy tale. He was not a prince. But he had a bona fide princess in his bed, and she just called him chef. A shiver slid down his spine.

He moved closer to her, pressing his lips against hers, opening his mouth to experience all that was Marlee. She was an early morning buffet, and he planned on sampling everything.

"Morning," he said against her mouth.

She leaned her head against the pillows, Eli poised over her. She reached for his arm, threaded her fingers with his, and lifted her mouth to his.

"Morning," she whispered against his lips before starting back up where they'd left off, tasting him like he was one of the German chocolate cupcakes she loved so much.

The kiss was deep. Tongue against tongue, naked body pressed against naked body, her nipples pebbled against his chest.

His erection went thick against her thigh, ready to take anything she was willing to offer. She squirmed so the tip of his erection ran along the bundle of nerves at her center. It took only the smallest movement on her part for him to slip between her thighs, right against her damp core.

Fuck him, he groaned with pleasure. She was ready to snap, and he wasn't even inside yet.

She sighed, her center wet and ready for him. Their bodies moved on their own accord, sliding against each other, the tip of him slipping against her entrance.

There was no control here for either of them. This wasn't drunk sex. Definitely not controlled intimacy. This was pure carnal desire. Two bodies doing what they were made to do.

He started to push forward, her wet warmth acting as an invitation he was not about to turn down.

"Eli." She ground herself down against the tip of his penis. Her mouth opened, small breaths coming quickly. "I need you."

The three words sucker punched him in the gut.

She needed him.

He was being totally irresponsible, mounted between her legs, his dick practically seated inside her without any protection at all.

This was a mistake. He withdrew faster than if he'd dropped a hot pan on his hand in the kitchen and scurried to stand next to the bed.

Marlee's forehead scrunched up. "What's wrong?"

His hands went to his hair. He was totally messing this up. Everything.

"Eli?" Her voice held a note of hurt.

Dammit. How was he supposed to fix this now?

He'd had sex with Marlee. Then he'd almost had unprotected sex with Marlee.

Now, she looked like her heart had been broken, and this time, he was responsible for that.

This is why he didn't do this shit. A quick hookup. That's

what he was good for. Not sex with someone who mattered, someone he absolutely couldn't hurt.

"Eli?" she asked again, confusion clear in her tone. He could tell the second she realized what they had been about to do. Her mouth dropped, and not in ecstasy. She scooted back, away from him. "Oh my God."

She swallowed hard, pulling the sheet to cover her breasts. Her lips stretched into a thin line, and she pressed her hand over her mouth.

What was he supposed to say to her? That he liked her? That he was cool with them as a *them*, but that she couldn't need him? He couldn't be responsible for her? They could have sex all day, but they'd almost had unprotected sex. And unprotected sex meant babies and babies meant responsibility, and now, his skin was flushing and his heart racing.

They didn't say anything, but their gazes never left each other.

His erection still jutted in front of him, completely unaware of his internal crisis.

Marlee gripped the sheet so hard her knuckles were white. "It's okay. We didn't…"

Heart pounding, breaths shallow, his fingertips numb, he was two steps away from a stroke. He needed to hit a wall, needed to shoot off his rocks, needed to get the fuck away from Marlee before he took the heart that Scotty had bruised and finished it off.

Marlee opened her mouth to speak, but in that moment, Eli did something he'd never done before.

He ran away.

Not literally, but he broke the connection of their gaze and bolted for the bathroom. Then he turned on the shower, ran his hand along his shaft, and refused to let his mind go to Marlee. This was purely a release. No thought involved. With one hand braced on the tile shower and the other on his erection, he finished himself off, letting the water wash away any remnants of what he'd done.

And when the water ran cold, he tucked a towel around his waist and cautiously opened the bathroom door.

It was silent.

No Marlee.

No Lothario waiting at the door for him.

Nothing.

This was exactly what he wanted. To be alone.

But Marlee's face when he'd turned away flashed in his mind. The hurt had been as clear as the sun shining through the blinds in the bedroom.

He got what he wanted, but what would it cost him?

HE HAD FUCKED UP. Eli couldn't think straight all morning at work.

"Who is this for?" his mom asked.

She'd stopped by on her way to Whole Foods. He packaged up the chicken cordon bleu he'd made especially for Marlee, plating it as best as he could in the little box.

"I'm taking it over to Marlee. Are you hungry?" He added a second box of seven-layer bars to the brown bag.

"I'm always hungry, but I'm not going to stop you from going to see your wife."

"Mom." He leveled a stare at her. "Don't start."

"It may be the only time I get to say that. I want to enjoy it until the divorce goes through." She pursed her lips in the way that only she could.

She'd made it clear she was thrilled about the marriage, not so much about the divorce.

"I'll walk you out." She grabbed her wallet, heading for the door.

He grabbed a box of seven-layer bars for her and walked

with her to the curb, opening her car door so she could climb in. She patted his cheeks before she got in. "Tell Marlee we need to have a family dinner soon. You. Marlee. Me. Dad."

He would do no such thing. A family dinner was a bad idea and just another opportunity for his mom to try to convince them to cancel the divorce so she could have a daughter-in-law.

He shook his head, kissed her on the cheek, slipped the box of desserts to her, and headed next door to the flower shop to give Marlee his best peace offering.

He wanted to rewind the clock. All the way back to the night before when they'd first had sex so that he could push pause *then*. Not wait until he was nearly balls deep before coming to his senses about what a bad idea it was to fall for the woman he was divorcing.

Jase's cowbell clanked against the glass. No one greeted him.

"Mar?" He shifted the bag in his arm.

"Marlee has left the building." Jase ducked out of the cooler. "But I am here for all your floral needs. What'll it be? An I'm-sorry-I-screwed-up bouquet or a sorry-I'm-a-dense-dumbass houseplant?"

Marlee wasn't there? Not that she had to check in with him, but he hadn't realized how often they usually talked throughout the day until right then. Random texts, popping in to see each other. He'd gone nearly six hours without a Marlee hit. It was making him edgy. "Where'd she go?"

"I'm afraid I'm not at liberty to disclose that." Jase shrugged.

Eli set the paper food bag by the cash register. "Bullshit."

"Yes, it is." Jase lay out a vase and a bunch of purple flowers. "She went to lunch with her mom."

Fuck a duck.

"Why'd you let her do that?"

"Her mom showed up here. Nice lady. Asked Marlee if

she could buy her a meal. Marlee balked, but not much. Seemed like she wanted to go."

"When will she be back?" This wasn't Marlee withdrawals. This was just Eli checking she was okay after he walked out on her this morning and then she walked out on him right into the clutches of her mom.

"After lunch." Jase gave him a funny look. "What did you do? Judging by how quiet she was today, you fucked up something."

"Nothing." Eli should've headed back to his kitchen. He didn't. He pulled up a stool to Jase's design counter, because he was a masochist who didn't want to deal with his own head. So he'd let Jase deal with it. Which was probably worse. Much, much worse.

"Hold tight." Jase grabbed his cell, tapped out a message, and dropped it back on the counter. "We'll wait for Brek and Dean. They'll want in on this."

That was not what Eli had in mind to clear his head. "Why?"

"Because you've got a case of the Marlees." He clipped the ends off the purple flower stems. "And when I had a case of the Heathers, you all gathered around and gave me shit advice. Same with Brek when he had the Velmas. And Dean when he had the Claires."

Eli sighed. "There's no use lying—Marlee's burrowed under my skin nice and tight."

"Yeah, I realized that when you started bringing her lunch and busting my balls for stealing her." Jase shoved the flowers into the vase. Not shoved exactly, he took his time doing it.

Eli missed Marlee in the kitchen, but she was in heaven working for Jase, so he couldn't be pissed about it for long. Jase must've misunderstood his silence, because Jase didn't get serious often. Not taking anything serious was kind of his thing.

Right then, though, he turned to Eli, and in total seriousness, he said, "Have you seen how good she is at floral design? She could run her own fucking shop."

Marlee loved it. And Eli loved that Marlee loved it.

"And if Marlee ran her own shop, *my* shop would probably go under because she's that much better at this," Jase continued blabbing through Eli's internal crisis.

"I slept with her," Eli mumbled.

"I heard." Jase nodded and continued on like this was not news. "Vegas'll do that."

Jase had no idea what Vegas could do. But this wasn't about what happened in Vegas.

"Last night. I slept with her." Eli's cheeks heated at the thought of what had happened afterward. That morning.

Jase paused. "I take it you weren't in Vegas last night."

"Nope." Eli folded his hands together on the table. "Neither of us was drinking. We just decided to have sex."

"Like grown-ups." Jase nodded along with whatever he was thinking. "Doesn't sound like something that would be that big of a deal. You've had sex before, my friend. Not drunk, grown-up sex."

Eli had, but he'd never done what followed…

"And then I freaked out and ran out on her this morning."

Jase didn't move. He blinked hard. "You did a fuck 'n' run?"

Like half a fuck 'n' run. Like a just-the-tip 'n' run. "Something like that."

"Huh." Jase didn't say anything else. He scrunched up his face. Clearly, thinking too hard was going to break something in his brain.

"What do you mean 'huh'?" Eli fiddled with one of the purple flowers. "You never just say 'huh.' You are the king of opinions."

Dean shoved open the door, cowbell clanking away. "What's the problem that made me cancel two of my afternoon appointments?"

"Eli had sex with his wife," Jase said, recovering from whatever he had been thinking and sticking more purple flowers in the vase.

Dean pulled up a stool. "Isn't that kind of the point of being married?"

"Dude." Eli dropped his forehead to the cool stainless steel.

Dean clapped him on the back. "Anyway, I thought you two had sex in Vegas?"

"Vegas sex is not Denver sex." Jase tossed clippings on the floor at his feet. "We covered this already."

"'cause Denver sex means somethin'?" Brek asked from the door.

Fuck, how long had he been standing there?

"Because Denver sex is not a mistake," Jase said in reply, boiling down exactly what was wrong into seven words.

A lump caught in Eli's throat. This was all jacked.

Jase filled in the other two knuckleheads on the morning's activities. Eli didn't insert his opinions into Jase's commentary. Instead, he tuned out the conversation until Jase finished.

"Why don't you ask her out?" Brek suggested. "You've done everything backward. Getting married first. Having married sex. Moving in together. Having more married sex. This time, ask her out. Take her on a date."

"I think he's onto something." Jase turned the vase a full 360, checking all the sides.

"Doing something in the right order with her might get you out of all the knots you've tied yourself into." Dean stood. "And if we're good now, I should go back to making money. Claire's supposed to meet up with Velma to go shopping later. That always ends with a decent dent in our credit card bill."

"Ours, too," Brek added.

"And you both love it." Jase tied a bow around the vase.

"Wouldn't change it for anything." Dean grinned.

"Nope," Brek added.

Maybe they were right. The key with Marlee was starting at the beginning. Doing things in an order that made some kind of sense. Yes, Eli could do that.

If Marlee was still talking to him, which he wasn't totally clear on at the moment.

"You should use flowers when you ask her." Jase turned the vase toward Eli. "Purple orchids are excellent sorry-I-screwed-you flowers."

"I didn't screw her," Eli practically growled.

"Thinkin' you did," Brek replied for Jase.

"She looked pretty sad when she came in this morning." Jase's words landed the blow.

Shit.

"Fine." Eli nodded toward the finished bouquet.

"Good choice." Jase ambled to the cash register with the bouquet. "I made it just for you."

"I can't believe I'm buying flowers," Eli said with a huff, already pulling his wallet from his back pocket.

"Your other options are the discount florist, where you'll get shitty carnations, or the grocery store, where they'll die in two days." Jase tied a ribbon around the vase. "You ever taken care of orchids before?"

Eli leveled a glare at him. No, but he'd figure it out.

"That's what I thought," Jase continued as though Eli had actually given a response. "Give 'em a little spritz of water every day or so to keep them happy."

"Put them in water." Eli tugged out his wallet. "Got it." Marlee would know what to do with them.

"Add an 'I'm sorry' when you hand 'em over," Brek suggested. "Even if you don't think you did anything wrong. Just consider it pre-payment for whatever shit you're gonna say later that'll piss her off."

Eli had absolutely no intention of saying anything that would "piss off" Marlee. Not again.

"The order of the hand off and apology is important," Dean added. "You don't want to seem like you're using the orchids in place of the apology."

"You are all full of it," Eli said.

"You are now in the land of committed relationships. You are a dude. One plus one equals you always have something to apologize for," Jase concluded.

This shit was exactly the shit Eli had wanted to avoid by avoiding relationships.

More than avoiding relationships, he wanted to avoid making Marlee sad again. He'd do whatever he needed to do so that didn't happen.

Eli grabbed a fifty-dollar bill and dropped it on the little plastic mat advertising whatever online network the shop belonged to. His glance snagged on the corner of plastic sticking out from behind the rest of the cash as it tumbled out of the confines of his leather wallet. He hadn't thought about the yellow condom in a SpongeBob package since he shoved it in there over a month ago.

"What the fuck is that?" Brek leaned over the counter, catching a glance at yellow packaging.

"Souvenir." Eli snatched it up, shoving it back inside. "From Vegas."

Brek's lips pressed into a smirk. Jase raised his eyebrows. Dean coughed into his hand way too pointedly. They'd all gotten a good look.

"It's nothing," Eli grumbled.

"Aye, aye, cap'n." Jase was sporting a full grin now.

A laugh rattled Brek's chest. Dean just shook his head.

Eli took a deep breath. He was officially the guy who bought flowers for his wife as an apology. Because they were married.

"Marriage," he said it under his breath. Tested it out. Checked how it felt.

"You okay there, Romeo?" Dean asked. "You're looking a little pale."

"Paler than usual." Brek leaned forward, elbows on the table. "Those fifty dollars do something to scare the shit out of you?"

"It was SpongeBob. I'm pretty sure," Jase said.

"I'm fine." Eli grabbed the flowers and beelined for the cold air of the outside world. In the back of his mind, he vaguely heard Jase say something about change, but he was already forming an apology in his brain. Orchids. Apology. Then they'd see what happened next.

Chapter Sixteen

Marlee: Mom offered money so I don't have to work at the flower shop.

Sadie: Trust fund back on?

Marlee: No. Just money so I don't have to work at the shop.

Becca: You said you like it there.

Kellie: Take the money. Still work there. Done.

Becca: Kellie is giving bad advice.

Marlee: I don't want their money. I want my money.

Kellie: 😔

Becca: Talk to Eli about it?

Sadie: I don't think they're talking yet.

Becca: Still? It's been like four hours.

Marlee: Six.

Kellie: That's not very long.

Becca: For Eli and Marlee it is.

MARLEE USED her key to let herself into Eli's commercial kitchen to say thanks for bringing her lunch—even if she'd already been at lunch with her mom when he dropped it off. Since it was a slower week, it was just him working right then. He glanced up from whatever he was stirring on the stove.

"Mar," he said her name on a breath.

After he walked out on her that morning, she'd left the apartment and did something she hadn't done in forever. She bought herself a latte. Truthfully, it tasted like the best latte she'd ever had—it'd been so long since she treated herself. But she had steady employment and a four-dollar coffee seemed like an appropriate splurge given the details of what had happened with Eli. Then she delivered coffee to Bert and his friends. He'd asked what was wrong and she'd dodged his question. If her life was so messed up that even Bert noticed she was out of sorts, then she was absolutely failing at getting herself together.

She'd already decided not to be pissed at Eli about what had happened. She knew better than to expect anything from him when it came to relationships. He didn't do them, she'd known this. And still, she'd practically thrown one at his doorstep. Then she'd inserted herself in his bed.

All thoughts of anything more than just being his friend were tucked firmly in a box in the back of her brain.

After coffee, she'd gone back home and spent an hour getting ready—blowing out her hair, picking the perfect dress that would be both practical for work in a flower shop and also give her the little boost of confidence she needed. Pink flutter sleeves totally boosted confidence—which was excellent, because when her mom showed up in person to ask her to lunch, Marlee needed that lift.

"Hi." She headed toward the sink to wash her hands.

Even if she had no plans of touching anything, Eli got all worked up if people came to his kitchen and didn't scrub in.

"I'm glad you're here." He moved to her, grabbing a vase of purple orchids from the counter. "These are for you."

Huh. Flowers were unexpected. Flowers were very relationship-y. Not super friendship-y.

She finished drying her hands, tossed the paper towel in the trash bin, and took the orchids. "They're beautiful. Thanks."

What was she supposed to say now? Jase had said Eli brought her lunch, but she'd already left with her mom. Their lunch had been nice—they kept to safe topics, caught up with each other—but after her mother offered money for Marlee to quit her job? Well, Marlee left the meeting feeling more alone than she had when she agreed to go.

"I'm sorry." Eli stuffed his hands in the pockets of his chef jacket. "For running out on you this morning."

The look of terror on his face. The way her heart fell when he dropped her to the bed. All of it flooded her again.

He gave the sauce another stir. "We almost ruined everything."

They'd already had sex twice, gotten married, and she'd lost her fiancé and her trust fund. What more could they have done to ruin the everything he was talking about? "But we didn't."

"We weren't paying attention." His voice held a panicked tone she'd never heard from him before.

"We would've stopped." She was pretty sure. They had just gotten caught up in the heat of everything and she had been barely awake. So had Eli. The feelings got too much for them. But they would've realized it before any damage was done.

He stepped toward her. His expression unreadable. "It's the kind of mistake you make when you've been with someone for a long time. Not the second time you hook up."

Her cheeks got hot at the term he chose. "Last night was just a hookup?"

"No, that's the problem. You make me feel too much."

"I'm...sorry." Her stomach got all twisted again. "What do you want me to say?"

"Go on a date with me." He was breathing heavy, like he'd just climbed a mountain.

Marlee was very near checking to see if he was feverish. "Eli, you are making zero sense right now."

"I want to date you." He turned a bit pale. "I want to start over. Do things right. Take you out to dinner. Spend time together because we want to, not because you have nowhere else to go."

Oh.

She bit at her lip. "You want to be a couple?"

"I want to give us a chance at that."

Then why the hell did he look like he'd just told her they were over? He had that same look that Scotty had the morning he broke it off. The one that was trying to be upbeat, but mostly looked like he was about to puke.

Truth was, she felt the same way.

The idea of getting serious with anyone after what had gone down when her last relationship ended? Yeah. That was a hard no.

She already knew she was falling toes over nose for Eli, but up until this point, she hadn't really given any thought to their future. Her relationships had a pattern—one she thought she'd broken with Scotty. Things would get semi-serious, she'd be having a great time, and then everything would fall apart.

"Do you still want the divorce?" she asked.

"Yes." He nodded. "And no." He shook his head.

Well, that made no sense at all.

"I want you to have the opportunity to see if this is what you want first. What I want. Let's give us a chance to do things in the right order. Date. See where that takes us. Go slow. No worries about timelines and trust funds and who gets what bed." Eli was getting way too intense for his own good.

"Can we count hanging orange dildo decorations as our first date?" she asked in an attempt to diffuse the intensity taking over his kitchen.

He grinned at that. "Why?"

"Because I plan on putting out tonight, and I don't really do that on the first date." She winked at him.

"You're not taking this seriously at all." He was back to being way too serious.

She fiddled with the petals on an orchid. "I have feelings for you, Eli. The fact that I'm feeling things for the guy who is divorcing me scares the crap out of me."

His eyes went soft.

"So now you want to date me, and that's amazing," she continued.

"Mar."

"But you want to start over, and I don't want to do that." She didn't. The last thing she wanted to do was start anything over again. Moving forward was the only way she'd get through the next few months. Going backward would only take her back to the place she'd been with Scotty.

"You don't want to start over?" Eli's soft expression hardened around the edges.

"Not even a little." Marlee shook her head. "I'd rather pick up right where we are. Move forward from here. Let's not try to erase what we've been through, even if it's messy."

Eli stared at her for a long beat in that way of his. If she was anyone else, she would've thought he was pondering how to end it. To break her heart. But this was Eli, and she knew better than anyone he was just taking a moment to hear what she said. Really let it sink in before he responded.

"Right where we are," he confirmed.

"All the messy. The divorce. The things that happened this

morning. I don't want to erase them. They're part of our story." And hopefully, they were part of a story that wouldn't shred her in the end.

He reached out to run the edge of his index finger along the apple of her cheek. "Okay, Mar."

"And I like you, Eli. I like you a lot. I don't know where we're going to end up. If I'm totally honest here, I don't know that I'll ever want to get married and plan a wedding again. But I like who I am when I'm with you. And I like who you are. And maybe that's enough?"

"Is it enough for now?" he asked.

"Yeah." It really was.

"Then that's all that matters." He took another step toward her.

"Scotty used to say all the time that he loved me more. That I was the best thing that ever happened to him. But Scotty didn't like the messy. He liked things to be precisely how he liked them. I feel like I'm still recovering from all that, from trying to be exactly who he wanted and still not being enough."

"You're enough for me," Eli said.

He seemed to mean it.

"And right now, I'm enough for you," he continued. "So what do you say we do this relationship thing moment by moment?"

"No future?"

"There's no future. There's no past. There's just who we are because of the things that made us this way. I'm not erasing the past. I'm not planning the future. I'm just letting this moment be what it needs to be for both of us."

Wow. Eli could be really deep when he wanted to be.

"Okay," she said.

He wrapped her in a hug, and it made the world fall away. In that moment, things were fine. And that was enough.

Palms against his chest, Marlee pulled back so she could

see his face. "I know you're not planning the future, but do you think you could make me some more of that chicken stuff from the other day? It was really good."

He chuckled. "Yeah, Mar."

Standing on her tiptoes, she brushed her lips against his. The light kiss only lasted half a second before it heated up.

His tongue slid against hers. Eli might not always have much to say, but boy, oh boy, could he use his mouth for other things.

She gripped the collar of his chef jacket, fisting her hands in the polyester. She wasn't paying attention to anything other than his mouth, his body, and the way her nerves were hot-wired for his touch. So she missed that he'd been backing her into his office.

To the couch in his office.

She made quick work of unbuttoning his jacket, pulling his white undershirt out from under the belt around his jeans, and unhooking the belt.

"I have to go back to work," she said against his mouth.

"After," he replied in that chef tone of his that pissed her off in the kitchen but, here in his office, didn't have the same effect. Here? It just added kindling to the fire already building. "I want you naked."

Right then, she decided not to argue with Chef Eli when he told her what to do—as long as it involved sex, him, and immediate access to both.

She shimmied out of her panties, thankful that she'd decided to dress cute that day. He had his jeans around his thighs, boxers right there with them, and dug through his wallet, emerging with a yellow condom and that goofy grin on his face.

She giggled. "That's not…"

He couldn't be serious. They weren't actually going to use it.

"It's what we have." He ripped open the package.

Apparently, they were going to use it. Yellow was the color of the day.

"On the couch, chef." It was Marlee's turn to order him around.

He sat on the couch, his erection standing at attention, and held the condom up between two fingers. The unspoken question hung in the air—did she want to do it?

Hell yes, she did.

She grabbed it like he was offering one of the seven-layer bars he had left over at the flower shop and sank to her knees in front of him. She ran the latex over his shaft. His head dropped back, his eyes closed, and he moaned as the condom fit snugly all the way down to the root.

Her hand still gripped him, and his gaze caught hers. She gave a light squeeze just so she could watch his eyes roll back that tiny bit. He didn't disappoint.

As if she weren't already turned on enough, his hand went to her neck and he pulled her mouth to his. She straddled him, his erection against her slick core, while he took his time with her mouth. Urging him on, like he was a shoe and she was Lothario, she lifted herself up, lined them together, and sank on top of him. Slowly. Letting him fill her.

He was making noises now deep in his throat. "Mar."

"Eyes open, chef."

He did as she instructed.

She moved up on her knees, still fully clothed except for her underwear, and then sank down again.

He didn't close his eyes this time. His hands rested at her waist, letting her pick the pace. Her nipples contracted to tight buds, the bundle of nerves at the top of her sex rubbing against the fabric of her dress.

There was something freeing about being the one in control. Eli was all about constraint. Control. Doing things himself. But he let her set the pace, let her move on him at her own speed. She'd never been so turned on in her life.

He lifted his hips to meet her on each thrust down. The Adam's apple in his throat pulsed.

"I'm almost there," she said, nearly ready to spin out of control.

There was not a breath of space between them, but somehow, he moved his hand to where they were joined. One flick at the bundle of nerves and she was done. She dropped her head against his shoulder and rode the wave that crashed over her. Mid-wave, he gave one last thrust and everything in him tightened.

"Maybe I should come work for you after all." She pressed a kiss to his swollen lips.

He brushed a stray hair from her face. "Maybe you should just come visit more often."

"Maybe you should hang curtains or something so we can make this an everyday occurrence?"

He barked out a laugh.

She pressed her face into his neck. "I really should get back to work."

He helped her ease herself off of him.

"I'm meeting up with Velma, Heather, and Claire after work. We're going to Brek's. You should come." Finding her land legs again, Marlee pulled her panties back on under her skirt.

Eli dealt with the condom and readjusted his own clothes so seamlessly that no one walking in right then would've ever known what just went on.

"I'd like that." He lifted the hair from her shoulder, tucking it to one side. He kissed the line of her neck where it met her shoulder. "How about you tell Jase you need the afternoon off?"

"What?"

"If I can't take you out tonight, I want to take you now. There's something I want you to see."

"I can't just bum off work. Jase needs me." But there was

something in Eli's expression. Something different. Something that told her that she should ask for the afternoon. She dropped her forehead to his. "I'll ask."

"See if Lothario can hang with him while we're gone?" Eli asked. "I want your full attention this afternoon."

A sly smile tipped the corners of her mouth. "What on earth do you have planned?"

"You'll see." He kissed her quickly. Then it heated, and it wasn't so quick.

Turned out, he burnt the shit out of his sauce.

He didn't seem to mind.

Chapter Seventeen

ELI LOOKED up at the old industrial building in LoDo—the building he'd had his eye on for months. It was old, it needed a bunch of work done, and it was overpriced. Hence why it remained on the market for all these months. But the location was spot on, and the place had character.

The perfect location for a restaurant. His restaurant.

He was willing to pay the price tag once he had the cash.

Marlee took his hand. "What's this?"

"I want to buy it," he whispered. He hadn't said the words out loud to anyone. Not even his real estate agent when she'd shown it to him three times.

A few more huge events and he would have enough for the down payment.

Marlee ran her hand along the brick exterior. "It's beautiful."

It wasn't, but it would be.

"Come on." He tugged her hand and opened the door for her.

She walked through, a layer of dust and musty air assaulting them.

For the briefest of moments, he wished he hadn't brought

her to the building. She should see it when it was complete. When it made sense. Right now? Right now, it was an over-priced building with stale air and red graffiti tagged on the inside walls.

When he was done? When he was done it'd be one of Denver's best hot spots.

"We can just walk in?" Marlee asked.

"Trish?" he called.

"I'm here," his real estate agent hollered back.

"I'll introduce you to her in a little bit. She's my Realtor, but she knows I prefer to check things out alone."

Trish got him. Understood that he didn't need the sales pitch. She unlocked the doors, showed him around the new properties, and then disappeared while he dreamt.

"The bar will go over here." He strode to the area on the west side of the room. "Bar tables here by the big windows so guests can have a drink and watch the sunset over the Rockies."

Marlee didn't move as he jogged up the stairs to the landing. "This will be the room for events. Not huge, but it'll work."

She followed, cautious on the stairs. They were rickety, but they'd hold—for now.

"The kitchen will go back behind the bar. We'll need new plumbing, get everything up to code, but when it's done..." He shoved his hands on his hips. "Yeah. It'll work."

Marlee still hadn't said anything.

His heart dropped. She hated it.

The building was a wreck, for sure, but he had a vision for it. And for some reason, he wanted Marlee to get it. To love it, too.

"You're not going to paint the brick, are you?" Marlee asked, running her fingers over a batch of graffiti on the wall. "I think you can get this off pretty easily."

He placed his hand over hers on the wall. "No, I like the exposed brick."

"It's beautiful, Eli." She turned so her lips were millimeters away from his. "It's perfect."

She wasn't lying. He saw it in her eyes. She got it. Knew what he was trying to do. And that meant everything.

"Can I decorate it?" she asked.

His lips parted. She wanted to help?

She shook her head. "I mean, if you don't want me to, that's fine. But I have some ideas. I'm thinking we go with dark wood accents—bannister, stairs, bar top. And really deep colors for the artwork. Maybe even a little red as a nod to the…" She tilted her head toward the graffiti.

"We?" he asked. She wanted to be a *we*, wanted to be involved in his project. He should've been scared as shit, but he just felt warm all over.

"I mean, if you want my help. You don't have to have my help."

"Yeah, Mar. You can decorate the place." The words were rough. He swallowed hard. "If I get it."

She turned her back to the wall, her chest to his. "You have to buy it. You know that, right?"

"I'm still saving." He stepped back, did another scan of the space. Took the dream out of its box long enough to let it live before he shoved it back inside and locked it up tight.

"I bet Sadie would invest. And Nicole. And Megan. And Rachel." She listed his sisters. "Sadie would help you like you helped her."

"I can't ask them for that." He shook his head. Buying law books wasn't the same as helping him buy a building.

"Your mom and dad would help you out, too," Marlee said softly. "After everything you did for them."

He shuffled on his feet. Truth was that when he was a teenager, his mom had gotten sick. The kind of sick that took a toll. The kind of sick that meant she was out of commission for two years. The kind of sick that started with a *c* and ended with chemotherapy and radiation. The doctors—and there were a lot of them—weren't sure she'd beat it. His dad—a great man—had worked his ass off during those years. Two jobs to pay for the health insurance and the bills. A third to put food on the table. Needless to say, Dad wasn't home.

Eli had four little sisters and a mom who needed more care than his dad could provide working three jobs. Eli was the oldest. He stepped up. Dropped out of everything that sucked up any extra time—guitar lessons, his job as a prep cook at a high-class restaurant downtown, the after-school French classes he'd needed to study gastronomy in the heart of the Parisian culinary world. He had dropped it all so he could take care of his mom and help out with his sisters—run them to ballet, get them to gymnastics, make sure they occasionally ate something that resembled a vegetable.

Marlee knew all that. She'd been there.

She'd even helped him out with a little French after she got back from a monthlong vacation at a villa in Bordeaux.

"Laisse-les t'aider," she murmured to him, the French filling the air in the musty, graffiti-filled room.

"What does that mean?" he asked.

"It means let them help." She squeezed his biceps.

After he'd lost the scholarship to Europe, he graduated high school, applied to the local culinary school, and thanked fuck he at least got in there. Then, he became a caterer so he could help put his sisters through college. He wouldn't ask them for money. He knew how hard it was to rub two pennies together, he wouldn't ask them to do that for him.

They had their dreams, and now, he was finally going to have his.

Marlee's hand found his as she dropped her head against his shoulder. "What are you going to do with the other kitchen when you buy this place?"

"I figure I'll keep the catering company. The restaurant

and catering company can work together. Two sources of income are better than one, you know?"

She squeezed his hand. "Look at you, building your own empire."

He shook off the emotion clogging his throat. "C'mon, I'll introduce you to Trish. Show you the kitchen space."

Marlee followed him to the kitchen, their hands still tethered together. She pulled at his hand to stop him. Then, on her tiptoes, she pressed her mouth to his.

"This is the best first date ever," she said against his mouth.

Yes, yes, it was. He sifted his hand through her silky hair.

He'd always liked being alone. But he hadn't had one of his end-of-autumn camping trips since he got married. And he hadn't missed it, because Marlee filled all the space in his world.

Everything was fine, and he took time to savor it because he knew better than anyone that moments like this could change in an instant.

Chapter Eighteen

"THEY MAKE TUXEDO CONDOMS?" Velma asked before taking a sip of her ginger ale.

"Yeah. I swear, it's a thing. Who knew? They have little white bow ties printed on them and everything." Marlee really wanted a glass of red, but the stress of her new life was getting to her and she elected to join in on the fizzy ginger, letting it settle her stomach. Sometimes a girl wanted a dash of merlot, and sometimes she didn't. A little over a month ago, Scotty would have usually made Marlee's beverage decisions when they were out and about. Marlee had actually thought it was cute at the time. Nice. He knew what she liked and made sure she had it.

Funny thing about that...she was learning that what she liked was changing. Like drinking ginger ale instead of a glass of red.

Besides, it was probably against the rules to order wine in a dive bar. Even if it was Velma's husband's bar and she probably made him stock the good stuff. Or at least the decent stuff.

"I want tuxedo condoms. I'm going to order some."

Claire had her cell in hand, searching novelty condoms. "I mean, can you imagine Dean's face?"

Straitlaced Dean? No, Marlee could not imagine that. She reached to pat Lothario on the head. He lounged next to her in the booth, noshing on a piece of steak Brek had tossed his way when they'd arrived.

"Brek wouldn't even wear a tuxedo to our wedding, I'm pretty sure this is totally out of the question in our marriage." Velma twirled her straw between her fingertips.

"What's out of the question?" Brek ambled up to their table, a bar towel slung over his shoulder.

"Tuxedo condoms," Velma said before taking a deep gulp from her drink. "I said I don't think you'd wear one."

Brek stopped mid-stride. He gave them a solid stare, the little crinkle what-the-fuck lines prominent between his eyebrows. He glanced from Velma to Claire, then at Heather and Marlee.

"I don't understand women," he declared.

He must've been talking to Lothario, because he was the only other male in their vicinity. Brek didn't wait for Lothario to reply. He just turned around, walked back to the bar, and said something to one of the waitresses.

She sauntered over to their table, notepad in hand. "Brek says you're my table now. How are you, Velma?"

"I'm fantastic." Velma giggled. "We're probably ready for another round."

"I gotcha covered." The waitress gave her a wink, picked up Heather's empty glass, and headed back toward the bar.

"So, tuxedos," Heather said when she was out of earshot. "Where were we?"

Yes, these were Marlee's kind of friends. Less than twenty minutes into girls' night, they were already searching tuxedo condoms.

Focusing on her phone, Claire's eyebrows pressed together

just like Brek's. Well, the lines between Claire's were not nearly as prominent.

"When did you use one of these?" she asked, tapping at the screen.

Um.

"You and Eli used the tuxedo condom thing when you were in Vegas?" Claire confirmed, the fun seeping out of her tone and getting replaced by strangely intense concern.

"That's a tad personal, don't you think?" Velma swatted at Claire's phone.

"It's not that private. I mean, you all know what happened there. So, yeah, in Vegas." Marlee sipped at her fizzy ginger ale.

"I wonder if we get a discount if we order extra?" Heather asked, ignoring Claire's concern. "I have some bachelorette parties that would go crazy for these."

Heather's cookie company had a solid underground following for penis-shaped cookies she called cockies. Marlee had been pretty certain within moments of meeting Heather that they were destined to be friends. Once she'd learned that little tidbit about the cockies? Their friendship was signed, sealed, and delivered.

"A bulk order of tuxedo condoms was not where I thought this evening was going." Velma giggled against the edge of her palm.

Marlee should get in on that order, just for nostalgia. Especially since she and Eli were officially doing this—whatever *this* was—and she already knew he'd wear one.

Claire set her phone facedown on the table. She rubbed at her temples, her hands framing her face. "Marlee, when was your last period?"

"Okay, seriously, Claire. Stop." Velma pulled Claire's drink away from her. "How many of these did you have before we got here?"

"They were recalled." Claire pushed the button on her phone so the screen lit up. "The condoms were recalled. Was it one of these?"

Marlee wasn't really listening to what Claire was saying because she hadn't had her monthly since a week before her wedding date. She'd been so relieved to have it over and done with so she wouldn't have to deal with it on her honeymoon. Then her life fell apart and she hadn't given it any thought. Stress had caused her periods to stop before. She'd assumed that's all that happened and it'd show up any day.

Besides, one actually had to have unprotected sex to get pregnant.

One actually had to have sex at all, and up until very recently, Marlee did not fall into that category. Except…in Vegas. With a recalled condom.

"Oh my God." The blood drained from Marlee's face.

"Marlee?" Heather rubbed at her back. "Was it one of these?"

Marlee didn't need to look to know, but she glanced at the screen anyway.

She nodded.

"She hasn't had her period," Velma said on a breath.

Marlee shook her head in a short, quick burst.

"Oh honey." Velma grabbed her hand across the table.

There was a moment after one got unexpected news when it kind of just sat there, not sinking in. This was that kind of moment. The buzzing in the bar went quiet, everything muffled. Marlee'd had sex with a recalled condom, and she hadn't had her period since.

It sunk in.

Her lungs constricted. She started wheezing.

Lothario barked at her. She grabbed her inhaler from her cleavage, taking a hit. The problem with her rescue inhaler was that while it opened her airway so she could breath, it also made her heart beat faster. Which in this instance wasn't the best thing, given that it was racing anyway.

"Even if you're not pregnant, you should probably talk to Eli about it." Claire's concern was the genuine kind. "I mean, I'm sure he's clean, but you might want to have that conversation."

"I…" Marlee opened her mouth. Closed it. "I thought my period stopped because I was so stressed."

Lothario nudged her arm in chihuahua solidarity.

Claire leaned closer. "That might totally be the case. It's going to be fine."

"How do you know?" Marlee asked, her voice oddly calm given that her heart was beating about a zillion beats a minute. "Nothing's fine. It's like my life is one big ball of not fine. And every time I try to make it fine, it gets *less* fine."

"Let's go to the drug store." Heather was already standing. "There's only one way to find out for certain. And if it's what it could be, you know you have options."

Yes, of course, she had options. But this was Eli, and if she was pregnant with his baby…she couldn't give that up.

"I don't want it to say yes. But I don't want it to say no. This is so confusing." Marlee focused on one of the Bud Light signs on the wall. "We just had a whole conversation about taking things slow." The neon flashed the tiniest bit every so often. She couldn't pull her gaze away from it. "Eli talked about how he's scared of having to take care of someone, but he's willing to try a relationship with me." She glanced between them. "Me. I mean, he's opening up to me and he's practically taking care of me already and now…"

He had his restaurant to buy. They couldn't afford a baby in the midst of that.

"Eli is a great guy," Velma said. "Give him a chance to be the guy we know he is."

"Or maybe don't tell him?" Claire rummaged around for her stuff, shoving everything into her handbag.

"You don't think he's going to notice when her stomach starts showing and then a kid shows up?" Velma asked.

"We don't even know if she is." Heather grabbed her purse. "Velma, you're gonna have to drive."

"I mean, if it is what it might be and you decide to do this, don't tell him right away," Claire continued, scooting out of the booth. "Give him some time."

"Starting a relationship by not disclosing something like this seems like a really bad way to start a relationship." Velma scooped Lothario up. Which was good, since Marlee couldn't really focus on anything but a Bud Light sign.

Velma headed toward the bar, probably to tell her husband so he could tell Eli and Marlee wouldn't have to. Eli who was supposed to arrive any moment.

Suddenly, Marlee understood why he'd run out of the room that morning. She wanted to do the same thing.

"Here." Velma handed over a bottle of Dasani. "Drink up."

"Huh?" Marlee pulled her gaze from the flashing neon.

"You've got a lot of peeing to do." Velma glanced at the bottle of water and then back at Marlee. "Drink up."

Oh.

"Did you tell Brek?" Marlee asked. For some reason, it seemed important to know who knew this information.

"Are you kidding?" Velma asked. "He stopped serving us because we were talking about tuxedos. If I mention anything about babies, he'll take off for a month with Dimefront. I mean, I only told him I was pregnant with Lily because I was pretty sure he'd figured it out before I did."

"So, no." Heather pressed against Marlee's back, propelling her forward. "She didn't tell him about our situation."

Marlee paused. The way Heather said it was like Marlee wasn't in this alone. Even when everything made it feel like she was.

"Thank you." She tried really hard not to let the tears well up.

She failed.

"For what?" Now, Heather had the what-the-fuck lines between her eyebrows.

"For not making me do this by myself." Marlee sucked in a big breath of air.

"We're your friends." Velma's arm came around Marlee on one side, Heather's on the other. Claire held the door. "You're not doing any of this by yourself."

"Except the actual peeing on the stick," Heather added. "Just to clarify, that's all you."

Marlee hiccup-laughed. "I can handle that part."

"I should clarify." Velma dug through her purse, her hand emerging with a set of keys. "Brek was over the moon about Lily. If you're pregnant, Eli will get to the excited part, too." They reached Velma's Prius, and Velma leveled her gaze right with Marlee's. "No matter what any test says, I believe Eli cares about you. And I don't think anything will change that."

"He's a good man," Heather added. "I mean, he doesn't really talk, so you think it'd be hard to know. I've seen it, though. The way he takes care of his friends. The way he looks at you. He's one of the good ones."

He was one of the good ones, and she was probably pregnant, and he'd probably run away. Marlee shivered, but only because it was autumn and nearly winter and it was Denver. The outside temperatures had dropped. That's the only reason she shivered.

In other words, she lied to herself.

Kellie: Scale of 1 - 10, how sure are you?

Becca: No matter what you decide, you know we have your back.

Sadie: ...

Marlee: It's going to be fine, right?

Kellie: ...

Becca: ...

Sadie: ...

THE DRUGSTORE DIDN'T MAKE BUYING a pregnancy test easy, that was for sure. Marlee's head was about to explode with all the choices. She only needed a yes or no. Was that so hard?

Yes, yes, it was.

Marlee set Lothario on the polished floor so she could do a thorough analysis of all the brands. There were so many. All different prices. They said they tested at different times.

The elevator music coming over the speakers was not helping her focus.

Why was this so confusing?

"The digital ones are easier to read, but this one uses lines and says it's more accurate. Also, cheaper." Heather held up the two tests, one in each hand.

"I took, like, six just to be sure." Velma started stuffing pregnancy tests in the red shopping basket she held on her forearm. "We'll just buy a bunch."

"Drink up." Claire held another bottle of water for Marlee.

Marlee's bladder was already through with this game of drink all the water. Could she just pee on something already? "Let's just grab a couple. Whatever. The pink one, I like pink."

Pink could be her lucky color.

Lothario, apparently feeling the stress of the day, started going to town on a cardboard tower display of Durex condoms. Which, Marlee might add, was a really stupid thing to have right next to the pregnancy tests. A not-so-gentle reminder that if you forget this, you'll need that.

"Not the time, Lothario." Marlee tried to pick him up, but he wasn't having it. He scurried from her reach, attacking the opposite side of the display with gusto. Apparently, he was really into *Intense, Ultra-Fine, Ribbed and Dotted Condoms with Delay Lubricant.* Too into them. The cardboard display started to rock.

"No," Marlee whisper-screamed.

There were moments in a person's life when it seemed things just couldn't possibly get worse. Those moments when their fiancé left them, when they woke up married to the caterer, when they were pretty sure they got knocked up by said caterer. In those moments, one should always remember that a chihuahua with a single-minded determination to defile a condom display can, in fact, make things worse.

For Marlee? That moment was happening in real time. Right then.

Lothario got going so fast the whole display tilted. She lurched to grab it, slipping on the polished floor and falling face first into the display.

Surprisingly, condom displays made for a fairly soft landing.

Not surprisingly, condom boxes went flying. Twenty-four count Durex flung clear down to the Hershey's bars in the candy aisle.

"Shit." Marlee scrambled to clean the mess, scooping boxes into her arms.

Velma and Heather scooped right along with her.

"Are you okay?" Velma asked. As if Marlee could even possibly answer yes.

She had an armful of condoms, a basket filled with pregnancy tests, and a dog who wouldn't stop humping that particular box of Durex. "I don't think I know what okay means anymore."

Claire tried to get the cardboard stand to…well…stand. It wasn't working. The thing was bent beyond repair from Marlee's spill onto it.

"Try this." Velma scooted a case of Pampers to hold up the display.

And, really, the store should thank Marlee for this illustration of what could happen if you didn't go with the twenty-four count pack.

Now, there are moments when you'd really like to be alone. And then there are moments when you'd really like to be with your girlfriends. And then there are moments when you're not sure what you'd like, but you absolutely know that the one thing that could make this moment worse was—

"This is my dream. I'm going to be a great-Babushka." Babushka stood with her hands pressed to her cheeks.

Marlee's lungs totally stalled out. She gulped for air. Lothario barked. She glanced at the abundance of condom boxes in her arms, Velma's, Claire's, and then she looked at Heather. Heather who held the red plastic basket brimming with pregnancy tests.

Apparently, Marlee had a full night of testing ahead.

Babushka's hands were now pressed together like she was praying on Sunday. Two elderly women Marlee hadn't met yet flanked either side of her. One leaned against a cane, the other held on to a walker with two bright yellow tennis balls stuck to the bottom.

"Babushka, hi," Velma said like this were a totally normal situation.

Heather's jaw went slack, and she dropped the basket. A dozen pregnancy tests skidded across the aisle. Not quite to the Hershey's bars, but Heather hadn't had the same running start as Marlee trying to catch Lothario.

"This is dream come true." Babushka shuffled to Heather. "Ve vill move the vedding up. No vone vill know."

"Nooo." Heather shifted her gaze to Marlee.

Marlee shook her head in a disjointed sequence of quick jerks.

"Please," she mouthed.

Heather's eyes went softer. "It's not official." She squared her shoulders. "I just thought I'd be...prepared." She squatted to scoop up the tests. "So it'd be great, fantastic, amazing if you didn't mention this."

Marlee wanted to hug her. Heather was totally taking one for the team. The team being all women everywhere who wouldn't want a nosy Russian grandma to know their business. Marlee owed her, big time.

"We went through this same thing with Etta. Except she wasn't really pregnant. Just a good pregnancy scare to round out game night that week," tennis ball lady said.

"That was a crazy few days while we waited long enough for her to pass the test." The other old woman ambled toward them at the speed of an eighty-year-old with a bad knee.

What kind of retirement home did these ladies live in, anyway?

"Heather has the glow." Babushka grabbed one of the tests from the floor and scooped up a box of condoms. "I knew it. I am so proud of my Jase. He does good vork."

"He sure does," Heather said from the side of her mouth.

Velma held her hand out for Babushka's haul. "I'll put those away for you."

"These are mine." The old woman gave Velma a serious once-over. "Get your own rubbers."

Velma's lips parted.

Claire chuckled softly under her breath.

Marlee was just super glad she wasn't sprawled on the floor anymore.

Babushka reached for Heather's stomach and gave it a rub. "I vill check-in tomorrow."

Heather looked like she was about to pass out.

"You." Babushka zeroed in on Marlee.

For real, if Babushka rubbed Marlee's stomach, she would probably throw up on her.

"Ve vant to decorate trees again. I need your number." She dug through her oversized Louis Vuitton handbag, pulling out a legal-sized notepad and a pen with a fake flower taped to it with floral tape—like they had at the bank on Hampden Avenue so patrons didn't accidentally walk off with them.

Marlee scribbled her cell number on the pad, the flower bobbing with each swoop of ink.

The other elderly ladies grabbed their own boxes of Trojan and Durex. Cane lady even snagged a box of ovulation test strips.

"Wha—" Velma started to ask, but then she smacked her mouth closed.

Marlee's mouth wasn't open, so she mentally slapped it closed. No way was she going to ask what those were for— besides the obvious checking for fertility.

They were for arts and crafts time at the retirement home. That's what Marlee was going with, and that was the end of it.

"Ve vere never here." In the smoothest of moves Marlee had seen in a while, Babushka directed her chin toward the cash register, lifting it just a tad at the end.

It was officially official, Marlee wanted to be Babushka when she got old. All who-gives-a-fuck and no-one-will-take-me-down. Hell, she wanted to be Babushka now.

She should begin Babushka training immediately.

The elderly brigade moseyed off to do whatever they planned to do with around a hundred condoms and thirty-plus ovulation test strips.

And a ridiculously large Pixy Stix—walker lady grabbed a blue one right by the register.

"I'm not sure what to say right now." Heather's shoulders slumped. "She's totally going to call Jase and tell him. Then she's going to call his mom. His dad. His sister. His brothers —even the one deployed overseas."

Marlee tried to pretend that this was all a dream. She closed her eyes and, in her mind, she was happily sipping a vodka tonic at Brek's Bar, listening to the cover band, and cuddling up against Eli's side. No pregnancy scare. No condom disaster all over the drugstore floor. Just a relaxing night out with her friends.

Unfortunately, when she opened her eyes, she was still at the drugstore. Lothario was not defiling anything, but she needed to remember to grab his vest next time so they could do it sans condom disaster.

Also, she was still probably pregnant. Still definitely not sure how she'd ever tell Eli if the test came back positive. And still totally unsure what she was supposed to do from there.

"Okay. Where do we do this?" She lifted the basket from Heather. "We cannot go back to Eli's place. Definitely not my house."

Scotty had probably de-dildoed the trees, but he would definitely ask too many questions if she showed up to use the bathroom with a basket full of pregnancy tests. Questions he'd relay to her dad, who would then blow a gasket (or ten).

So the question remained, where the heck were they going to go so she could take a dozen pregnancy tests in peace?

"I have a babysitter. If I show up at home, there's no way the baby will let me leave again," Velma said. "And depending on how this goes, we'll probably want to leave again."

Okay, so Eli's place was out of the question. Scotty's wasn't even a question. Velma's was a no go. There was no way Marlee was taking pregnancy tests in the bathroom of Brek's Bar. First of all, because it was a bar and that seemed like not the best place to do it. And second, because Eli was probably there.

Crap.

Eli was probably there. He was expecting her to be there. Which meant he was probably worried.

Marlee grabbed her cell from her bra.

Double crap.

He'd texted her three times. Called twice.

She didn't particularly want him to know she was living her own personal freak-out of epic proportions. She also didn't want him to worry.

Thus, the problem with being Marlee in that moment.

What was a girl to do in the middle of a pregnancy scare? Marlee did the first thing that came to mind. She pushed the button on the side of her phone until the screen went black.

Now, Marlee wasn't an idiot. She absolutely understood that this wasn't solving anything. But at the same time, right then, it seemed to solve everything. So she went with it.

"Let's go to my place. Dean's out with a client tonight." Claire tossed a couple of condom boxes into the basket.

Marlee raised her eyebrows toward the haul.

"My treat." Claire grabbed a mascara, tossing it in with the rest.

Heather sauntered toward the cash register, grabbing a giant Hershey's bar and a can of barbeque Pringles along the way.

Marlee followed with a basket filled with way more pregnancy tests than anyone could possibly pee on in one night, two boxes of condoms, a Voluminous Mascara, and a gigantic blue Pixy Stix. The last one only because it seemed like something Babushka would do. And Marlee was now sworn to be the new Babushka.

Velma, Claire, and Lothario followed close behind. Marlee didn't turn to see what they were carrying.

They did the cash register thing, loaded up in Velma's Prius, and darted off to Claire's.

Marlee peed on a shedload of sticks.

She lined them all up on the counter. Her heart beat

against her chest wall, thumping so loud Eli could probably hear it across town. Her mouth went dry. Her knees started to buckle. She lowered herself to the edge of Claire's kickass soaking tub, and she waited until the results rolled in.

A dozen tests all came back with the same result.

Then she texted her best friends.

Chapter Nineteen

WHERE. The. Hell. Was. Marlee?

They'd had plans to catch up at Brek's. So far, he was the only one catching up. There was no Marlee to be found.

No Marlee picking up her phone.

No Marlee answering his texts.

Which meant an Eli who was getting more and more concerned by the second.

"You said they all took off together?" Eli asked, swiping his thumb across the rim of his untouched beer.

"Said it three times now." Brek mixed up what appeared to be two fingers of whiskey on the rocks. "Didn't change in the last twenty minutes."

"They weren't with Babushka?" Eli was pretty sure Babushka could get Marlee to do anything at this point.

"Nope." Brek shook his head.

"You're still not the least bit worried?" Eli wasn't an especially jumpy guy, but he was officially in a relationship, and call him crazy, but once they'd sealed the deal that afternoon, his nerves went haywire.

"Nope."

"They're supposed to be here."

"Yep."

"They're not."

"Nope."

This was ridiculous. Eli was ready to be a search party of one if he had to be, since no one else was taking this seriously. Well, no one being Brek. He had no idea where Jase was, and Dean was meeting with clients.

He just needed to find her, check in, and make sure she was okay. Then he'd be better. The silence felt louder when Marlee wasn't there.

"Uh-oh." Brek glanced at the door.

A crackle lit the air in the bar. The kind of crackle that usually preceded life-changing news.

Eli turned, hoping it was Marlee.

It wasn't Marlee.

Jase shoved through the masses. He sat his ass on the bar stool next to Eli. "Heather's pregnant."

Say what? Eli didn't say anything, just stared at his buddy. They were dropping like flies—marriage, parenting... Pretty sure they'd all start driving matching minivans.

"She's pregnant and she hasn't said anything to me." He pointed to a bottle of Jose Cuervo. "I'm gonna need a hit of that before I go home and she delivers the news. Officially."

"How'd you find out she's having a baby if she hasn't told you she's having a baby?" Eli asked.

"Babushka. She's planning a bridal-slash-baby shower and she'd like to know if we want to do girls only or girls and boys." Jase scraped a hand down his face.

Oh, well. That sort of made sense. In a world where nothing made sense.

"What did you decide? Because if you make me go to a bridal-slash-baby shower, there better be fuckin' beer." Brek grabbed the bottle of tequila from the backlit shelf.

"I didn't know you were trying to get pregnant," Eli said.

Although, given the fact Jase wanted a shot of tequila, maybe it wasn't so planned.

"We were waiting until after the wedding. Not long after. But after." Jase tossed back the shot Brek had poured. "It's not that I don't want a kid. I just don't want to deal with planning the wedding and planning for a baby all while wrangling the insanity that is my family. I like my insanity in nice tidy boxes. All separate from each other."

"It's not that bad." Brek leaned against the bar top. "The planning a baby and a wedding. Velma and I did it."

"Your family is not my family. You have a very sane mother. Velma has two totally normal parents. Have you met Babushka? My mother? My sister? You might as well call in the ringmaster now, because my life is about to become a full three-ring circus."

Eli had met them. Jase was right. He was fucked.

"How'd Babushka find out before you?" Brek asked.

"Said she caught Heather taking pregnancy tests at Rite-Aid."

Eli had heard the stories of Velma testing for a baby in the bathroom stall at Target. At least now he knew where Marlee'd gone. Why she hadn't responded.

She'd been too busy helping out a friend.

Jase would be a great dad; Eli had no doubt. Just like Brek. And Dean, if that's what he and Claire decided they wanted to do. Eli? Eli was barely ready for his first real relationship. Did he want kids? He let that thought ferment in his mind.

Maybe.

Yes.

Someday.

If it was a little girl and she looked like Marlee.

Shit.

This is why he didn't think too hard about things like this.

He was two inches away from nailing down his

restaurant. This was his dream, and he was finally following it. He wasn't going to screw it up by losing focus.

"This is gonna be awesome," Brek said with a grin. "Let's hope your kid is blessed with the beauty that is Heather and not…" He gave Jase a once-over.

Jase gave Brek the finger.

Eli smiled down at the bar top. His phone buzzed. He glanced at the screen. Marlee. His chest went warm.

"Mar," he said into the receiver.

"Hey." She sounded breathless. "Sorry. I had to go with the girls. I was thinking I'd just head home from here."

"Where are you?" he asked. "I can come get you."

She'd left her car at the apartment. He'd seen it when he ran home for a quick change of clothes before meeting-not-meeting her at Brek's.

"Already called a car." Her voice got muffled as she said something to someone in the background. "I'll see you at home."

His gut turned funny when she called his apartment home. And not in the sour way. In the warm way his chest had also felt when he saw she was calling.

Fine. Eli liked that Marlee referred to his apartment as home.

Yes, he was making progress.

MARLEE WAS pregnant with Eli's kid. A dozen pregnancy tests confirmed it. So she resolved to do what any sane woman would do when faced with the knowledge she carried the baby of Eli Howard.

> Marlee: I'm not telling him yet.

> Becca: Ever?

Kellie: I'm really bad with plans, but even I
know this is a bad plan.

Sadie: Hang on. I'm calling you.

Becca: Conference call?

Kellie: Don't leave me out!

It's not that Marlee *wouldn't* tell him.
Of course, she would.

Marlee: Today just isn't the day to bring
this up.

Not on the same day that he finally opened up to her and
decided that maybe they shouldn't look toward a future that
only included the demise of whatever it was they had.

Marlee: He just needs some time to adjust to
things before I throw this in the mix.

She would simply give him a bit of time to adjust to the
fact that there was a them. Then she'd tell him about the
baby so he could adjust to the fact that there was a *them*.

She did her best I'm-pregnant-and-everything-is-fine
saunter through the breezeway to the apartment. Her Sadie
ringtone started going off right as she reached the door.

"Hey," Marlee said into the receiver.

"You have to tell him," Sadie said gently.

"I…" Marlee's voice cracked.

"Are *you* okay?" Sadie went into concerned friend mode.
Concerned friend mode was a lot like concerned lawyer
mode, but without the threat of legal action.

"No." Marlee sat on the concrete bench surrounded by a
flower patch in the courtyard outside the apartment. The
flowers were long dead, the concrete cold as winter started to
creep into fall.

"I'm in trouble," Marlee murmured, her throat getting

thick at the acknowledgement. Lothario hopped out of the purse, snuggling his head against Marlee's thigh.

Sadie went quiet. "I know."

"I think I'm falling for your brother." And by falling for him, Marlee meant she was pretty sure she was all in with him.

Sadie sucked in a breath. "Well, given everything, that's not so bad."

"He's Eli. And he's started opening up to the idea of a relationship. He wants to go slow, try it out." Absently, she stroked the top of Lothario's head.

"Do you know how long we've all hoped he'd get over his shit and find someone?"

Actually, given that she and Sadie shared everything, Marlee did know that Eli's family hoped he wouldn't always be alone.

"I'm pregnant, Sadie," Marlee whispered. "This is happening."

When the tests had come back positive, she couldn't say the word. She understood how Eli felt about the "married" word. That's how she felt about the "pregnant" word. Velma had seen the tests first, so she's the one who told Heather and Claire.

"I'm coming home," Sadie announced. Marlee could practically see her pulling out her suitcase and throwing in clothes. "Like now."

"That's not—"

"I'm coming home." Sadie's words were final. "I'll just stay with Mom this time. We'll get things settled."

Marlee's heart dropped. Sadie knew Eli as well as anyone —better than anyone. She wasn't coming home to console her brother when he found out he was going to be a dad. Marlee sucked in a broken breath. Sadie was coming home to scrape Marlee off the floor when Eli broke what was left of her heart.

"Okay," Marlee said. "I've gotta go inside."

"I have your back," Sadie said.

"Do you think there's any chance Eli might come around on this?" Marlee asked, hopeful. Needing some kind of reassurance.

There were times in a girl's life when she needed her friends to be straight with her. There were times when she needed them to blow hot air and assure her everything was going to be fine—even if fine was a relative term.

Right then? Marlee didn't know exactly what she was looking for from Sadie.

Sadie didn't respond right away. Which said everything that Marlee already knew.

"I'll call you when I land tomorrow," Sadie replied, not addressing Marlee's actual question. The line went dead.

Marlee pressed the cell screen against her forehead.

Then she pulled herself up, scooped her dog into his purse, and marched to the door. She'd just put all this out of her mind until she absolutely had to face it.

That wasn't this night.

She stepped inside. Eli sat on the sofa. He scowled at his phone. Then he glared at an open notebook in front of him. Then he scowled back at his phone as though willing it to ring.

"Hi." Marlee put the purse down so Lothario could hop out and go snuggle with Eli's shoes. Look at her, sounding perfectly normal even when things were not normal at all.

"Hey." He didn't pull his eyes from whatever weird ritual was going on with the cell. It looked like something would've done when she was fifteen and really wanted Bobby Martino to call her back.

"I'm sorry I missed you tonight." She sat next to him on the couch. Not super close, but not weird far either.

"Jase told us what happened." He kept his focus on the phone.

No glance toward her.

Shit.

He knew.

She swallowed hard and cleared her throat, fidgeted with the hem of her dress.

"Kids are good." He shrugged. "Glad it's not me, but good for them."

What?

He glared one final time at the cell before glancing at her, his stone face melting a bit with the movement. "Jase'll be a great dad."

"Jase told you he's going to have a baby?"

"Jase told us Heather's going to have his baby."

Shocked silence was becoming a thing that night.

"Oh yeah?" she asked as nonchalantly as she could manage, what with the current night's activities and now this.

"You ran into Babushka at Rite-Aid?" he asked.

"Uh-huh." To put it mildly.

"Babushka spilled. She's got the baby shower practically all planned to go along with her bridal shower."

Damn. Damn. Damn.

"Did he talk to Heather?" Because something told Marlee he'd had the Babushka conversation but not the Heather one.

"Not yet." Eli dropped back against the couch. "He was waiting for Heather to tell him."

Marlee sucked her lips between her teeth. Jase had no idea and neither did Eli.

Eli's phone rang. He immediately grabbed it, accepted the call, pressed it to his ear, and said, "Eli here."

Then he got scowly again.

"Totally understand. Don't worry about it. Thanks again." He hung up the phone.

"Problem?" Marlee asked, grateful for a reprieve from the Heather-Babushka pregnancy discussion.

"Three waiters are out for tomorrow's gala. They've got the flu. I can't come up with replacements, everyone's booked." He dragged a hand over his face. "I was on a skeleton to begin with to save money. Now, I'm gonna be cooking *and* serving."

"Is that even possible?" Marlee asked.

"No." He dropped his forearms to his knees.

He needed help. Help for a solvable problem. A problem Marlee could assist with. She may have been not-so-great in his kitchen, but she had done fine when she served at his other events.

"I can do it," Marlee said.

His scowl lightened. "You don't mind?"

"I like you. I like people. I like your food." She gave him her best let's-not-talk-about-babies-anymore smile. "I think I'm probably overqualified, if anything."

"That'd be amazing." His hands held out, he gripped hers and pulled her so she tumbled against him on the sofa. Then he pressed his forehead against hers in a move that made her knees turn melty and her stomach flutter.

"I can call Velma, Heather, and Claire. I bet they'll help out if you need it. The guys, too."

"I don't want to bug 'em." Eli's eyes heated, his fingers massaging her temples. The right amount of pressure eased a headache she hadn't even realized was brewing.

"You've never helped out at Brek's?" she asked, already knowing that he'd volunteered a load of time to get Brek's kitchen set up.

"That's not the point." His mouth had now moved to her right earlobe, pressing a small kiss there, raising all the hairs on her neck.

"Never helped out Jase on Valentine's Day when he gets the last-minute rush?" Jase had told her that Eli always showed up to kick in extra time at the cash register or for overflow deliveries.

"Still not the point." He kissed lower, light kiss after light kiss along the column of her neck.

"Claire said you helped Dean put together her new dining room table last month when it came in a giant box with no instructions." Marlee ended on a squeak as Eli's hands slid down her back and over her tush, lifting her skirt.

He didn't say anything for a moment, just focused on laying tingle-inducing kisses on her shoulder.

"You're making a lot of points here," he finally said.

She ran her hands through his hair, lifting his face so he had to look at her. "Ask your friends. Ask me. We want to help."

Something changed in his expression, something that took that heat she'd seen earlier in his eyes and spread it over his entire face. The muscles went soft, his expression turned serious.

Then, before she could say anything about the fact that he'd taken her into his apartment and given her a job when she needed one, plus all the other things he'd done for everyone, she was in his arms. Like she was precious cargo, he adjusted his grip—her arms around his neck, one of his arms around her back, the other under her knees in the bridal-threshold carry.

He crushed his mouth against hers, silencing anything else she was about to say. Carrying her was an excellent choice, because she was more than a little certain that there was no way she would be able to walk after that kiss. Her brain had turned to gelatin.

With the kind of care she'd only ever seen from him when he pulled a soufflé out of the oven in his kitchen, he set her on the bed. She'd gone with strappy heels that night, but he had no problem untying, unlacing, and slipping them away from her feet.

True story, she'd never thought that removing shoes was particularly sexy. It'd always been that utilitarian thing that had to happen so they could get to the good stuff. With Eli? Just then?

Whoa.

As though he had all the time in the world, he undressed her. He used his mouth, his hands, his body to turn her into a mess of aroused desire.

Finally, he got to her panties. He took his time sliding them down her legs, past her thighs, over her knees. She lifted her hips, willing him to end the torture and have his way with her. Take her deep, like he'd always done before.

It didn't work.

She was naked before him, more ready for him than she'd ever been ready for anything before. With her eyes closed and her mind pretty sure she'd never been this turned on before, her breath caught as he stroked her thighs, planted kisses on the inside of her knees, and moved his way up to her core.

And then Eli Howard's mouth did things to her body that she didn't know were possible. His hands hitched under her thighs—baring her, opening her, lifting her to him.

There were few coherent thoughts going on in her brain. Not when his tongue, mouth, and hands were telling her a story without using any words. She understood, somewhere deep down, that he was trying to communicate something important. Something that mattered to him enough that he was practically worshipping her. But the only thing that mattered was the crest of the wave pulsing over her, washing her away.

Marlee was not loud during sex. Despite the fact that she was generally a pretty loud person, when it came to climaxing, she was surprisingly quiet.

With Eli? Different story.

She cried out, her moan cresting into a crescendo while the "Hallelujah" chorus seemed to play in her mind. Yes, that sounded dramatic. Overly so.

It wasn't.

Eli wasn't using words, because there were no words to describe the sensations. The feelings. The way her legs were heavy, but her heart was light. Her mouth was parched, but she had everything she'd ever needed.

The sensation of floating back into herself had her opening her eyes, meeting his. He was naked, sheathed, and poised over her. She was nearly all the way down from her pleasure when he spread her legs, centered himself, and then went inside her.

They'd had sex before.

They'd had amazing sex before.

That was not this. This was not just sex. It felt less like something carnal and more like a promise.

This time, there was no driving into her, pulling out nearly all the way, and then taking her over and over. This time, Eli's strokes were slow, measured, lazy. His mouth was on hers, mimicking there what he was doing below.

Her arms gripped his back, her legs wrapped around his waist, and with ankles hooked, she held on to him with everything she had.

This build took less time, but when the wave took over, Marlee continued holding on to Eli. Knowing he would catch her when she landed.

And when he met her there, his own orgasm overtaking him, everything in the world righted itself—like they'd just been tilted and then everything was fine. He fell against her, his weight pressing her into the memory foam.

Her heart swelled.

They'd be okay.

She pressed a kiss to the dark hair at the crown of his head. She fiddled with the hair at his temples, both of them sated. Neither saying a word.

Still inside her, he lifted himself onto his forearms, gazing at her like she was chocolate cake filled with fudge icing and vanilla crème.

This was the moment. He needed to know about their baby. What they'd made together without even trying.

"Eli—"

He cut her off with a kiss.

It was a *good* kiss.

An after-sex, *he's-still-inside-me* kiss.

She wanted to lay like this with him forever, but he had to know. "Eli—"

He tickled the tip of his nose against hers. A move that was so gentle and silly, it seemed out of place after the intensity of what they'd done and totally normal. It wasn't the Eli everyone else got. This was the Eli who was only for her.

"Is what you're about to say gonna piss me off?" he asked.

Well… "Maybe."

"Then don't say it." He kissed her again, withdrew, dealt with the condom, and then settled next to her. He rolled her to him, fitting her body against his like it was made only for that purpose.

She didn't say it.

Perhaps going all Scarlett O'Hara on the situation made the most sense. *Gone with the Wind* and "Tomorrow is another day." That worked out okay for Scarlett. Mostly. Okay, it hadn't really worked out at all for her.

Maybe it'd be different for Marlee.

Chapter Twenty

ELI HAD NEVER BEEN good with words. They'd always eluded him when he needed them most, so last night with Marlee, he'd used every other part of him to show her how he felt. Every sensation he could use to bring out the feelings in her that she did in him. How he was feeling about her. The way she was shifting his perception of the life he thought he wanted and bringing in sunshine when he didn't even realize he'd been in the dark.

And it scared the shit out of him.

He needed to get to work early for the big gala. That's why he was going to slip out of bed early that morning to head to his kitchen. The only reason why.

With that plan in mind, he wasn't entirely sure why he kissed Marlee good morning.

Okay, so he kissed her good morning because she was Marlee and she was in his bed and they'd had sex that spoke volumes.

Marlee's eyes fluttered open. He recognized the moment the fog of sleep drifted away and she knew he was him, and she was her, and it wasn't a dream.

And she smiled. She fuckin' smiled.

"My turn," she said, voice husky from sleep.

Eli needed to get to work. He had a boatload of food to prepare for the day. He was going to be on a graveyard staff and needed to figure out the logistics of what that meant for the evening.

Marlee rolled him onto his back, her palms pressed against his pecs.

He let her.

He had work to do, sure. He was also many things—an idiot not included. Marlee pressed her lips along the column of his neck, down to his collarbone.

His blood heated, nerves fired, throat went dry. She licked his nipple.

The breath he inhaled was filled with Marlee's scent.

She reached below the sheet, wrapping her palm around the length of him.

Annnnd he was about yay-far from blowing his load before they'd even truly started. What he needed to do was get his head in the game. Regain control. Be the one handing out orgasms that morning.

Marlee had other ideas.

And if he were being totally honest? They turned out to be exceptional.

"I FOUND YOU HELPERS," Marlee singsonged, sauntering through the door of the kitchen at the event center where Eli was presently sweating his ass off trying to pull together an impossible evening. Five more of his servers had called in sick.

The kitchen staff was on a skeleton crew and the waitstaff was pretty much Marlee and his head server—who swore she got her flu shot early. Eli needed to pull off a miracle.

He glanced up from plating what felt like his two-hundredth plate of surf 'n' turf in about thirty minutes.

Brek, Jase, Dean, Heather, Velma, and Claire all followed Marlee into the kitchen wearing his uniform of black slacks and a white top. Well, Brek's black jeans were ripped to hell and back, and he had a formfitting white tee that would probably make the event chairwoman go bonkers with the amount of tattoos it showed—he'd be working kitchen staff, Eli decided—but everyone else looked the part of server for his gig.

Then his sister Sadie waltzed through the door like she was supposed to be there.

He couldn't help the smile spreading across his lips. "Sadie."

"I hear you got yourself in a pickle." She marched forward to give him a hug, totally ignoring the fact that she needed to wash her hands before she came any farther into the kitchen.

Still, he hugged her. "You flew five-hundred miles because I needed help serving?"

"No, I flew five-hundred miles to see Marlee. Helping you is just part of my penance for being a brat when I was a kid." She gave him a peck on the cheek.

Then his mom and dad traipsed through the door.

"We're here," his mom chimed. "Where are the aprons?"

"Mom." Eli gave her a definite what-are-you-doing-here look. "Dad."

"Put us to work," his dad directed.

And that was that.

Eli divided up the serving responsibilities. His head server was still there, so she took to training Jase, Dean, Claire, Sadie, his mom, and Marlee. Velma and Heather were on kitchen duty since they both were fluent in all things culinary. His dad got kitchen duty because he could be bristly when he didn't know people. And Brek got kitchen duty because there was no way Eli could put him and his ripped jeans out on the floor at the fundraiser for Denver's most beloved charities.

The Consolidated Means event didn't raise money for one charity; no, this group went all out and raised money for them all.

Chefs all over the city were willing to drop down on their knees for the chance to cater this shindig. No way was Eli going to blow it.

Everyone found their groove, Eli finished plating, and the ballroom started to buzz loud enough that he could hear it all the way in the kitchen.

The night was going to be fine.

Marlee bolted through the swinging doors of the kitchen, her heels—why the hell had she worn high heels to waitress?—tapping across the tile floor. *Click. Tap. Click.*

The color was gone from her skin.

"Mar?" he asked.

She waved him away with a flick of her hand, heading straight through the door of the walk-in cooler.

He followed.

"Mar?" A blast of cold air smacked him in the face.

"Mom and Dad are here." She pressed her palms against her forehead. "They have a whole table for the office, and Scotty brought my ex-friend Brittney as his plus-one."

Fuck.

"I mean, I know that I told them to take a flying leap, but I didn't expect to have to smile and serve them steak while they rub it in my face." The color was starting to return to her cheeks, a good sign.

"You don't have to serve." He tipped his forehead to hers. "We'll assign someone else."

That's when he caught it. The spark that hit her eyes. A fire that he understood meant Scotty, whoever Brittney was, and her parents were in for a show.

She jutted her chin up. "You know what?"

"Bet you're about to tell me."

"I'm doing it." She firmed her shoulders. "And I'm going to have fun doing it."

As long as that fun didn't cost him the client, he was good with it.

"I wasn't expecting them. They don't like these things, so they never attend. I'll be good. Promise. But I'm going to go out there and enjoy myself."

He understood her. Knew she'd do it with the professionalism needed for him to keep the client and the sass that would ensure her parents regretted carting Scotty and his date along with them.

"You want this? It's yours." He stroked the sides of her neck with the pads of his thumbs. "You don't want it? I'll assign Jase."

Jase took no shit from anyone.

Then again, pissed-off Marlee didn't either.

"I want this." She wrapped her hands around his wrists.

"Then you've got this." He kissed her quickly—he had a buttload of dessert prep to finish so he could get this night over with and get Marlee home and naked underneath him. Or on top. He wasn't picky.

SCREW. Scotty.

Marlee was about to make a point with a bread basket. She marched through the kitchen, grabbed a basket of rolls, and headed straight for her parents' table. Tonight, they'd probably be the king and queen of Denver's elite fundraising community. They'd spend way too much on the auction. And they'd hate, absolutely hate, the idea of their daughter serving them dinner so publicly.

But they were the ones who cut her off.

They could deal.

Carefully, like they were truly important VIPs, Marlee slipped the basket onto the table at Scotty's left.

"Drop off at the left, remove at the right," the head waiter had said.

Of course, Scotty, Brittney, and her parents hadn't noticed she was there. She was one of the faceless servers for the night.

"Enjoy the meal," she said as brightly as she could.

Her dad startled and glanced at her. He did a double and then a triple take.

"Dad, I think you'll really like the steak. Eli did an amazing job with it." She winked at him. "Mom, let me know if you want a refill on the wine."

"Marlee?" her dad's business partner, Jim, asked.

Jim was a silent partner, an investor, who never had his own kids, so he'd doted on Marlee when she was younger. He'd never particularly liked Scotty. They had that dislike in common now.

"Hey, Jim." Like the good server she was, she refilled his water glass. "Let me know if you need anything, too."

Jim gave a pointed look to Marlee, then the pitcher, then his glass.

"What are you doing?" he asked like she was Lothario and she was hooked to his pant leg.

Her parents and Scotty had gone silent—with shock, she hoped.

"Working." She filled Scotty's water glass as well. "Mom and Dad cut off my bank accounts after Scotty dumped me."

Scotty sucked in an extremely audible breath.

"Leelee," he said low.

Well, it was true.

"It's Marlee." She pointed to her nametag—black matte with white engraving. "And I heard you got some new landscaping." She pulled a *yeesh* face. "Orange is an interesting color choice."

Scotty blanched. Then he got it. She caught the moment he registered it'd been her that did the decorating.

"We need to talk." He started to stand. He'd placed the swan-folded napkin from his plate across his lap. He tossed it back on the plate.

Jim glared Scotty down. "I'd like to hear more about the breakup. I understood the cancelled wedding was a mutual decision."

"Oh, it was mutual. After he got done dumping me." Marlee held the pitcher like it was a dozen roses from the time she had been a finalist for Miss Teen Colorado. "Take me to lunch sometime. I also work over at The Flower Pot in Cherry Creek. You can find me there. I'll make Janet an arrangement of daisies. She likes daisies, right?"

Janet was his wife. She straight up refused to come to these events.

"I'll do that." Jim's expression was both tense and soft at the same time. How he managed that, Marlee couldn't know.

"Marlee." Scotty's tone was clipped. "A word."

"We can go to the kitchen." She glanced over her shoulder to the swinging doors leading to Eli. She shook her head. "But that's not a good idea. Eli's in there." She quickly glanced at Jim. "He's my husband. You'll love him. He's amazing."

She gave a pointed look to Scotty.

Sadie grabbed Marlee by the elbow. "Hey, Eli said I should check on you. Looks like maybe I should take this table?"

"Good idea." Marlee started to move aside. "Mom, Dad, you remember Sadie? She's my attorney."

"And as her attorney, I'm telling her to stop talking." Sadie gave Marlee what could only be described as a shut-the-hell-up stare.

"Marlee, honey." Her mom started to stand. "I think there's been a very big mistake here."

"Marlee's a waitress?" Jim's glare was equal opportunity between Scotty and her dad. "And her attorney is serving me dinner?"

"I've got to get back to work. You all enjoy your fundraiser." Marlee didn't flee to the kitchen. There was no need. When Scotty had dumped her, she set out to make a new life. She'd done just that. A life she was proud of. A life with Eli.

So she didn't escape to hide in the kitchen, she just moved to the next table. Filled the water glasses. Made sure the wine flowed abundantly. And then she did the same with the next, chatting it up with anyone who felt chatty. Sinking into the shadows around the ones who didn't. She didn't mind.

Everything was fine.

"Marlee." Her mom touched her elbow when she was mid-move between tables. "We didn't know he was bringing someone. It's very distasteful. Your dad never would have allowed it if he'd known."

"You picked him." Marlee met her mother's eyes and made it perfectly clear how she felt about that. "You picked him over me."

"No." Her mom shook her head. "Dad's transferring him out of Denver. Scotty doesn't know yet, but we didn't pick him. He picked us. But, of course, we always pick you."

"Miss?" A random man at the next table over held up his glass. "We could use a refill."

She smiled at him and nodded, then focused on her mom. "I've got to get back to work."

She'd process the rest of it later.

Much later.

Chapter Twenty-One

ELI HAD NEARLY SURVIVED the night. A night he'd worried he'd never make it through. They were at the dessert portion of the evening. From here on out, everything was on autopilot. Things had finally slowed down enough to focus on something other than food. That something being the conversation Jase was having with Dean.

"Heather's not pregnant." Jase loaded up a tray of ginger layer cake with poached pears at the wait station set up in the corner of the big ballroom.

"Then who the hell is?" Dean asked, arranging plates on his own tray. "There were a ton of positive pregnancy tests in the trash when I took it out."

"Claire?" Jase asked.

Given that they were found at Dean's apartment, Claire seemed to be the top choice.

Dean shook his head. "It's not us."

"It's not Velma." Brek joined the fray, preparing a tray for Sadie and one for Marlee.

He stayed behind the table so his ripped jeans weren't on display. Eli's dad was right beside him, helping get the next dessert round to the waitstaff.

"You sure?" Dean asked, his eyebrows drawn together.

Brek gave a curt nod. "One hundred percent."

"Then who the hell *is* pregnant?" Jase asked, looking around as though the culprit would bounce by any second.

Eli didn't have spider-like senses. He had caterer senses, and when it came to women, those were total shit. Still, the little hairs on his arms started to raise.

No one said anything, but three pairs of eyes settled on him.

Absolutely not. It couldn't be Marlee.

"You don't think…" Jase scanned the room for Marlee.

All four of them tracked her as she served dessert to the table next to her parents.

"Sonofabitch, it's her." Brek looked as shocked as Eli felt. "It's gotta be Marlee."

"Is it even possible?" Jase asked.

Sadie paused next to Marlee, said something in her ear. Marlee grinned.

Marlee'd been pale that day. Marlee'd had an upset stomach more than once recently.

Marlee was pregnant.

His wife was pregnant, and while they might've been smashed beyond all reason the night they got married, they'd used protection. Every time after was way too recent to count, and even those had been protected. They could practically pose for the yes-we-make-bad-decisions-but-we-always-have-safe-sex poster.

But Marlee had been engaged to someone else a month ago. Marlee had lived with that someone else. Eli hadn't grilled her on their sex life—why would he? But she'd been engaged… Of course, it was possible.

The idea that she was pregnant with Scotty's kid made Eli want to throw the pears across the room.

The woman of the moment breezed through at that precise moment. They all stared at her.

"What?" she asked, glancing down at her white shirt. "Did I get something on me?"

"Maybe you should get off your feet?" Jase asked. "I can take your tables."

Marlee gave him a total what-are-you-talking-about look.

"Mar?" Eli used his calm voice even though his blood pressure was up to the ceiling. "Can we talk?"

Her expression was odd, which made sense given that they were in the middle of his big job and he wanted to pull her aside for a chat.

"What's going…" Her expression changed. She glanced to Jase, Brek, and Dean. Then she got it. They hadn't been together long, but he knew. And she knew. She swallowed. "You know about the baby."

"Fuck." That was Brek.

And that was precisely the word Eli wanted to use in that moment. The clattering of the plates, the voices from the dining room, all the noise zipped to the pinprick of a stop. There was no feeling anywhere in his body. The thing was a shell.

"You're pregnant?" He heard himself ask. He must've asked, because it was his voice. His lips were moving. He just didn't seem to be in control of them. Somewhere deep inside, he needed confirmation.

Marlee's gaze darted between the boys again.

Sadie moved behind Marlee, ready to refill her own tray. "Eli, don't do this here."

"We'll handle everything." Brek took her tray. Tried to take her tray. Marlee wasn't letting it go.

"Brek." Velma said her husband's name but slid her gaze to Eli. "We need to finish the job first."

"Who all knows?" Eli asked. The words came out harsher than he'd intended, but why did everyone else seem to be in the know? Given that he shared her bed, maybe he should've been clued in when she found out?

Marlee focused on him and he felt that gaze cut straight to his spine. "The girls know. They were there when I found out last night."

The ballroom floor seemed to fall open. He was in a freefall.

"Not Sadie," Marlee continued. "She wasn't there."

"But she's here because you told her." He couldn't seem to process anything that was happening after the words left his mouth.

They'd never even had a real shot.

Scotty would find out. He'd want her back. Marlee might've been pissed at him, but she couldn't spend a decade with a guy and not have any feelings for him. Marlee felt everything. How could Eli even compete with that?

He studied Marlee's face, steeling himself for what was to come. Letting her go would be the hardest fucking thing he ever had to do.

"Eli?" his head server asked. "We need to keep dessert moving."

Given the tone of her voice, she'd heard the whole thing. Everyone within ten feet had. Eli still hadn't taken his eyes from Marlee. Memorizing her face was all he'd be left with.

He'd finally decided a chance with Marlee was worth the risk, and the opportunity was being swiped away.

The one time he finally opened himself up? She was going to break him in two anyway.

The thickness in his throat nearly choked him. He wished beyond anything that he could hold on to the numbness for a bit more, but feeling was already starting to return.

He fought against it, knowing it was a fight he wouldn't win.

"Go," Brek said. "You two need to talk."

The committee chairwoman tapped a glass at the microphone. The room went silent just as—

"Marlee's pregnant. What are we supposed to talk

about?" Eli asked louder than he'd intended, zeroing in on his wife.

Shit.

The ballroom's attention shifted to him.

"Marlee?" An older version of Marlee stood from a table, the man in a tux on her right standing as well. Eli recognized him as Jackson Medford from the media box on Altitude Sports Network.

"You're pregnant?" Jackson asked, his face drained of color.

"Seriously?" Scotty asked from beside Jackson.

The whole family came out to play.

"Maybe we should take this to the kitchen?" Eli's dad slid his gaze to the doors leading to the kitchen.

Marlee's jaw dropped. She took in her family. The ballroom. The silence.

"Is it mine?" Scotty asked in front of God, Eli's parents, her parents, and the upper crust of Denver's elite.

That's when Eli's freefall ended and reality smacked him right in the face.

Chapter Twenty-Two

SHIT. *Shit. Shit.*

This was not how Marlee had wanted Eli to find out. She'd hoped to tell him gently after she'd had time to think of the best way to break the news.

She shoved the swinging doors into the kitchen, Eli following behind. Everyone else on staff shuffled in behind him. Her parents and Scotty *and* Brittney brought up the rear.

"Scotty'll never let you go now," he said, his volume higher than normal.

"Why would Scotty have any say in this?" she asked, ignoring the fact that Scotty was right there. "And he already let me go."

"I didn't know you were pregnant, Leelee." Scotty pushed through the small crowd, placing his hand on her shoulder.

Eli looked like he was about to cut it off with a butcher knife.

"Scotty." Brittney's tone was ice.

"It's Marlee. Not Leelee." Marlee kept her focus on Eli while she addressed Scotty, shaking his hand from her shoulder. He could take his stupid nickname and shove it right alongside the unused thank-you cards for their wedding gifts.

"Maybe you two should talk this out." Eli pulled the bandana from his skull.

"Why would you think I want to talk to Scotty about this?" None of this made any sense. Unless…

Seriously?

Eli thought the baby was Scotty's? He thought she wanted Scotty? "Eli, I haven't been with Scotty in forever. Not like that. I've been with *you*."

Eli didn't say anything. *Gah*. He didn't get it.

"I haven't had"—she nearly said *sex* in front of her parents—"relations"—there, much better—"with Scotty since weeks before the wedding. He claimed that he wanted the night to be special, so we took a break."

"Perhaps you should take this someplace more private?" Sadie suggested.

Marlee glanced behind her. Sure enough, her parents stood wide-eyed next to Scotty.

"The kid's mine?" Eli asked. The apparent shock kind of pissed her off and hit her like a right hook to the jaw.

For a smart guy, he was being really stupid.

"Who else's could it be?" she asked, her voice cracking.

"Even when we weren't careful, we were careful," he said, the expression on his face one of genuine confusion.

"I guess that doesn't always matter." She lifted her shoulder even as her stomach plummeted. She needed to get out of there.

She pushed passed the group, her heels clicking against the kitchen floor toward the heavy brown door under the green *EXIT* sign.

The door slammed shut behind her. She took a gulp of air, her eyes getting warm with tears that she refused to let fall.

"Mar." Eli jogged to catch up with her.

She paused in the alley, a security lamp on the building spilling fluorescent light on them. The air was chilled, but she crossed her arms around herself and ignored it.

"You didn't tell me." He was clearly hurt.

"I *was* going to tell you. You said not to tell you if it was going to piss you off." She tossed her hands to the side. "You don't have to do anything."

"Why wouldn't I do anything?"

"You don't want kids."

"Who said I didn't want kids?"

"You did. Last night when you thought Jase and Heather were pregnant. You said, 'Glad it's not me, but good for them.'" She did her very best impression of his deep voice.

He reeled like she was the one tossing out right hooks. "I didn't know the baby was mine."

"Exactly." He had been more honest because he didn't know. He couldn't change that.

He stepped forward like she was a scared Lothario and he had to be cautious. "You don't keep something as important as this to yourself."

Now, she was just getting mad. "Yes, Eli. The time to tell someone he's going to be a dad is directly after his declaration that he is so relieved that it's not his kid."

"No, that's the time to have sex instead," he clipped.

Her fingertips pressed against her lips.

He was lashing out. Yes, she should've figured out how to tell him. How was she supposed to do that when she knew it'd ruin everything they were building? "That's not what it felt like, Eli. It didn't feel like just sex. It felt to me like the start of maybe you wanting me. It felt like you were trying to tell me something when you couldn't find the words. And I thought maybe if you wanted me, you'd want our baby, too."

She had to finish. This wasn't the time, but it was what they had. So she'd see it through.

"I mean, you've barely started to want *me*," she continued. "I didn't want to scare you away with the rest of it."

"Barely want you?" His expression got dark. Heavy. He closed his eyes and he dropped against the wall, his head falling back so it hit the plaster.

"I get it, Eli. You're scared that you're going to care for people and those people might need you. You're terrified that you'll have to take care of everyone like you did when you were a kid. You're scared beyond reason that you'll have to give up your restaurant dream." Marlee stepped closer, reached for his jaw, stroked the little bit of stubble there. "And I get you. Which is why I wanted to give you some time to get used to us before I added in a complication."

He turned his chin to the inside of her wrist.

"Fuck." Eli pressed his hand against his forehead.

"You don't have to do anything for me. For the baby. I've got a job with benefits. The baby will be well taken care of, and you can be as involved or uninvolved as you want." She took in a deep breath of cold air, letting it fill her lungs, wishing it would freeze the pain of this conversation. "You can go do whatever you want to do. You don't have to worry about us."

This wasn't exactly how Marlee had planned on getting her life in order, but it's all she had to work with.

"Fuck," he said again.

Marlee's breaths came out shaky, but she'd get through this night. Then she'd get on with her life. He always wanted to start over, go back, and try again. On that thought, she asked, "If you could rewind time, not go to Vegas, not marry me, not find out we're pregnant, what would you feel? Deep down."

He didn't respond. Glanced away. Apparently, the little pebbles along the edge of the asphalt were suddenly intriguing.

His not saying anything? It said everything.

A tear slipped from her eyelid. "You'd feel relieved. That's the emotion."

"Yeah," he said, short. A quick dagger straight through her heart.

That? That acknowledgement? That right there killed her. Murdered any hope that she'd had that they could make this work.

"I'm going to take off." She started toward the parking lot. Toward her car. Away from Eli.

He hurried to catch up with her. "Mar, this has been a lot. It's a lot to process. I wouldn't be human if I didn't need some time to process it."

Sometimes, taking the time to figure out how something would affect you costs the future. Because sometimes, there was no going back. No do-overs.

"Do you believe in love at first sight?" she asked.

Because she hadn't. Not before the morning they woke up together in Vegas. Maybe she hadn't known that's what she was feeling, but she understood now.

"That's how it is with you," she continued, "but not the first time we met. Not when I was in high school. For me, it was the morning we woke up married. It felt right. Like it was always supposed to be. I'd seen you a million times, but that morning? That morning was love at first sight."

His gaze sliced to her. Settled there, exposing her. "You were lonely. You don't know how to do alone. And I was there."

Ouch.

"That's really what you think?" she asked.

The thing was that Eli wasn't being a jerk. She knew that, understood that this was Eli calling it like he thought he saw it. But still, his words cut to the bone.

He really believed that. That she'd just loved him because she couldn't be alone.

Screw that. "Loneliness is all you know, Eli. And that's sad. You're so scared that people might need you that you can't see everybody already does."

He glanced away.

"And the craziest part?" she continued. "The craziest part is that you need us, too. You need me, and I need you. That's our love story, Eli. It may not be the story I'd have written for myself. It may not be anything you even thought you wanted. But it's *our* story."

"Mar." He had a look like she'd gut-punched him. "You've had a load of shit to deal with lately. We both have feelings for each other, but I think they're getting all twisted in the craziness."

How could she stay and just hope that someday he'd feel the same way about her? She started walking again. He didn't get it. He was too wrapped up in being scared of all the baggage that came with relationships to see what he was missing and what he was going to miss. She stopped, turned one more time.

He stood next to the streetlamp over the parking lot, the halo of light flooding the asphalt around him. The image was branded in her brain—the way his eyes seemed to have more lines than before, the way his lips pressed together, the way his hands slung low on his hips.

"Do you know how scary it is to be the one who loves you more?" she whispered. "The risk is even more than I ever imagined. And I get it now. I get why Scotty held on so long. He wanted to get back to this. To the way I feel about you. To have this and then lose it? I thought I knew devastation before. I had no clue." Another tear fell over the edge of her eyelid, making a trail down her cheek.

"Mar." His voice was low. Warning. Jaw clenched. His posture drooped. He started to step toward her, paused, and then stood right there. Never able to truly move forward.

"You don't need me. And I need you. And I can't be the one who loves you more." She hurried toward her car. This time, she didn't look back.

Eli didn't think she knew how to be alone, but if she were

totally honest? She'd spent a good deal of the past years alone. It might not make any sense to anyone else, because technically she'd *been* with Scotty. Spent tons of time with him. Looking back? She'd been lonelier than she'd ever realized.

"Marlee." This time, her name wasn't a warning. It was a plea. But Marlee couldn't go back. The time had come for the future. Her future. Their baby's future. Even Eli's.

She shook her head.

The ball was in her court. But she was done playing.

She dug the key fob from her bra and clicked it. She didn't need to glance behind her to know that Eli would wait for her to be safe in the car before he went back inside.

Because despite everything Eli ever said—all the starts and stops, everything she knew to be true about him—deep down, he was always watching out for the ones he cared about.

Until he realized it for himself, he'd always be stuck. Always going backward.

As long as that was happening, she had no place in his life. There was only forward for Marlee.

"SORRY, DUDE." Marlee gave Lothario a snuggle. "He's got to figure out what he wants. Until then, it's you, me, and Thumper."

Velma had sent Marlee some magazine articles on pregnancy. One of them encouraged her to give the baby a cutesy name. The idea was that if the baby had an adorable-sounding name, then giving birth to it wouldn't scare the crap out of her so much.

So far, it'd only worked minimally. Since she was still in the first hours of the experiment, she figured she'd withhold judgement on whether this actually worked or not.

Lothario stuck his nose in the air. He seemed to understand they were moving out of Eli's apartment, and he was not happy.

Marlee had packed her bags, loaded them in the car, and now, she was waiting. Waiting for Eli. Because even if she was moving forward and he was standing still, this was his Thumper. He deserved to know where she was going to be—a long-term motel until she found a real apartment.

After she'd left the fundraiser, she'd picked up Lothario from Babushka and then texted Sadie, Velma, Heather, and Claire so they'd know she was fine. Then she'd texted Kellie and Becca, but Sadie had already filled them in.

She was as fine as she could be, given that she was pretty sure she and Eli were over. Over-ish. She held hope that he'd come around.

Someday.

Maybe.

She curled herself into a ball on the sofa, and she waited. Her eyes got heavy, her breathing steady. There was that space between being awake and being asleep, not fully conscious but not unconscious, and that's where Marlee had settled when a knock on the door startled her awake. Her heart did the just-woke-up-not-where-I-should-be race.

Eli still wasn't home.

Toes in the carpet, she padded to the front door where Lothario currently snuggled with one of Eli's flip-flops. He gave her a don't-you-dare-move-me look.

Winning his regard back after they left would take some time and probably an abundance of Pup-Peroni.

She glanced through the peephole.

Her dad.

Along with her mom.

Damn.

Still dressed in their black-tie attire—Dad in a traditional tux and Mom in her version of a little black dress. The LBD was floor length (not so little), but it had a slit up the side, which her mom totally pulled off. Marlee fully expected that they'd be angry after everything. Instead, they just looked worried.

Marlee pressed her forehead against the doorframe.

Her dad knocked louder, right next to her forehead.

Marlee opened the door.

"Hi." She stepped back to let them through. "You two are out late." She said this as though they hadn't witnessed her confession of being pregnant, who the father was, and the fallout in a ballroom filled with their peers

"Marlee." Her dad's edges were often sharp—he wore suits to the office, polo shirts to the country club, and he took no shit from anyone. Well, except Marlee, but it could hardly be considered taking her shit when he had essentially cut her off and cut her out. So, yes, his edges were often sharp. Tonight, they weren't so harsh. "May we come in?"

"Sure." She gestured to the living room. "Yeah." She pressed a hand through her hair, doing a finger-comb she hoped would settle her just-awake hair.

Lothario, apparently pissed at her parents, raised his chihuahua nose in the air and marched his furry butt to the bedroom.

"Come sit down. Can I get you something to drink?" she asked.

"Maybe in a bit," her mom replied, tone soft like cotton candy.

This was new. Usually, when Marlee screwed up, they took a hard line with her.

Marlee might've expected a lot of things to happen that night. What she did not expect was her dad to wrap her in a bear hug and not let go.

"We messed up," he said into her hair.

"What?" She pulled back.

"Is he here?" her mom asked. "Eli?" She took in the

apartment, nowhere near the glitz they were used to. "We'd like to apologize to him."

Marlee's heart did a little dip. "No. Not yet."

Her mom nodded. "We'd like to meet him. Officially."

"I transferred Scotty to Cincinnati. Talked to Jim, got it all settled." Dad dropped his arm and pulled a key from his pocket. "After everything tonight, we sat down with Scotty and told him. He agreed to sign the house over to you. He'll be out of there tonight."

The cool metal of the silver key pressed into Marlee's palm.

"We also made some calls." Her mom cleared her throat. "Your cards are turned on. We'd like to start some paperwork to transfer control to you early."

"We don't like that Eli could get a chunk of it," her dad added.

"Eli won't want it." Eli was a lot of things. A jerk, he was not.

"We believe that," her dad said. "Had a nice talk with his friends after you left. You said he was a good man. We believe you."

"We just forgot you're not so little anymore." Mom squeezed Marlee's hand. "We thought being firm when you came back married was the thing to do. We didn't realize it'd cost us...you."

Marlee tightened her grip on Scotty's key in the other hand. Her eyes had gotten hot.

"We'd hoped that you and Scotty would work things out." Her dad's voice was rough. Which made sense, he'd adored Scotty. "We hoped he'd see he made a mistake calling things off."

"And we thought if you had no other choice, you'd come around to see that he made a mistake, too," her mom added. "We shouldn't have gotten involved."

"It's pretty clear if you're waiting tables in defiance and

Scotty is dating again, the two of you won't be finding your way back to each other." Her dad was apparently resigned to the idea that Scotty wouldn't be the son he had always hoped he'd be.

Of all the things that made her sad about her breakup with Scotty, that was the thing she couldn't forgive. That Scotty hadn't just broken it off with her, he broke it off with her and then tried to hold on to her parents.

There was one thing that needed to be clarified. "I waited tables because Eli needed the help. His staff was all sick. I would've done that if I had Grandma's money or not."

Now that? That surprised them. Clearly.

"Then you must care very much for him," her dad said.

She did. She really did. "I do."

"Then I'm certain we'll love him, too." Her mom gave her hand a squeeze.

"Eli needs some time to get used to the idea that he's going to be a dad." Marlee glanced around at the apartment he still hadn't returned to. "I'm not sure he'll ever get there."

There was a time in the very recent past when having her parents show up at her door ready to give her money back would have put Marlee over the moon. Tonight, she just wanted to know where Eli had disappeared to.

"Marlee, we saw the man when he came back without you." Her dad tucked a chunk of her hair behind her ear. "He'll come around."

She hoped, really hoped, Eli would see that all he needed to do was stop going backward.

She'd just have to keep hoping…

Chapter Twenty-Three

MARLEE HAD LEFT.

"She said she's going back to her old house." Sadie held her phone up to Eli, showing the text.

Scotty had moved out. Marlee had her money. She had her house.

Marlee was set.

She may have been the one with chronic asthma, but Eli was the one who couldn't catch his breath.

"You're just going to let her move out?" Sadie asked, all sass.

The fundraiser was complete, but the committee chair had been frosty with him after everything—who knew if he'd ever get another job with them. Afterward, he'd driven Sadie back to his parents' house. Then he stuck around, telling himself it was because he hadn't talked to his mom and dad in a while.

If he were being more honest with himself, he stuck around because he didn't know what to say to Marlee. This was confirmed when he realized his mom and dad were already asleep, but he still stuck around.

He was having a kid.

With Marlee.

And she was moving out.

Eli held his hand at the back of his neck, rubbing the knot there.

He'd fucked up a lot of shit in his life. Never anything that mattered this much.

"Eli?" His mother came from the back bedroom, tying her robe around her waist. "What are you doing here?" His mother's eyebrows furrowed. "Where is Marlee?"

"I don't know." He went with the truth.

"Elias Santiago Howard," his mother said, her words low. "Have you lost your mind?"

Sadie crossed her arms. "This ought to be excellent."

"You're nicer when you're not in Colorado. You know that?" he asked.

"You're nicer when you're not knocking up my friend," she replied in a huff.

"Eli." His mother clapped her hands together like she'd done when he was a child. "Sit."

He sat his ass at the table as directed.

"Sadie." His mother pointed toward the hallway leading to the bedrooms. "Time for bed."

"I don't think so." Sadie shook her head. Instead of listening to their mother like any of the other Howard children, Sadie grabbed her purse and marched out the front door.

Eli probably should've been worried, what with the way the blood vessel in his mother's forehead was pounding. He wasn't, only because he knew Sadie was going to Marlee.

He didn't want Marlee to be alone.

His mother dug through the cupboards. His parents' house hadn't been remodeled since the eighties—the appliances were old, but they worked, the carpet was old, but it worked. All the times he'd tried to do any updating had been firmly yet politely declined.

"I like Marlee." His mother placed a pan on the stove, poured milk from the Meadow Gold container, and turned the flame on low. "And I love you."

He knew better than to reply. His mother had a point to make, so he knew his job was to sit down, hush, and let her do it.

"When you got married to her, I thought, 'This is not a mistake. This is a good thing for Eli, and he will be good for Marlee.'"

She'd thought that? He hadn't realized—

"She is wild, and you're stable." She smiled a flash of white. "Balance."

"And then I messed it up," he said. "I'm not who she needs me to be."

"Eli." She sat across from him. "You are always what anyone needs you to be. It's time you are who *you* need you to be."

He stood, unable to stay still. "I don't understand."

"When I got sick…"

Eli flinched. He couldn't help it.

"When I got sick," she said again. "You were there for the girls. You were there for me. You were there for Dad. Not once during those years did you put yourself first."

She wasn't wrong.

"And in the years that followed, you continued with this." She stood to stir the milk, adding a handful of chocolate chips. "Then you tried to cut everyone out of your life. But in attempting to cut everyone off, you continued putting yourself behind. Because you never really cut anyone off, you only told yourself you did."

Was she right?

"Being alone is not the only cause of loneliness." She pulled two thick ceramic mugs from the cupboard. "Sometimes, it's being afraid."

He took the offered mug, wrapped his hands around it.

"You love her," she said. "And you don't know what to do with that."

Did he? Did he love Marlee?

"Maybe," he said to the mug of hot chocolate before him.

She tipped his chin up so he had to look at her. "Then you tell her."

He took a sip of the rich chocolate.

"You tell her how you feel," she continued. "You tell her that you're scared. And you stop hiding your life from everyone else under the disguise of protection."

"She's already gone." He glanced down then back up to catch his mother's gaze.

"I doubt that." She clinked her mug against his.

They finished the cocoa. He went home.

And he was right. Marlee was already gone.

Chapter Twenty-Four

IT WAS MONDAY, which meant coffee on the corner. Marlee distributed about twenty cups of java along with cookies Heather had given her to hand out.

She may have had her money back. Sadie may have been back in town. Heather, Velma, and Claire may have all checked in on her regularly. But Eli had been incommunicado.

He was in the middle of buying his building. Marlee knew from talking to Sadie that he had finally asked his sisters to come on as investors. They'd been thrilled to finally be able to pay him back.

Marlee picked up her Lothario purse—he was hanging on to his pissy mood for a lot longer than she'd expected. All the Pup-Peroni at Wal-Mart wasn't swaying him to her cause.

Empty drink carriers in hand, she headed back toward her SUV. She was due to work at Jase's in fifteen. Money woes may have become a thing of the past, but she liked working at The Flower Pot. Liked making pretty things that brought others joy. She'd just donate her paychecks to Babushka's retirement home and Babushka's pet projects—whatever those might be each day.

She'd have to ask her CPA if purchasing a batch of sex toys in bulk for a senior citizen's project was an effective write-off.

That thought had her smiling.

Seeing Eli and Sadie milling around her Jag? That had her frowning.

"What are you doing here?" Marlee asked.

Of course, she knew she'd be seeing Eli again. She had just hoped it would be when she expected it and had time to prepare her heart.

"I'm not here as your friend. I'm here as his attorney." Sadie was in full legal mode.

"Aren't you my attorney?" Marlee asked. Also, best friends couldn't be the attorney of the other best friend's ex. Even if the ex was the attorney's blood relative. Marlee was pretty sure that was written in the manual.

"Not on this case." Sadie slid her gaze to her brother and then back to Marlee. "Sorry, he's making me."

Marlee moved to get past them. "Today's not a good day for this."

She worried no day would be.

"Give us five minutes?" Sadie set her hand on Marlee's arm.

Marlee looked at Eli. His gaze was burning a hole right through the icy veneer she'd sworn she'd hang on to when he was around.

"Eli?" Marlee asked. "What are you doing?"

"He's not allowed to talk." Sadie was back to attorney mode. "When *he* talks, things go wrong. So he's going to not talk for the duration."

I'LL JUST MESS *it up*. Eli did his best to telepathically reassure Marlee that he wasn't there to screw her over. He was there to win her back. *That's what Sadie keeps saying anyway*.

"Is there a place we can go sit?" Sadie asked, gesturing to the tables and chairs outside of Starbucks.

"Sure." Marlee led the way, Lothario whining in Eli's general direction.

He'd missed the little dude, too. Marlee looked good. Not that she ever didn't look good, but she didn't look like the miserable pile that he felt like. She looked like she was going to be just fine.

That's what worried him. She'd be just fine without him, and he was convinced that was not the case for himself.

Marlee sat on one of the black metal chairs, her posture precise.

Sadie spread out the documents she'd had Eli sign earlier across the table.

"Now, my client wanted to let you know, in person, that he's contesting the divorce." Man, Sadie as an attorney on the other side was scary—she held her posture firm, her eyes sharp, and her words hard as granite.

Marlee sucked in a breath.

Eli wanted to reach out and hold her. Reassure her that this was a good thing. He didn't. Sadie told him to zip it, so he would.

"Eli?" Marlee asked, her voice cracking.

He just shook his head. The lump in his throat practically clogged his esophagus with the pain reflected in her eyes.

"He doesn't feel that the current structure is fair to both parties." Sadie slid one of the documents to Marlee. "He wants you to have half of his estate, the catering company, and his future restaurant. Half of the profits from both will belong to you."

"It's not a lot, Mar. Not what you're used to. But it's yours." Eli's voice was smoother than he felt. "Yours and the baby's."

"Thumper," she said.

"What?" he asked.

"I'm calling him Thumper." She pushed one of the documents away with her fingertip.

His heart beat hard in his chest.

"You think it's a boy?" he asked. He'd thought he wanted a little girl with her, but a boy…a boy would be just fine. He would love a little boy.

Her breath shook on the way out. "Yeah."

Sadie gave him her best shut-up look. The one he'd known since they were kids. He took the hint and zipped it.

"I don't understand." Marlee skimmed the first page of the packet.

"He's also signed a post-nuptial agreement forfeiting any claim on your trust, income, and any future inheritance that may be left to you." Sadie handed over that document next.

He was giving Marlee everything. He just hoped that in the end, she'd give him her heart. To keep this time.

"What do you want then?" Marlee asked cautiously. "From me."

He couldn't blame her for proceeding with caution. He hadn't done much in the recent past to warrant her trust. But he'd been working double time to make things better—get things set up for them.

"I want you, Mar." Eli shifted, the seat suddenly uncomfortable. He just had to get it out there. "If you still want me, I want you. And if you don't want me? I'll wait and pray that someday you do. And I want to know our kid. I want to help raise him. I want to be the one he comes to when he needs things."

"I'm a mistake, though. And he's a complication." Her hand fluttered to her stomach in a move that made Eli melt.

That she thought she was a mistake and their kid was a complication? That was on him. The fact that she believed such a lie? He'd spend the rest of his life proving it wasn't true.

"That may be how we started. That may be how he came to us. But I refuse to let that define who we are as a family. I refuse to let that define him. That's not our story." He glanced at Sadie, pretty sure she was going to tell him to shut up.

"Go on," she mouthed and nodded toward Marlee.

"That's not our great love story, Mar." He braved on. "Our great love story is you bringing coffee to these guys every Monday morning while I watch our baby. It's me opening up to you when I screw shit up. Especially when I screw shit up. It's both of us sticking around, no matter how hard it gets."

"What happens if the spark fizzles?" Marlee asked. The question she'd clearly been thinking about.

Their spark burned so bright he knew it'd never fizzle. But if it did?

"Then we'll relight it. And if it goes out again? We'll relight it again. As many times as we have to." Eli reached for her hand. He squeezed it. "When you find something like what we have, you don't let it burn out. You do everything in your power to make sure it shines bright."

"Which is the post-nup and the one that says I get half of his stuff?" Marlee asked, still holding his hand, her question directed toward Sadie.

Sadie slid the documents in question across the metal table to Marlee's outstretched fingers.

Marlee dropped Eli's hand, took the papers, arranged them so they were carefully stacked, and then ripped them in half.

He stilled. "Marlee."

This was literally all he had to offer her.

"New terms." Marlee dropped the ripped pages on the table so they fluttered here and there.

"We're listening," Sadie replied for him. Which was good, seeing as how he couldn't find any words right about then.

"You promise we'll be together for always." Marlee took his hand again. "And we stop the divorce. And we face each day as it comes to us, but we face it together."

"Marlee Medford?" He relaxed for the first time in days. "I accept your terms."

Her eyes were watery. Fuck, his eyes were watery. He didn't check Sadie's, but he could guess hers were, too. Even his badass kid sister had a soft heart when push came to shove.

"Are we done here?" he asked, standing.

"All done." Sadie collected the ripped papers into a pile. "I'll handle the changes to the divorce."

He kicked his chair back with the ball of his foot. Then he went to Marlee, held her hand like she was made of porcelain, and helped her stand.

"Sadie?" he asked.

"That's me," Sadie chirped.

"Go away," he said.

Then he tilted Marlee's face to his. "We good?"

Her lips parted.

"Yes," she said on a breath.

"And you'll marry me?"

"We already are, silly." Her eyes misted further.

His gut clenched. "Feels like I should ask the question. We'll go pick you a ring, if you want one."

She nodded. "I want one."

"I want one, too." He ran the edges of his thumbs over her cheeks, wiping the tears, praying he'd never make her cry again.

"And I can kiss you?" he asked.

She smiled a watery smile. "Whenever you want, chef."

He took that opportunity to take her up on that. His mouth met hers, and the world was perfect.

"I love you," he said against her lips.

"I love you, too." The edges of her mouth tilted more.

"You don't love me more, Mar." He touched his fingertips to the apples of her cheeks. "We love each other exactly the same."

That got him a full smile.

And that was perfect.

Epilogue

"I'M FINE," Marlee mouthed the words to Eli from across the restaurant.

His restaurant. With the help of his family and his savings, he'd bought the building. She'd personally ensured every other expense was covered, enjoyed the heck out of picking out the decorations, and Eats Grille was ready to open less than a year after they'd found their way back together.

Not to say it was nice to have money again, but it was really nice to have money again.

One thing money couldn't buy was Eli's peace of mind. Marlee was due any day—any minute, really. Eli had been on edge about it for weeks. He'd tried to convince her to stay home and skip out on Heather and Jase's wedding. But this was their reception—the first time the restaurant served guests—and she wasn't going to miss it. Thumper would have to stay put until after the festivities.

It was a good thing the festivities were about over. She was spent.

Heck, the kid was over a week past due. If he were a library book, he'd be racking up the fines. They'd fully expected to bring a newborn to the reception, but Thumper was nice and content where he was, much to everyone's—mostly Marlee's—dismay.

"He's worried about you." Sadie passed her a ginger ale and gave a jaunty wave to Eli.

He scowled back.

He was very scowly lately.

Heather and Jase stood in the middle of the bridal party, the sun setting on the Rockies behind them while the photographer snapped away. Jase said something that made Heather laugh like crazy. The vibe was definitely one of happiness.

Heather had gone with a formfitting satin wedding gown that looked amazing with a pair of strappy heels peeking from the hemline. The way Jase had looked at her when she walked down the aisle of the church made Marlee choke up.

Jase went with his dress whites, the rest of his groomsmen in tuxedos.

"Do you wish you would have had this?" Sadie asked.

Marlee shook her head. "I wanted the party. Not the man. Now, I have the man. I don't need the party."

Sadie was Marlee's designated wedding babysitter since Eli was on groomsman duty with Dean, Brek, and Jase's brothers, Zach and Roman.

Zach lived in Denver. Roman had just moved back after a stint in the military.

He kept glancing at Sadie. She didn't seem to notice or care.

Interesting.

Marlee could tell Eli was on edge—his gaze kept sliding to her all throughout the ceremony at the church. Now, he kept finding her around the restaurant, catching her gaze, and waiting until she gave him some sign that she and the baby were both A-OK. They'd both been fine the entire pregnancy. That didn't stop Eli from worrying.

Eli had worked his tail off to get his restaurant in order before the baby came. They were hosting Jase and Heather's reception that night, but they didn't officially open for two more weeks. Tonight was more of a dress rehearsal for the restaurant.

A dress rehearsal where the chef wore a tuxedo and stressed out way too much because he was in the bridal party and not in his kitchen.

He'd left one of his sous-chefs in charge there.

Another contraction—she'd been having them for weeks —took Marlee's breath away. She waited until it passed, gripping the edge of the bar top until her knuckles turned white.

"What do you say we take a breather in Eli's office?" Sadie asked super gently once the contraction was over.

That was an excellent idea. Marlee nodded and followed Sadie through the room filled with Jase and Heather's friends and family, past Babushka and her boyfriend, Morty, and down the hall to the kitchen. Eli's office was just off the kitchen here.

This one had real walls. Marlee liked to think it was innocent, but she was pretty sure he'd ditched the glass this time so he could have conjugal visits whenever Marlee popped in.

She turned the handle to the door and slipped inside, Sadie two steps behind her.

"We should text Kellie and Becca, see what they're up to," Marlee said as another contraction swiped her breath clean away.

Lothario took one look at Marlee from his perch on Eli's chair and yipped. He trotted toward her. She waited until the contraction passed before she knelt to pick the little dude up.

She'd chosen the green maternity dress because it had loads of room to move around and it went well with Jase and Heather's wedding colors. Funny thing. Three months ago, it had loads of room to move around. Tonight, it was extra tight around the waist.

"Why don't I go catch Eli, let him know he needs a break from pictures?" Sadie asked, helping Marlee to the sofa.

Marlee didn't need help to sit on a sofa.

"I'm. Fine," Marlee said as an answer, setting Lothario beside her.

The truth was that the contractions were coming closer together. But they weren't so close that she was ready to head home, grab her bag, and insist they head to labor and delivery. She'd already been there twice. Both times were false alarms.

Both times were also over a week ago.

The door flung open before Sadie could even get past the desk to go find Eli.

"Mar?" Eli asked, breathless, heading straight for her.

"I say, 'I'm fine,' but no one listens," Marlee said, readjusting herself on the sofa so the pillows gave her some support.

"They're closer together," Sadie whispered. Not so quiet that Marlee couldn't hear, but loud enough to make her grumpy.

"How close?" Eli asked like Marlee wasn't sitting there able to answer herself.

"I wasn't timing, but three minutes, I'd guess," Sadie replied like Marlee wasn't the one actually having the contractions.

"Hey," Marlee called to them.

They both looked at her. Finally.

She gave a wave she hoped was reassuring. She was at Heather and Jase's reception. Eli was supposed to be posing for photos. Thumper was already a week overdue—what was a few more hours?

"I'm. Fine," she said, just as another contraction made her pause.

So she might've grunted with this one. Sue her.

"She's not fine." She heard Sadie say on the periphery. This contraction took all her attention. Not painful, not really, just intense. The kind of intense that required her attention, that was all.

Except this didn't feel like before. She couldn't quite put her finger on why, but this wasn't the same.

She focused on their baby, just like they'd learned in birthing class, waiting for the contraction to finish. This one just seemed to keep going. She might've made some noises, she couldn't be sure. Probably. Definitely. She'd made noise.

The wave receded. Sadie stood beside her, concern etched in the lines of her forehead.

"Marlee." Eli kneeled in front of her, gripping her hands in his. "It's time to go."

She shook her head, her lips pursed.

No way was she leaving before they'd even cut the cake.

Sadie kneeled beside him. "Marlee, you need to not have your baby in Eli's office. It'll stain."

For some reason, that popped Marlee right out of the haze. "Is it time?"

Eli's palm rested against her cheek. "It's time, Mar."

Oh.

He was probably right.

"Okay," she said, trying to lift herself off the sofa.

"Okay," he repeated, helping her up and holding her tight when another contraction started.

"I'll bring the car around," Sadie said somewhere in the background. Marlee was trying really hard to focus, but everything seemed to be wrong.

"Eli?" she asked, needing the reassurance that he was right there.

"You're okay," he assured, helping her to the door, through the kitchen, and out the back exit.

"I want to name him Lucas," she said, drooping against him. For some reason, that was the important thing that needed to be said. "His name is Luke."

She couldn't say why, not really. The name had just been nagging at her for days.

Eli paused as they waited for her SUV.

"I like it," he said, his voice gravelly. "Lucas."

She liked it even more when he said it.

Her hand found its way to her stomach. She stroked up her abdomen and pressed against the foot lodged at her lungs. "Hang tight, Luke."

Sadie drove the car right up to them. Eli helped Marlee into the passenger side. Once he'd buckled her in, she stopped him with a tug on his hand.

"I love you," she said.

"Same." He pressed a kiss against her lips. "Exactly the same."

Do you need more Eli and Marlee?
Sign up for the bonus scene at:
ChristinaHovland.com/takeitoff-bonus

Acknowledgments

I'm often asked if the heroes in my stories are modeled after my husband. Up until this story, the answer was…not really. There are pieces of him in every hero I write, but they're not *him*. This time there is a whole lot of Steve in Eli. Thank you Steve for supporting my dreams, for loving me as I am, and for being an amazing father to our kids. I hope readers love Eli as much as I love you.

Thank you to my bestie, Karie, for getting tipsy with me and brainstorming antics for Babushka. The silicone tree decorations were *all* Karie's idea. Oh, how we laughed and laughed when she said, "You know what Babushka should do…"

I am so grateful to my mom, Shirley, and my sister, Sereneti, who put up with my random ideas and love my books.

Kiele, as always, thank you for keeping me grounded. You are my person.

Courtney, Dallas, Leeann, Lindsay, Sarah, Shasta, Stephanie thank you for supporting me, always.

Thank you to A.Y. Chao, Dylann Crush, Colette Dixon, C.R. Grissom, Jody Holford, Diane Holiday, and Renee Ann Miller for being my beta readers on this project.

Todd I so appreciate your answering random questions about the legal needs of fictional characters. And Victoria thank you for seeing to their fictional medical needs.

Beth, thank you for being the best author assistant ever. (Truly, I am grateful for you.)

Thank you to my agent, Emily Sylvan Kim. I don't know what I did to deserve you on my team, but I remain grateful that you are Team Christy.

Thank you to Holly Ingraham who is so much more than an editor. She listens to me brainstorm and helps me make my stories the best they can be.

Thank you to Tamara Beard of Wrapped Up in Writing for the exceptional job with copy edits and proofs.

And thank you to Shasta Schafer for being my *ahhh-mazing* final proofreader.

Deb Smolha, thank you for being my biggest fan. (I won't tell the others.)

Thank you to Delhia for helping Marlee with her French.

And, finally, thank you to you, the reader of my stories. Your kind words, e-mails, and reviews make my time spent crafting these characters worth it.

Also by Christina Hovland
THE MILE HIGH MATCHED SERIES

Rock Hard Cowboy

Going Down on One Knee

Blow Me Away

Take It Off the Menu

Do Me a Favor

Ball Sacked

The Mile High Rocked Series

Played by the Rockstar

From Entangled Publishing

The Honeymoon Trap

Rachel, Out of Office

April May Fall

About the Author

Christina Hovland lives her own version of a fairy tale—an artisan chocolatier by day and romance writer by night. Born in Colorado, Christina received a degree in journalism from Colorado State University. Before opening her chocolate company, Christina's career spanned from the television newsroom to managing an award-winning public relations firm. She's a recovering overachiever and perfectionist with a love of cupcakes and dinner she doesn't have to cook herself. A 2017 Golden Heart® finalist, she lives in Colorado with her first-boyfriend-turned-husband, four children, and the sweetest dog around.

ChristinaHovland.com

Enjoyed the Story?

**Turn the page for chapter one of
Do Me a Favor!**

Some days things just click. Today is not that day.

Love is a battlefield, and divorce attorney Sadie Howard is entrenched on the frontlines. She thought she might have met the right man once, but he was a career military guy who got shipped overseas and left her heart on the tarmac. These days, the only commitment Sadie wants is the one she's made to her Denver law practice.

Combat photographer Roman Dvornakov is back. Fresh out of the U.S. Army, he's using family connections to snap photos at a few weddings while he builds his civilian photography practice. After all he's captured on film, a few posed wedding shots should be a cakewalk. Seeing so much death through the camera lens, he's now ready to build something worth living for. A thriving photography business, definitely. But he's certain his new mission also includes Sadie, the girl who slipped away.

Sadie isn't convinced, and she's not willing to open her heart anytime soon. Besides, she's got a high-profile divorce case taking up all her attention. Winning the case for her client will make or break her practice. So what if it's a custody dispute over a ridiculously expensive fish tank? When Roman discovers the soon-to-be divorced couple are still in love, he and his slightly-nutty grandmother, Babushka, are determined to convince them to cancel the proceedings. He's not camera shy when it comes to matters of the heart, but interfering with Sadie's clients could wreck her career and any chance they'll ever have together...

Do Me a Favor -
Chapter One
BEFORE

NO. Absolutely not. *Sadie, don't do it.*

A million gazillion and one. That's how many reasons Sadie Howard had to slip her tush off the tailgate of the truck, toss her red plastic cup into the nearest bin, track down her brother, and get her butt home.

Roman Dvornakov stalked—yes, oh yes—he stalked her way. Roman didn't walk. He didn't run. He didn't mosey. No, Roman stalked. A muscled man always on a mission.

His mission at the moment? Given the way his gaze bore into hers? Yeah. That.

Do. Not. Do. It.

The last thing she needed was to dive into anything too distracting before she started law school in three weeks.

Three weeks and she would be totally engrossed in all things legal.

He grinned.

Shit. She was toast. Not just toast, but toast with butter and grape jelly.

Totally distracted grape-jellied toast.

"It's Sadie, yeah?" Roman asked.

Her heart was torn between doing a happy dance that he had remembered her name and a sad-panda waltz because he had to confirm it.

Which really meant that he didn't remember her name. But rather, he probably remembered that his friend Eli, her brother, had a sister named Sadie and he assumed that was probably her.

"Yes. Sadie." She futzed with the plastic cup she held between her palms. The beer had warmed a while back. She was better at people-watching at these sorts of desert parties than actually getting the soles of her shoes dirty and socializing.

"The attorney." Roman's tongue rolled against his bottom lip while he turned his matching cup in his hands.

"Soon to be. Not yet."

Another tongue roll and...oh dear, that time? That tongue roll? It did interesting things to her insides. Fluttery things.

He remembered she was going to law school. That was something.

"Roman Dvornakov." She stared straight ahead as she spoke, afraid that she'd spontaneously combust if she stared at him too long. "Photographer. Military."

Last she'd heard, he was on a mission that had taken him away from Denver and he hadn't been back in years. Not that she'd been keeping tabs. She'd been busy as hell getting her degree and working two jobs to help pay for it.

"This seat taken?" His voice wasn't smooth. It wasn't gravelly. It was Roman. And it could likely get a girl to drop her panties in two-point-five seconds.

He nodded to the empty space on the tailgate where she sat.

She was so *totally* gonna let him distract her before classes started.

Any thoughts of saying no vanished, and she scooted to her right to make room for him on the tailgate. Roman, however, didn't sit. No, he leaned against the tailgate—more like he propped himself there, crossing his ankles with an air of total relaxation.

"If you'd rather, I can find another seat." Roman gave her a look like finding another seat was not high up on his list of desires.

Wait. What?

"Why?" Sadie asked.

"I asked if this seat is taken and you didn't say anything. I can jet if you'd rather be alone."

"I scooted." She gestured to the empty space she'd cleared so he could sit. "The scoot implies that you are invited."

"Scooting isn't verbal confirmation."

"You need verbal confirmation that I'm okay with you sitting next to me after I pointedly scooted? That's ridiculous. When someone scoots, you know that it's an invitation. Unless there's some Russian thing where scooting means something else." She thought on that for a second. "But that doesn't make much sense, does it?"

"Fuck, you're cute." The edge of his thigh brushed against her calf. His jeans to her corduroy.

Still, he didn't sit. He just kept leaning. He was a leaner.

"Pointedly scooted," he said under his breath with a chuckle.

"Um…" Smooth, Sadie, real smooth.

Roman did this thing with his lips that wasn't really a smirk and wasn't really a grin. It was more like a please-let-me-take-your-panties-off-for-you smile.

He started to turn his prior lean into a full sit when Sadie set her cup aside and held up her hands, palms to him. "Hold up."

He held up.

"Why *do* you want to sit here?" Sadie asked, doing her best to put on a solid, untouched-by-all-that-was-*him* facade.

"I was thinking it's out of the way." He lifted his shoulder. "The party's getting crowded. Don't much care for crowds."

Oh. He was simply looking for a place to sit. Not because it was next to her. Well, that stung now, didn't it?

The party *was* getting crowded though. A desert party with a couple of kegs. They weren't high schoolers, so they didn't need to come to the desert to have a party. But Roman's brother Jase had decided this was what he wanted to do with this fine Friday evening. So they all tagged along.

Turned out, there were *a lot* of tagalongs.

Jase threw good parties.

"You wandered all the way over here because the party's getting crowded? What's wrong with sitting over by Jase? Don't you want to spend time with your brother?" Sadie never tried to be argumentative. But that didn't mean that her family hadn't been telling her from the time she could form a solid word-string that she had a future as an attorney.

Sadie was just…Sadie. She didn't like to think of herself as contrary, she just required an abundance of clarification. Was that so bad?

Roman didn't seem to mind.

He didn't move. He didn't sit, either. He just stared at her with the panty-removal grin.

"*You're* not sitting by Jase," he said. "And I've been thinking it'd be nice to catch up." Roman crossed his arms, amusement dancing in the gleam in his eyes.

That was a better answer, at least.

It wasn't, I'm just trying to escape the throngs of people. And this seat is available.

She turned fully toward him, which meant there was more leg-to-leg contact, but she was going to go with it.

"Catching up," she said, "would imply that we've spoken

more than two sentences to each other in all of the time we've known each other."

Spoiler alert, they hadn't. Sure, through friends of friends and friends of family, they had seen each other around. She was fairly certain that if he would run into her at the Cherry Creek Mall parking lot, then he'd probably help her out if her car didn't start. But given that Roman Dvornakov would probably never be caught dead at any place that involved shopping, that wasn't a likely scenario.

"Do you always argue like this?" he asked.

"I'm not arguing, I'm just asking questions. And yes, generally, I do ask a lot of questions. It helps me find answers."

"I'll play." Suddenly, he was the picture of intensity. "The first time I saw you was when Eli dropped my brother off at the house and you were in the backseat of the car."

Holy crapola. He remembered that? *He remembered that?*

Yes, she remembered that, but Roman was the kind of guy you didn't forget. Even if they're just kids, a girl noticed when a guy like Roman was around. Even if the attention was totally platonic. Even if the attention was only because she happened to share the same air with him.

"I asked how you liked the seventh grade," he continued. "You gave me a solid two-minute dressing down of all the reasons middle school sucked. You liked to argue back then, too. Glad to see that hasn't changed."

Sadie took a drink of warm beer because she wasn't quite sure what else she was supposed to do.

"Next time I saw you," he went on, "you were probably around sixteen, hanging out at the creamery place near your house. The one that blended all the stuff into the ice cream."

"Frozen yogurt," Sadie corrected. "Totally different than ice cream."

"Details."

Oh no, that's where you get into trouble—the details. "Details are important."

He scrunched up his forehead in clear question.

"Frozen yogurt is not ice cream. Like if you get the Oreo cookies blended in, then you have to get vanilla frozen yogurt. If you were to go with the Reese's Pieces, then you'd go somewhere they serve chocolate ice cream. Everyone knows that."

"Seriously?"

"You brought it up."

"I didn't come inside because I got a call. I'm still a little pissed Babushka chose the moment I was about to get my frozen yogurt fix to insist she needed urgent help. Turned out that she just needed someone tall enough to switch out the soft white light bulbs to brighten the dining room."

"Since we didn't technically speak, I don't think that time counts," Sadie said.

"You like the fine print, don't you?" he asked.

"It's my favorite." She raised her cup and clunked the plastic edge against his.

Here's the thing, she wasn't trying to be challenging. Not at all. But she'd been training to be an attorney for God-knew-how-long—it'd been her dream ever since she was five and her mother had watched some lawyer show on television —which meant that she had a predisposition to uncover holes in all theories, all stories, all…well…everything.

Her best friend Marlee now refused to take her to the movies because Sadie was the queen of drilling holes into any plot.

"You may not believe me, but I don't have a photographic memory." Roman uncrossed his arms, the muscled bulk bulging as he set his cup on the wheel well of the truck bed. "Sometimes there are people in your life who stick. You remember everything about every interaction," he said. "You ever experience that?"

Not that she was ever aware of. She shook her head.

"Every time you brush past each other. Every time you get a little piece of their attention, it sticks. Doesn't mean I had a thing for a kid when I was eighteen, but it means I knew that person was special. And she'd grow up to be someone special."

"You thought I was special?" She gave an inner high five to twelve-year-old Sadie.

"I thought you were special back then. Now, I think you're fucking stunning. And we've spoken at least a dozen or more sentences to each other, if you want to get technical. I can go over them, if you'd like."

Well. Okay, then. Her breath caught in her lungs.

"Seat's free." Sadie shoved the satchel she used as a purse behind her to create even more space.

The bed of the truck bounced with the addition of his muscle as he lifted himself up so that they sat thigh-to-thigh. Their thighs actually smooshed together—which seemed like an important note to make so she could tell Marlee later when they caught up after she got back from her family trip to the Maldives.

"I can't believe Eli still has this piece of crap." Roman bounced a little, the shocks creaking with the movement.

Her brother Eli's beat-up, blue Ford should've been retired about two decades ago, but he wouldn't let it go.

Speaking of… Where the heck had Eli gone? She scanned the crowd. No sign of him.

"You were also at the horrible party my parents threw when I enlisted," he mused.

She'd tagged along with Eli to Roman's going-away party when he went off to basic training.

"I don't recall it being horrible."

He leaned back and braced himself, one hand on the metal truck bed behind her back. Not making contact, but totally claiming her space. Which was super funny, given that she was Sadie and it's not like she got claimed often.

She wasn't a stunner like her sisters.

Sadie was just…well…Sadie.

"You're correct. Not horrible. Totally awful is a better word choice," Roman said.

"The party wasn't either of those things." She flicked her brown hair over her shoulder so her view of him wouldn't be blocked by her annoyingly long hair. She'd been considering a short, smart bob cut for law school. Something that might make her look a little older. She had a baby face that she'd never fully outgrown.

Roman scratched at the top of his ear. "As I recall, there was a brawl between my brother and me."

"That was actually pretty fun to watch." This was not a lie. The two brothers were so evenly matched that the fact that Jase was younger than Roman had no real bearing on the outcome of the fight—a draw according to their mother who lost her utter shit when the boys took out the catered buffet—chicken skewers and shrimp satay flew through the air to bounce off the guests and land in the swimming pool.

That part was pretty funny.

"Good times." Roman grinned a grin that made Sadie hope. Really hope.

Hope for what?

Well, that part was debatable.

"Now look at us," Roman continued. "Grown up, but still going to desert parties to drink beer from a keg." He jerked his chin toward her oh-so-warm beer.

"Where would you rather be?" she asked.

He caught her gaze then. Despite the chill in the air, she heated like she'd just slipped into a hot bath after a long trip.

Which made no sense.

And all the sense in the world.

"Nowhere else I'd rather be, Sadie."

Do it, Sadie. Oh yes, just do it. Perhaps a distraction was in order, after all. She'd never had a one-night stand before. Never wanted one until now.

"Do you want to get out of here?" She glanced up at him.

The intensity of his gaze sparked with interest at the implied meaning of her suggestion.

"That depends." His chest rose and fell softly with each breath he took. "Where are we going?"

"There's a movie playing that I've been wanting to see."

"Is that right?" Roman asked, angling his body so they faced each other. So their individual spaces became one. Not his, not hers, but theirs.

Sadie traced a fingertip over the curves of his knuckles. "Or we could go to my place."

A breath of a moment passed. The kind of moment when a girl had to pause to see if she was going to have a freaking fantastic night or if rejection would be her friend as she watched a hot movie star race cars on the big screen instead.

This was that moment.

And, goodness gracious, it was stretching into what felt like forever.

"Let's go to your place." Roman followed the line of her bottom lip with the edge of his thumb.

Sadie grinned, holding his gaze. Yes, distraction with Roman was going to be oh so very fun. She nodded.

Sadie took his outstretched hand and, tethered, followed him through the crowd to his car—an unremarkable, very respectable sedan with a rental company sticker on the back window. He held the door as she climbed inside, their gazes briefly melding together as the unspoken promise of what they'd both agreed to simmered between them.

Settled in the car, she shot a quick text to Eli so he'd know where she'd gone and that she was fine. More than fine.

Roman's hand found hers as they made their way to her apartment near the University of Denver. A heady buzz of adrenaline and lust wrapped around them in the confined space.

"Hungry?" he asked.

"Nope." She'd eaten before she went to the party. Even if she were hungry, she had many, many other things on her mind. "You?"

"No."

"You leave Monday?" she confirmed.

"Early." He tapped a beat along with the music, his thumb brushing against the fleshy spot at the base of her thumb.

"Big mission?" she asked.

He shook his head. "I don't usually know where I'm going until I'm halfway there. This one's an aid mission though. Not classified. They need a photographer to track their progress for evidence. Should be an easy one while I get back into the swing of things. Time off always screws with my head."

"What exactly is a hard one?" She cleared her throat. "Mission. I mean."

"Anytime bullets are coming at me, it's not an easy one." The words were serious and said without emotion—flat—but they were accompanied by a flash of dimples and relaxed shoulders.

"You like those, too, though, don't you?" she asked.

"Yeah." He kept his focus on the road, moving his hand away from hers to turn onto the street leading to her building. "Keeps things interesting."

Bullets? Nopers. *Interesting* was not the word she'd use. "Do you get to come home often?"

"Not a lot of time off for me. But I like what I do. Like that it's never the same thing twice."

She fidgeted with the zipper on her handbag. "I'm with you. I like to be moving forward. Toward something."

"Exactly." He looked her way, a camaraderie sparking between them at their mutual understanding.

"Next left, last building." She pointed at the gray building that housed her teeny tiny apartment.

Roman walked behind her as they climbed the stairs to her front door. They didn't touch—the promise of what was to come taunted her, making her skin tingle and her mouth water.

This was just one of those one-night—maybe two-night—things. Nothing serious. Nothing more than sex between two overachievers both waiting for the next move.

But once they were inside and Roman's hands landed on her hips, things felt a whole lot more serious than they'd ever felt for her before.

Palm against his jawline, she ran the tip of her nose against his.

He grinned, moving in. Sadie's body instinctively moved with his as he pressed a feather-light kiss to her forehead and then her temple before moving down to kiss her cheek, ending with her lips.

Sadie knew there were all kinds of kisses—the fast kind, the slow kind, the *meh* kind, the holy-crap-this-is-good kind—but Roman's kiss was unique in its ability to turn her legs to applesauce.

She gripped the muscles of his shoulders for support as his mouth moved in tandem with hers, his tongue sliding with hers, his body pressing against hers.

She led him to the bed, kissing him the entire way—heat and flesh and the carnal need to be with him propelling her forward.

"Sadie," he whispered as they fell against her bedspread.

God, he said her name like she was special. And that was the kind of moment a girl wanted to put a pin in so that she could come back to it over and over again.

The kind of moment when nothing would be the same.

The kind of moment that ignited the next, which would

lead to the next and the next until, eventually, everything would fall apart.

Everything always fell apart.

Enjoyed the sample?
Do Me a Favor is available now!

.